Scent—the scent of flowers. Ramsay was aware of that first. Then he was chilled by a flash of fear as his mind sluggishly fitted together events of the immediate past. That mountain road in the dark, his skid as he fought to avoid the man caught in his headlights. He must have gone over.

Flower scent—a hospital room? He tried to feel pain, something. There was nothing. A broken spine? Complete paralysis?

Sound returned. Very near him, a voice spoke. But he had no understanding of the words. Slowly Ramsay opened his eyes. . . .

He was lying on his back, yes. But above him was no hospital ceiling; it could not be. Arches swept up, to meet in peaks, and from the center of those peaks hung a chain with a pendant in the form of a cage of elaborate latticework holding a globe of light.

The chant continued at his right. He tried to understand the words—but there was no one word that he knew. There were only sounds.

What had happened? Where *was* he?

KNAVE
OF DREAMS

by
ANDRE NORTON

ace books
A Division of Charter Communications Inc.
A GROSSET & DUNLAP COMPANY
1120 Avenue of the Americas
New York, New York 10036

KNAVE OF DREAMS

Copyright © 1975 by Andre Norton

An ACE Book
by arrangement with The Viking Press, Inc.

Printed in U.S.A.

ONE

THE ROOM WAS large enough to breed shadows in its far corners, for the one light came from a globe set in the middle of the long table. The woman who occupied a canopied chair of state could be distinguished only with difficulty by staring straight at her cloaked form. Though the room was warm, she had drawn the furred garment close about her as if she were chilled.

However, the men, seated in less impressive chairs, were far enough into the glow of light for their features to be clearly visible. There were four of them, and they ranged in age signs from youth to more than middle years. For the moment they were silent, as if each were brooding upon some thought he did not want—or feared—to share with the rest of the company.

To the woman's right, the black-and-white robe of the Chief Shaman identified Osythes, a respresentative of Powers Unseen (but not unfelt) at this gathering. Beyond him was the slightly younger Privy Cokncillor Urswic. These two represented age and a conservative caution, to balance the youth and impatience facing them beyond the limited source of light.

Prince Berthal sat there, his tunic glittering as he

shifted impatiently, uneasily; the heraldic symbols emblazoned on his chest displayed glints of gemmed splendor. His neighbor was the least impressively clothed, for his tunic carried only the badge patch of the Household. Yet his face had a trace of arrogance that marked him as no common servant, but one who had a right to address those about him with equality. He was Melkolf, a delver into new ways of thought, an experimenter whose recently discovered knowledge made him a power to be reckoned with.

They all turned their faces now a fraction toward the canopied chair, as if willing its occupant to speak. Perhaps their concentration did act upon her, for she leaned a little forward as if to see them better.

Now her features were illuminated. She was old, her dark skin drawn tightly over the bones of cheek and jutting nose. But her eyes were not those of one entirely in command, reminding the other that it was *her* will that was paramount in their venture, whether they would have it so or not.

"You are certain?" The Empress spoke directly to Melkolf.

"The proof has been shown, Your Splendor Enthroned," he replied with complete confidence.

Berthal once more shifted in his chair. Osythes's wrinkled, large-veined hand, resting on the table top, began a tapping of forefinger, his thumb ring glinting red and green as the light caught the jewels in it. He might have been measuring the number of words spoken or the passing of time.

Urswic, although an elder usually taking a conservative course, reinforced the Younger Melkolf's statement, though there was a ring to his words as if he did not do so with entire willingness.

"There were three exchanged, Your Splendor Enthroned. All succeeded."

Once more a moment of silence fell. To be broken by Osythes: "This is wrong, an evil thing—"

The Empress's eyes fastened upon him alone.

"There are small evils and large. You yourself, Reverend One, have correlated the phophecy of what will happen to this land if matters proceed as custom decrees. My son lies on his deathbed. He breathes, and only while he breathes do we have this small space of time to amend or prevent that darkness which Ochall and his slave Kaskar will bring upon us.

"Can you deny that what they would accomplish is an evil," she continued, "a very large evil, enough to engulf all that my lord Hunold, my son Pyran, have wrought? Sometimes we have no choice between good and evil; rather, there is set before us a small ill and a great one. And in this hour we face that."

Osythes's eyes no longer met her fierce ones. His forefinger moved upon the table, tracing signs no man, except perhaps himself, could read.

"You speak only what is true, Splendor Enthroned. Still, the deed is evil." Then Osythes, the Shaman, was silent, as if withdrawing from what they were about to do here.

"You are sure"—this time Urswic spoke, addressing Melkolf—"that you have the right man selected?"

Melkolf shrugged. "Ask that of His Reverence, the Shaman. It is *his* knowledge that searched the worlds for us."

"Yes." The Shaman did not raise his eyes from his moving finger. "He who is twinned to Kaskar has been found. The dream sending has been very clear—it is all recorded."

"You see?" Melkolf demanded. "All is ready. We have only to move. And by the latest reports, we must move soon. His Supreme Mightiness fails fast. Ochall has his man in the outer chamber there. The moment breath fails, Kaskar will be heralded as ruler. And, think you, when that is done, any of us here will be safe for even a portion of an hour?"

Berthal ran his tongue over his lips. He glanced uncertainly at the Empress Quendrida in her cave of a chair. His fingers dropped below the edge of the table to close upon the hilt of a ceremonial short sword.

"For all Ochall's impudence," the old Empress said, "he will not move openly against *me*. But there are hidden ways—yes, I do not doubt that he intends to dispose of all opposition with his usual efficiency. And with Kaskar entirely in his power, there is no limit to what he can do. To see all that I and my lord have fought for, all that Pyran labored to make stable, go crashing down because of this—this man—!" She beat her first upon the table top, her voice rang deeper in an intense note.

"If the death of one man of whom we know naught, except that he exists, can save our land, then, to me, that death is a deed of worthy cause!" Her gaze centered again upon the Shaman as if demanding some answer from him. But he did not speak.

"Very well. Let it then be done. And as soon as possible. There is one other who must know—"

They all stared at her, startled.

"The Duchess Thecla. She is on her way here now for the ceremony of betrothal—to Kaskar. That she comes unwillingly and under threat, we are all aware of. However, she loves her country and would not see it under Ochall's fist—so she comes. We need Olyroun, but we shall not overrun it as Ochall would do. Thecla is well beloved. Her people would rise, even if it meant the blotting out of their land.

"My Eyes and Ears have sent me many reports. Already there is unrest in Olyroun. Rumors spread that Thecla comes under duress to this matter of a future wedding. Therefore, we must assure her that she does not have to see in Kaskar her betrothed—"

"Splendor Enthroned"—it was Urswic, the Councillor, who dared to speak as his mistress paused for breath—"is this wise? Need she know? When all will be done perhaps before her arrival?"

The Empress nodded. "She must know. She must understand what we are doing for the sake of the land. This will make her more amenable afterward to the suggestion that she be joined with Berthal. Let Kaskar die without her understanding and she may depart to Olyroun, there to make some other alliance that will not be to our liking. But if she is assured that she need not hand-fast with Kaskar, in her relief she will look to Berthal. It will be your duty"—now those hawk eyes were turned upon the Prince—"to woo her with that skill that I have heard much of—"

He flushed and his lips parted as if he would reply, but the Empress was already continuing: "You, Osythes, will bring her to my private chamber upon her arrival. I shall make plain to her what we do and why. I ask no other to say such a thing. Kaskar—" She hesitated for a breath's space, and then spoke on. "He is the son of my son in body, though surely not in mind or spirit. I could well believe in the ancient tales of possessed ones. How Ochall wrought this change in him I do not know. Perhaps that should be the subject of your searching, Master," she struck out at Melkolf. "Does Ochall also have the use of some machine which he may put into operation to change the spirit of a man? Or, Osythes, can he call up the Power Unlimited to do such a thing?"

"Perhaps he can," the Shaman answered quietly.

Quendrida stared at him, shock showing for the first time on her face. "You mean that, Reverend One!" Her voice held the same astonishment.

"In one way of thinking, yes, Splendor Enthroned. There are things of the mind that can overrule the identity of a man. Just as Melkolf can use his machine to exchange the spirit of one person into the body of another in an alternate world. Ochall is not of the Enlightened Ones. However, that does not mean that he may not have learned some trick of mind control that he has used to override the inner man in our poor Prince and make Kaskar only an echo of himself."

Councillor Urswic leaned forward. "But if that is so—could such an enthrallment not be broken? Why have you not said this before? As an Enlightened One, you could have—"

"Done nothing," Osythes interrupted him. "That which was free once in Kaskar was long ago killed. Do you think"—he lifted his head, looked from one pair of eyes to the next in that company—"I have not tried? I do not know what power Ochall has called upon, but it is such as cannot be broken now. But think not so ill of Kaskar, for he is but a helpless tool in the hands of a determined and evil man. And now we plot his death—and the death of another, who is wholly innocent. Also, we say that this must be done for the good of Ulad."

"You know that it must—" There was almost a pleading note in the Empress's voice.

Osythes nodded. "As you say, Splendor Enthroned, it must. Yet that does not make this deed any the less evil when it shall be weighed against us as we come to the Final Gate of all." He raised his hand and covered his eyes, his shoulders hunched under the heavy folds of his black-and-white robe. "I offer what excuse I may to the Power Unlimited in the name of all of you. Still, it will weigh—"

Now it was Melkolf's turn to move in his chair. There was a faint expression of distaste on his sharp features, as if Osythes were uttering nonsense that the younger man found hard to endure.

"Then we are to move at once?" he asked.

The rest looked to the Empress. A moment later she inclined her head in a nod, though her expression was troubled and she watched Osythes with a fraction of uncertainty she had not shown earlier.

"Reverend One?" Her mention of his title was half question.

Osythes dropped the hand that had masked his eyes. "Splendor Enthroned, the coordinates have been already sent to the machine. The dreams have prepared the selected one with linkage and for the necessary manipulation within his own time world."

"What is he there?" Betthal showed some curiosity. "Is he a ruler, one who will be missed? If we have out counterparts in these alternate universes—and we must or the experiments would not have worked—do they live lives such as we do? Is there another Berthal who is a Prince, and a Reverend One"—he nodded to Osythes—"a Councillor—a—"

"Circumstances alter with the world, Prince," Melkolf answered. "I think there are very few princes or emperors left in the world to which we send Kaskar."

"Then how do they govern?" Berthal asked.

"Through representatives elected by the people, I believe. We have only a few scattered readings picked up from our subject there. He is not connected with the government. He has been a student; now he seeks work—"

"And such as he is Kaskar's twin?" Berthal laughed. "No prince but a commoner who must work with his two hands to earn his bread? I wish that Kaskar knew! I wish I could tell him—" He laughed again.

"This is not amusing!" Quendrida's tone was cold, the snap of a lash. Again the Prince flushed. "You speak of a man who must die, and you do not jeer at death. From what Osythes has told me, this one who is not tied to Kaskar is far more worthy of wearing the Imperial Crown than he who is of my own blood. I wish that we might save him, but there is no way. Yes, Master, let it *be* done and speedily—while the Emperor, Kaskar, still lingers. We must not hesitate too long."

"The deed is—evil—" The Shaman drew a deep breath. "Yet the foreseeing is also evil. It is true we have no choice, but to say yes—that I cannot do. Agree you will. As I have agreed in spirit, may the Power forgive me!"

"It is agreed then?" The Empress kept her eyes away from Osythes as she asked.

The "yeses" from Melkolf and Berthal came quickly and firmly, followed by that of Urswic.

"Then I say it be so," Quendrida ended. "Make ready, Master. And that speedily. As you have pointed out—our time is very short."

Three of the men arose and bowed formally to the old Empress, withdrawing with some haste back into the shadows beyond the reach of the globe. Osythes remained where he was.

"My friend"—the Empress put out her hand toward him—"do not believe I cannot understand what lies in your heart now. It is through the Power Unlimited that this person to be sacrificed was found, and through your direction that he was entangled in the destiny of Ulad. Duty is a harsh mistress. I have spoken words that my heart would not have owned had there been any other way to achieve that which had to be done. Now I condemn one of my own blood because he is unworthy, because he would be only the face behind which an utterly evil and vicious man would rule. This is not easy—But it is what I must do so that all that has been built of peace and goodness here be not destroyed.

"When my lord came to the throne, you will know what measure of hardship there lay in this land. Small lord warred against his neighbor, famine and death stalked hand in hand. No man, woman, or child was safe. My lord used what forces he could summon to counter this chaos. He brought you and the other Enlightened Ones, and set up the Groves wherein you might teach your ways of peace and fulfillment. He tamed the outlaw lords, he fostered the trade of cities, he made Ulad a bright and smiling land.

"And after him Pyran carried out his father's work with the same will and dedication. But this wasting illness which was sent upon him, sapping his body and then his mind—that defeated him. Then came this devil Ochall who made himself so strong that he put hand upon the High Chancellor's key and none dared say him no. And Kaskar—Ochall enfolded Kaskar as a swamp serpent enfolds its prey, crushing out of him everything except his own will.

"I was in deepest despair, for I knew, as well as your fore-tellings could say, what would come to Ulad when Kaskar ruled. Then Berthal and Urswic brought Melkolf to me, and I learned to hope. Not for my own line—for now we perish—but for the land which was our duty to protect. Yes, I live by duty, not by my heart, old friend. And if indeed that fact weights ill upon me when I reach the Final Gate, then I can offer no other excuse for all the acts of my life.''

The Shaman lifted his eyes, and there was a sadness in them.

''Lady,'' he said quietly, ''I was at your handfasting to your lord, at the naming of our dear lord-in-chief who now lies so spent and helpless, at the naming of his son who is now a lost one. I know well that what moves you to this lies as heavily upon your shoulders as does the ancient Power weigh upon mine. We made our choices long ago and we must live by them. I do not doubt that this act will save the Ulad which your House brought into being. And I shall entreat the Power that good may come from ill, for there is no other way—''

''No other way,'' she echoed. ''Now I must go to Pyran and watch the life ebb slowly from him, praying for him to live, in spite of all his pain and torment, until we can make safe his country. And upon me that weighs heavily also.''

She pressed on the wide arms of the thronelike chair, levering up her body as if her limbs were so stiffened she found movement hard. Osythes also arose, but he made no move to help her, knowing well that her fierce pride would not allow her to acknowledge the infirmities of her aged body.

With effort, she stood erect, and now her back was very straight, her head, bound with an embroidered scarf over which was set a small diadem of Presence, held high. She walked toward the shadowed end of the room, moving with purpose, Osythes near but not touching her.

Another dream! Ramsay Kimble sat up in the bed

on which sheets were rumpled and tangled as if he had been fighting some hard-pressed battle against it. He was sweating, though the night was rather chilly; his black hair was pasted across his forehead. He looked around him, half amazed to find that he was really here, in his own well-known bedroom—not in that other place that had been so real. Then he snapped on the reading lamp and reached for the notebook and the pen placed to keep the pages open at that point.

"Get it down right when you wake up"—that was what Greg had told him last week. "The longer you wait, the more the details can recede." Ramsay set the notebook on one knee and began to write.

"Big room," he scrawled, "machines of some sort—never saw them before. Two men—" He must remember details. "One young—queer clothes—a kind of body suit something like a leotard, close-fitting, all over—color—" Ramsay closed his eyes and tried to center a memory that was already growing fuzzy around the edges. Yes! "Color green—dark green. Over the suit a kind of loose-fitting vest—sleeveless—fell to about the mid-thigh—but not really a vest because it was not open in front. There was a design on the chest—looked like gems and gold—very intricate—" Only he could not remember more than the general impression of that.

"The other man—a little older—body suit, too—gray, and over it some type of jacket—but also gray—no fancy trimming except a small patch of red on the right-hand side of the chest. Both men dark skinned—but not blacks—dark hair and eyes, too—Indian?" He underlined the questioned word. "Man in gray busy with the machines, going from one to another. Feeling of excitement—as if they were very tense about something that was going to happen. Impression that this was another room in the same building or place I dreamed about before. Old man not there, though. What came through most was *their* feeling—all tense—as if a lot depended on what they were going to do.''

He did not add his last impression as he closed the book and laid it down—the impression that he had an important part in what was going to happen. Of course, that was normal. It had been *his* dream.

Ramsay snapped off the light, thumped the pillow straight, and lay down. There was a streak of moonlight reaching from the window. He lay watching it with no desire to go back to sleep now.

Perhaps he was feeding all this from his own imagination because of Greg Howell's interest. Subconsciously, he wanted to please Greg, maybe make himself important, so he dreamed. But he was sure these were not ordinary dreams. In the first place, they were like fragments of a play. He saw a bit here and a bit there—though the plot eluded him. They seemed to be in a kind of sequence, though, and the reality of the people moving through the scattered bits of action, the background, was certainly stronger than he had ever found in any dream before.

Greg had been excitied, of course, because of his project, and because Ramsay was half Iroquois. He kept talking about how an Indian had to dream up a spirit guide or something of the sort before he was considered a man. Sure, that happened in the old days. But a medicine dream, as far as Ramsay could learn through reading, was about an animal or some kind of object a man could afterward claim as a totem. This collection of strange scenes certainly could not be included under the heading of any ancestral memory.

The Dream Project at the university was new, and Greg was all wrapped up in it. They worked on dream telepathy—with a control studying a picture and the dreamers trying to pick up what he saw. But Ramsay had not been interested. After all, he had graduated and it was time he was working. There were no funds to expand the project—

If he had only *not* mentioned it to Greg when these dreams began! Ramsay grimaced at the moonlight. Now Greg was after him all the time—keep an account, try to find out what spiked them. Certainly nothing he saw on TV or read or encountered during the days had any relation to these dreams. Greg had questioned him exhaustively, and they were both convinced that that was so. Then—why did he dream? And they—the dreams—grew more vivid and real each time. He had felt in this last one as if he could reach out and tweak the coat or vest or whatever it was that the man in green had been wearing.

Ramsay was oddly restless, as if the excitement he had sensed in the two dream men were beginning to infect him also. There was no chance of getting back to sleep; he was sure of that.

He pulled out of bed and went to the window. The bit of moonlight had vanished; so had the moon. There were clouds rolling up. Ramsay shivered and glanced back over his hunched shoulder. He had an odd sensation of being watched, which intensified as the moments passed. All his imagination! This settled it! He was through trying any more experiments with Greg.

Thunder muttered low in the distance. Ramsay began to dress with a furious haste which a part of him did not understand. He could not stay in this room another minute! He looked at his wristwatch.

One o'clock. It was Greg's night to monitor at the lab. All right. He himself would go over there right now and say he was through—

As Ramsay tightened his belt, he shook his head. Why was it so necessary to talk to Greg now, at this hour of night? He must be going crazy—those dreams—Yes, maybe if he told Greg it was over, he could come back and get some reasonable sleep. He had that appointment to see the personnel manager at the Robinson place at ten tomorrow. And he was not going to blow that. Tell Greg that he was finished, come back and take an aspirin, and get a good night's sleep.

He was down the hall, realizing he was nearly running, yet unable to account for this urgency that moved him. Ramsay only knew that he must get out of the apartment, down to the lab. He found the car keys clenched in his hand, though he did not remember picking them up.

Outside, the banners of the storm were very dark across the sky. He got in the car in the parking lot, was pulling out before he forced himself to take it slow. There was no need for all this hurry. Why—

But there was! The unease inside him was growing, insisting on speed, while the unease itself was swiftly developing into a kind of fear that made him glance twice into the back of the car, almost expecting to see someone crouched there behind him, willing him to hurry.

What had happened to him? He had to see Greg—find out if this was some normal reaction to the type of intensified dreaming he had been doing. But—this was not the way to the lab! He should have turned right at Larchmont, and he was two streets past now. Now he deliberately swung left into Alloway, which would take him straight on up to the lake and the park.

He did not want to go that way—what made him—?

Fear dried his mouth. His hands were on the wheel of the car, his foot on the gas—but he did not want to go this way! Yet he could not will himself to turn, to elude the control that made him drive on and into the dark.

The storm broke, and it was a furious one. Driving rain walled him in; his headlights could not cut far through that flood. The sensible thing was to pull up and wait, but whatever possessed him now would not allow that. He could no longer see the lights of any house—or street lamp. He must be already approaching the park, and the road was climbing. Its curves were not to be negotiated in the rain, not such a rain as this.

Still, he could not stop.

The headlights picked out dimly the white paint of the railing to his left, he was above the river ravine here with a drop—

Then—

In the faint reach of his headlights a figure. Ramsay yelled involuntarily, swerved to avoid the floundering shape. The car skidded straight for the fence. There was a crash. He had a last moment of utter fear when he knew that the car was going over and down.

TWO

SCENT—THE SCENT of flowers. Ramsay was aware of that first. He might be slowly climbing some steep hill out of the darkness into a garden. Yet this scent was more concentrated, stronger than the fragrance of any garden he could remember.

He tried to remember more, then was chilled by a flash of fear as his mind sluggishly fitted together events of the immediate past. That mountain road in the dark, his skid as he fought to avoid the man caught in his rain-dimmed headlights. He must have gone over.

Flower scent—a hospital room?

Now he tried to feel some pain, some sign that he had been smashed up in a wreck. There was nothing. Again fear struck—hard! A broken spine? Complete paralysis? His acute terror at that thought made him afraid to try to move arm or leg.

As he lay, immobilized by his own dark suspicion, sound returned, as scent had earlier. Very near him, a voice spoke. But he had no understanding of the words. There was a rhythmic pattern to the flow of those sounds which was not unlike a chant.

Slowly Ramsay opened his eyes. He was lying on his back, yes. But above him was no hospital ceiling; it could not be. Arches swept up, to meet in peaks, and from the center of those peaks hung a chain with a pendant in the form of a cage of elaborate latticework holding a globe of light. Though its glow was not brillant, Ramsay blinked and blinked again.

He could catch designs in color that were painted or inlaid between the arches with a flamboyance and richness unlike anything he had seen before. The chant continued at his right.

Ramsay edged his head around, seeking the source of it. The flower scent was almost overpowering. He could see a massing of blooms near him. They must be banked against the bed on which he lay, but—why—?

Beyond that massing of flowers, someone was kneeling. Ramsay could make out only a rounded head, the suggestion of shoulders, for the figure was enshrouded by thick veiling, completely hiding it from his sight. Only hands, small dark hands, were raised to the level of his vision. Clasped between those was some object that glinted when the light reached through the encircling fingers.

He tried to understand the words the veiled figure was saying. But there was not one word that he knew. There were only sounds. What *had* happened?

Now he was determined to test the mobility of his body.

Try his right hand— To his overwhelming joy, he could raise his hands. Though it moved oddly, stiffly, as if it had lain in one position long enough to cramp a little. As he raised it, he dislodged whatever his fingers had been clasped about, and that in turn slid across his body into the bank of flowers.

The veiled figure started—went silent—pulled away from his side—stood up. The veil fluttered as one hand lifted it and revealed the face underneath.

A girl—but one he had never seen before. Yet there was something familiar about her face. If he had not seen her exactly, he had seen someone like her in cast of features, dark color of skin. In the dreams!

He was back in the dreams again. Perhaps he was actually in the hospital and unconsciousness had returned him into that series of subconscious-triggered imaginings that had grown so vivid over the weeks just past.

However, Ramsay was shaken out of his own thoughts by the expression on the face of the girl. She had eyed him first with—he supposed fear would be the best description. Now that was easing, and there was something else, though he could not read the emotion that made her eyes narrow a little, her lips press tightly together.

Her skin was smooth and delicately flushed beneath the brown. She could have been full-blooded Amerindian, except that she lacked the width of cheekbones. Rather, her face was a delicate oval, her nose high-bridged, perhaps a fraction too prominent for real beauty. But her eyes were the most remarkable of all. As Ramsay gazed straight into them, they seemed suddenly to grow larger and larger, until, in an odd way, he was aware only of them.

Then there came a delicate touch against his cheek. He realized she had lifted one hand, her fingertip sliding down to rest at the pulse point of his throat.

"Kaskar?" A single word asked as a question.

Only it was one Ramsay could not understand. This was the most vivid dream he had ever had. Could it be born from some drug, used to help his hurt body, that had this effect on intensifying his dream?

He found that he could not willingly break the gaze with which her eyes held his. She might have been probing him in some way, trying to awaken a response that she needed desperately.

Then once more he saw her frown of surprise. Whatever response he could not give had alterted her to danger. He knew that as well as if she had audibly warned him of peril. She glanced to right and left and then back to him. The finger which had sought for his pulse was now set to her lips in a gesture that he could readily understand.

She drew her veil tightly around her, though she did not hide her face, and pressed out of his range of sight in a quick movement. Because she had made him deeply aware of some peril, he obeyed her command and remained quietly where he was.

But where was he?

The ornate ceiling above him, the flowers, their scent now so strong as to make him feel rather sick— He tried to deduce what these meant. Ramsay did not remember ever being aware of smells in a dream before. While the touch of the girl's finger on his cheek and throat—somehow he could still feel it.

Where was he? What had happened?

Desperately he recalled as best as he could those final few moments before he had crashed out into the dark maw of the river gully. The rain, that figure blundering into his headlights. Both of those were clear. But no clearer than this present scent about him. Only this could not be real!

Wake up, he told himself firmly. Wake up—right now!

If this dream was drug-induced, would such tactics work? It seemed not. He was not waking; the flowers, the place remained. Would the girl come back? What had she said? Ramsay tried to shape the word correctly with his lips but not utter it aloud—

"Kaskar." Was Kaskar a person, a state of bodily being, a place? What was Kaskar?

And why should he lie here?

He brought his right hand up into his line of sight. The skin was certainly a shade or two darker than usual, and on the thumb was the wide band of a ring, a ring with an elaborate casing of what must be gold holding a dark stone-carved intaglio, as if meant to serve as a seal. There was a band of gold about the wrist also, folding in the bottom of a sleeve of a rich coppery shade—a color he had never worn in his life.

Always before in dreams he had been aware of others, but never of his own body or clothing. In those dreams he had seemed a disembodied spirit of some type, watching the action before him, but not caught in it. But this reality of the hand with its ring and wristlet was awesome.

There was a flutter of movement; he looked up quickly. The girl stood there again. Now her hand advanced to clasp his with a commanding firmness, pulling toward her. Her message was clear enough. She wanted him to get up and come with her.

Ramsay levered himself up. That stiffness that had cramped his hand and fingers seemed to have spread throughout his body. He realized he had not been resting on a bed's comparatively soft surface, but rather on a long slab as hard as stone, over which there was only a thin draping of crimson cloth. At head and foot stood candlesticks as tall as himself when he at last reached his feet, where he wavered unsteadily, clutching at the flower-rimmed slab to keep erect. Each of those sticks held a candle as thick as his forearm from which thin ropes of scented smoke coiled lazily.

Again the girl tugged at his hand, urging him away from the slab—back into the shadowy space beyond the reach of either overhead lamp or candles. He was startled to see four men, their backs to him, one at each corner of the place where he had lain. Their heads were bowed, their hands clasped upon the hilts of swords which rested, bared point, on the pavement.

None of them stirred as Ramsay lurched forward in obedience to the girl's guidance. As he passed the nearest man, he could see that, though the man's eyes were fully open, he stared only at the sword hilt in his hands with a curious fixed intensity. Yet this was no statue, but a living man. Ramsay could see the rise and fall of his chest as he breathed.

Their complete stillness, the fact that they were ignoring any movement made by Ramsay and the girl, did not strike him as peculiar. After all—this was a dream. And in a dream one expects the unusual. What bothered him was the continued feeling that this whole episode was far too vividly detailed. His dreams of the past few months had never equaled this.

All four of the men, Ramsay noted, were dressed much like those he had seen in the lab scene, with form-fitting undersuits and loose vest jackets coming to mid-thigh. Their undersuits were a dull black, the overvests gray with a large device of red stitchery spread almost completely across the chest. He looked down at his own body to find it clothed in a similiar fashion but with other colors.

The undersuit, which appeared to have all the elasticity of a finely knitted garment, was the coppery color. His vest, a deep gold with a red breast device, was embellished by what could only be small gems sewn into a highly intricate piece of embroidery. On his feet were smooth, soft boots, ankle high and of the same coppery shade.

The girl had drawn her veil back over her face, and now only the hand that gripped his so tightly was still in evidence. Like his own, her thumb was encircled by a massive ring bearing a blue engraved stone. But she wore two other rings as well. One on the forefinger was formed as an odd mask of a horned creature in gold, the eyes green gems; the other, a wide band around her little finger, had a deeply incised design which Ramsay could not distinguish. Otherwise, she was only a moving shadow among other shadows as they drew farther away from the light around the slab on which he had awakened.

They passed pillars, which he could only half see in the gloom, to approach a wall covered with stone panels carved with figures he could not clearly distinguish. The girl went to the middle one of these and thrust the fingers of her other hand into a deeper portion of that carving. Perhaps she released some fastening, for under her touch the tall length of the panel swung outward like any other ordinary door. Thus they came to a narrow flight of stairs lighted by a globe at the top.

There was a hallway at the head which the globe more fully illuminated. It ended in a door resembling those Ramsay had always known. This his guide pushed open, that they might enter a chamber far more clearly lighted than the scene in which he had awakened.

His interest won over his conviction that this was some drug-induced dream. Instead of any uneasiness, he felt an avid and growing curiosity about what would happen next. As the girl dropped his hand, left him standing just within the chamber, he stared about him.

There were some features of the room he found familiar. These had appeared in early dreams, such as those that had been dominated by an elderly man wearing a long black-and-white robe.

The walls were paneled, covered here and there by long strips of what must be embroidery. The subjects were plainly fanciful, with oddly shaped and improbably colored vegetation and beasts which were not of the world Ramsay knew. There was a fireplace with a large hearth on which crackled a fire that did not a quarter fill its black cavern. Flanking that stood two long seats covered with a stiff cream-white cloth on which was sprinkled a glitter of gold dusting.

A long table with carved legs stood between him and the fireplace. On that was a medley of things, including bronzed candlesticks, goblets, a plate with what he thought were apples, though they were very large, and the like.

Except for the long seats, there appeared to be no chairs. However, here and there were piles of large square cushions made of different materials in colors that blended subtly. The light came from four of the suspended globes in their filigree containers.

The girl had gone to the nearest of the long seats. Now she lifted the veil that cloaked her so thickly from head to foot. She drew it up from her feet and shoulders and tossed it across the end of the divan before she turned to face Ramsay straightly.

Her dress was akin to his own clothing, except that her overvest was near ankle length. It was split on either side, so that when she moved one could see, more than thigh high, those limbs covered by the lighter, clinging undergarment. The color she had

chosen was a rich green-blue, near the shade of the
gem in her thumb ring, in startling contrast to the
cloak veil she had shed, which was an ashy gray.

The embroidery on her breast was in silver, the
design being far simpler than that which he himself
wore. It showed only the head of a cat, the eyes of
which were yellow gems, perhaps as large as his own
thumbnail, having a bar of light across the surfaces,
as if they were indeed the living eyes of the creature
they represented.

Her hair was thick and black, cut short and kept
sleekly in place by a silver band that held another
smaller cat's head just above and between her eyes. It
was an outré dress, but it became her. And there was
about her an aura of presence, as if she had been used
to giving orders all her life and having them unques-
tioningly obeyed.

She was still watching him with that searching,
measuring look, which was a reflection of the gaze
she had turned upon him when he had first seen her,
when there came a faint rapping sound. Without
turning her head, the girl spoke. Her voice carrying,
Ramsay was sure, the inflection of a question.

She was answered by a voice which came more
faintly. At that she spoke again and, to Ramsay's
right, a second door opened to admit another woman. Though she wore clothing not too different
from the girl's, it was plainer and of a dullish russet
brown. The cat's head was repeated on the tunic vest,
only in a much smaller size and lacing the gemmed
eyes. Her face was plump and broad of feature, her
short hair coarse, having only a russet ribbon to
control it.

She halted just within the door which she had
closed behind her—her attention on Ramsay. Her

generous mouth fell open in the most exaggerated expression of surprise he had ever encountered. For a long moment she simply stared. Then the girl spoke, swiftly, her words sliding into one another, so that Ramsay could no longer separate one strange sound from the next.

As she talked, the woman's gaze shifted from Ramsay to the girl, then back again, her first complete astonishment fading as the girl continued. Then the girl looked once more at Ramsay.

Slowly, as if determined to make him understand, she touched the cat's head on her breast with a ringed forefinger.

"Thecla," she pronounced. That must be her name. She was waiting now for some response from him. Was he Ramsay Kimble in this dream? But, of course, who else could he be—no matter how he was dressed or how bizzare the circumstances surrounding this encounter.

In turn, he pointed to himself. "Ramsay Kimble," he replied.

Again, the older woman displayed confusion. She shook her head violently and spoke that same word the girl had used earlier:

"Kaskar!"

It was if she were trying to deny the identity he had claimed, and force upon him another.

"Ramsay Kimble!" he returned, more loudly, and with all the emphasis he could center on those two words.

Thecla made a gesture that Ramsay read as urging the woman to understand him. Then she pointed at her companion and said: "Grishilda."

Though such manners were not of his own world and he was a little surprised himself at his instinctive response, Ramsay inclined his head in a slight bow and repeated: "Grishilda."

The one he addressed came closer. Her survey of him from head to toe and back again was both searching and slow. Then she shook her head, threw up both hands.

"Kaskar!"

Thecla smiled, the first time he had seen her expression lose all tenseness. It was as if the reaction of Grishilda were in some way amusing.

However, Grishilda herself broke into rapid speech, her air that of one raining questions, without pausing for a breath to catch any answer. Again the girl gestured—this time raising her hand palm up as if to urge silence. She spoke a single sentence. Grishilda gave a quick nod and hurried toward the door where she had entered. There she tugged a small bar into place, effectively locking it.

Thecla beckoned to Ramsay, bringing him to join her on the long seat by the fireplace. What followed was a language lesson. First, she pointed to the objects in the room, repeating words which he echoed as best he could, though she often corrected his pronunciation. There was about her an air of urgency, as if they must learn how to communicate as quickly as possible for some reason. And he caught her uneasiness.

A long dream, he thought fleetingly. And the most consecutive as to action he had ever had. This very strangeness gripped his complete concentration, and he gave himself to following Thecla's lead as best he might.

Ramsay did not know how long they sat there, repeating words. He was more tired than he had realized when Grishilda broke in upon their study session, bearing a tray on which she had two brimming goblets, small squares of what looked like a yellowish bread, as well as one of the huge apples sliced into several portions.

The drink was, Ramsay decided, some kind of unfermented fruit juice. The squares were slightly sweetened, more than the bread he knew, but less than the cake of his waking world. The firm-fleshed apples were the most refreshing of all.

They ate and drank. Thecla stretchd wide her arms and made a comment to Grishilda. Then she touched his own hand lightly.

"Sleep—Sleep—" She repeated the word she had pantomimed some time before with closed eyes and her head resting on one palm.

Ramsay almost laughed. Sleep, was it? He was asleep—and dreaming. Could you sleep within a dream? Apparently Thecla believed that you could. But, of course, she was a character in his dream, not in the least real.

He nodded to show he understood. She motioned to Grishilda.

"Grishilda—take—sleep—"

The russet-clad woman nodded emphatically and beckoned. She did not lead him to the door she had so cautiously barred, but back to the passage through which they had come from the place where he had "awakened" (if one could awake into a dream). Ramsay wondered if he was now to be returned to the flower-encircled slab and the four unseeing watchers.

However, Grishilda turned left, pressed open another panel, and so brought him into a small room in which there was a bed, not unlike a stripped-down cot, with only a single covering folded at its foot.

Here was no window, but a slit high in the wall, through which, apparently, some air found its way, for the room was not too musty.

Through the slit came now a sliver of daylight, enough so that, when Grishilda abruptly left him, Ramsay could see to slip out of the stiffly fashioned vest-coat. Then he lay down on the cot, dragging the cover up over him.

Oddly enough, he did feel sleepy. But he did not yield to that. There was too much to think about. And since he no longer had the stimulation of Thecla's language lessons, his self-erected barrier against doubt began to melt away.

He knew enough of Greg's research—had listened to tapes and seen dream telephathy in action—to realize that this adventure of his was certainly unique. But to believe, to accept it as real was a step he shrank from. There was too much that could not be explained in any logical fashion.

Now Ramsay began to reconsider every small detail of what he had seen since he had first opened his eyes. That slab on which he had lain, with the tall candles and the seemingly entranced guardsmen— the whole scene haunted him somehow. He had seen its likes before. Not in any dream, no— Had it been on TV, in a film? Not in real life, no.

Ramsay began a methodical memory search for the answer. Perhaps if he could identify one small bit of this whole episode, he could unravel it all. Where *had* he seen such before?

A picture— It must have been a picture. All right. What picture? When and where? He tried to visualize a book, turning the pages, looking for that all-important illustration. No use. That did not work.

Maybe it had not been in a book, but a magazine.

Now his memory picture produced larger pages, began to turn them as he searched. Yes!

Ramsay sat up on the cot. He had remembered!

That—that had been a bier, the kind a king or some royalty personage would lie on in state. Guardsmen at the four corners, the candles. A little different from the picture he could now recall, but enough like it to make him sure he had hit upon the truth.

That meant—he was dead!

But he wasn't! He was sitting right here. Anyway, in his own waking world, Ramsay Kimble would never have been laid out in state with guardsmen and those candles, with a strange girl like Thecla coming to mourn him. He might have been in a funeral home—in a casket—yes. But not with all those trimmings.

However, he could not rid himself of the idea that that had been the way that a dead man might be treated. And this Kaskar—he knew now from Thecla's tutoring that Kaskar was a proper name. Kaskar was the man she had expected to find lying on that bier—a dead Kaskar.

He was not Kaskar! He was Ramsay Kimble, a perfectly normal American who had gotten mixed up beyond his depth in a screwy research project of some sort and was now having hallucinations. Yet he had never been involved in the drug scene. If some dude wanted to blow his brains clear out of his skull, popping uppers, downers, all the rest was just the way to do it the quickest. No, he was not on drugs, and he had been all laid out for a funeral—

Ramsay drew a deep breath and tried to control hands that were suddenly shaking. This was the time to wake up. And the sooner the better. Let go, dream, let go!

THREE

BUT THE NIGHTMARE part was that Ramsay could not wake up!

The small, dim room remained as clear as ever. He pinched his own arm viciously. That hurt—but he did not wake. Fear dried his mouth, made him gasp for breath. He was fast caught in his hallucination!

"Don't panic now!" He said the words aloud, as if the very sound of them in his ears could somehow calm him. He had to get hold of himself, rationalize in some way what was happening.

But there was no way to rationalize all this!

Ramsay looked about him, at those solid walls, at the slit through which a scrap of daylight reached him. He stood up and jerked at the cot bed, bringing it as close to the wall under that slit as it could be moved. Then he mounted on it, tried to see out. He could sight another wall some distance away that was bathed in sunlight. But there was nothing else to be seen, except an ordinary-looking strip of blue sky.

A suspicion possessed him, and he went to try the door. But Grishilda had not locked it. He was able to peer out into the narrow corridor. There, at the end, were the steps leading down to where Thecla had found him. In the other direction, nearly within his arm's reach now, was the door to the chamber where he had been with her. However, he had a strong feeling that to prowl about on his own would be dangerous.

He had to do something! If he just sat and thought—he'd go completely crazy! He had to *know* where he was and how he got here. For somehow the reality of his surroundings had impressed themselves on his mind. If this was not a dream, then something completely beyond understanding had occured. They had to *tell* him!

Ramsay took a hasty step toward the door to Thecla's chamber. But he did not raise his hand to the latch. Thecla had definitely dismissed him. Until he knew more, he would abide by the rules she had apparently set. And to know more he must be able to communicate.

He returned to the cot and relaxed on it. Now he began to mumble the words she had impressed upon him, summoning with each a mental picture of explanation. He knew the names of each piece of furniture in that chamber, and the words for simple action, but he needed more vocabulary. And, against his will, he was growing tired now. Suppose he did sleep— would he then dream himself back into the normal world?

That was the last thought of his waking, but his sleep was dreamless, or else he did not remember what dreams he had had when he awoke to a slight shaking and opened his eyes to see Grishilda bending over him.

"Come—" She shaped the word with extravagant lip movements, as if to make her order perfectly clear.

Still sleep-dazed, Ramsay sat up. The woman had looped over her arm the richly embroidered vest-coat he had discarded, and she was watching him impatiently.

They went back once more into the chamber where the girl had taught him words, but there was no sign of Thecla. The older woman did not linger there, but beckoned him on into a second room.

Here the walls were tiled with shining pale-green blocks through which was a drifting of silvery motes. And in the center of the chamber a tub, like a small pool, had been sunk. It was now filled with water, and he caught a pine-like scent.

On a bench at one side lay a pile of what could be only towels. And the other appointments of a bathroom were enough akin to those of his real world that he was able to recognize them at once.

"Wash—" Grishilda waved a hand toward the waiting bath. Then she pointed to a pile of fresh clothing at the other end of the bench from the towels. "Clothes—on." She made gestures of dressing.

But how did one get out of this skintight underclothing? Ramsay could see no form of opening at all. He pulled it a little away from his throat, and it snapped promptly back. Then he heard a sound that could only be laughter.

Grishilda, her mouth stretched in a wide grin, advanced on him. Her hand reached to his right shoulder, pressed there for an instant, and there was an even splitting of the fabric, peeling open across his chest.

"So—" she said, and guided his own fingers to a button-like spot imbedded in the fabric. Then she turned briskly and left him to it.

Ramsay had peeled off the undersuit before he was aware of the long mirror panel. But he caught a glimpse of his movements in it and, once stripped, went deliberately to stand before it. Even though he had somehow known that he would not look exactly like himself, what he saw there was a shock.

His features were the same, but he missed the small scar along his cheekbone that had marked his encounter with a wooden splinter the summer he had worked with the logging crew. His hair was brushed back and fairly short in front, down to his neck in back. And he wore around it a broad band of what could only be gold, set with red stones. Also—his ears—he had on stud earrings of large red stones.

There was no trace of beard on his face; in fact, he had very little hair anywhere on his body. And across his chest was a red pattern, a tatoo, his rubbing finger advised him, in the form of a fierce-looking bird, perhaps an eagle or hawk, its beak half open, its wings mantling.

So—this was Kaskar! The dead Kaskar, except that he was Ramsay and he wasn't dead in the least.

He pulled off the headband, detached the earrings. But he couldn't wipe away the bird which was a part of his very skin. For the rest, he thought he looked much as he always had.

But he wanted to know—he *had* to know!

Ramsay lowered his body into the water. There was a bowl of some solid green substance—reminding him of jade—and in this was a soft cream that gave off the pine scent. He scooped out a generous fingerful, and when the water touched it foam appeared. Soap! So equipped, he proceeded to luxuriate in the largest bath he had ever seen.

As the water cooled, he came out and rubbed dry with the waiting towels. Then he investigated the pile of clothing. These pieces were different in texture and embellishment from those he had discarded, being far less rich.

The undersuit he fumbled his way into and sealed via shoulder button was the same dull russet shade as that of Grishilda's over-robe. And the vest-coat that went over it was green, with no elaborate spread of thread and gem across the chest. Rather there was only a small patch of a silver cat's head near the shoulder to the right. It was shorter, too, than his golden tunic had been, by at least three inches.

He made no move to pick up either the headband or the earrings he had shed. And he was standing before the mirror, sleeking down his hair with his hands, since a brush was one appointment he had not found, when Grishilda came back. This time Thecla accompanied her.

The girl was dressed much as he had seen her the night before, but her expression was less serene. She came directly to him, surveying him from head to foot, as if there were something very important in the appearance he made.

"Trouble—" she said. "You—go—with Grishilda—go to Kilsyth. They hunt for Kaskar— find"—she shook her head vehemently—"find— kill!" She repeated that word, stabbing a pointed finger at his breast as if that were a knife. "Ochall— angry—hung—you must go."

Before Ramsay could either protest or question, her hands on his shoulders pushed him back and down on the bench. Grishilda rustled forward, a box open in her hands. She held it ready, and Thecla frowned at the contents, which appeared to be a selection of tubes and jars.

The girl selected one of the tubes and uncapped it. Inside was a thick pencil-like projection. She took

Ramsay's chin in a firm hold, turning his face more to the light, and with swift strokes marked his brows with the pencil. With another tube she dabbed along the line of his hair, and finally smoothed his face with a cream. Then she gestured him toward the mirror.

She had not made any great changes with her cosmetics, but the effect startled him for the second time. His skin was much darker in shade, his brows thicker, nearly meeting above his nose. His forehead was lower, and somehow his whole face was coarser, appeared older.

"Good, good!" Grishilda complimented the girl on the effect.

But Thecla shrugged. "Little," she said, "But all one can do. Listen!" She caught Ramsay by the sleeve, drew him away from the mirror. "You must go—with Grishilda. At Kilsyth safe—there I come. You learn speak—Grishilda teach. Must not be taken by Ochall—or"—she hesitated—"others. We plan—you do. Eat—go—" She made shooing motions with her hands.

Ramsay wanted to protest. But her uneasiness was so manifest that he knew he would have to trust her. For she was able to convey to him not by her scattered words but rather by some reaching of emotion that she was in deadly earnest. There was a direct danger to him here, and her plan was his only hope.

He ate hurriedly of food from a tray in the outer chamber. While he chewed and swallowed, Thecla walked up and down, talking to the older woman. Perhaps she was giving orders, but she spoke so fast Ramsay was not able to catch more than a word or two. Twice Grishilda seemed to raise a protest but was straightway overruled.

At length the older woman pulled a cloak around

her shoulders and signed for Ramsay to put on another. Then she pointed to him and a small chest sitting on the floor. It had a rope handle on its top, and he understood that he was to carry it.

"You"—Thecla once more addressed him directly—"Grishilda's man—servant. She goes to Kilsyth—safe there."

"Thank you," Ramsay said, "but why—"

"Do I do this?" She completed the sentence for him swiftly. "You know later. Learn—speak—then we talk, I tell you. You stay here—Ochall—others find—like Kaskar—you then be dead."

That she thought her fears were based on truth he was certain. And he could not produce any protest she might heed or understand. Better go along with this, at least for now, until he could learn enough of their language to find out just what was going on, where he was, and perhaps even why.

He was turning away, having picked up the chest in his right hand, when Thecla caught his left, holding it tightly between both of hers. Ramsay was startled, even more than when he had seen the changes they had made in him reflected in the mirror. For there actually seemed to be a kind of energy flow that spread from those two palms clasping his fingers so tightly, passing into his own hand and arm.

Nor was that contact a physical sensation alone, for, at the same time, there built up in his mind a need for haste and caution, a warning of danger, the suggestion that he must follow any leads Grishilda might give him or else be betrayed in some way to an unexplained but very real peril.

"All right," Ramsay said in answer to that mental warning. "I will do as you say." Some of his answer was in her tongue, some in his.

She nodded vigorously and dropped his hand, breaking the communication, so odd because he never had known it before. He wished that she had continued, if only for a short space. Perhaps so he could have learned more— But he guessed that now haste was imperative, and he turned obediently after the woman out of the door Grishilda had fastened so carefully at their first meeting.

They came into a wide corridor, carpeted and paneled, with globe lights at regular intervals along its length. Grishilda walked fast, suggesting with a gesture that he keep behind her, the proper attitude, he suspected, for the servant role he was now playing.

Twice they passed others, both times men wearing a shorter vest-coat resembling his own. But those tunics were yellow and the small badges on them the red hawk or eagle which he bore concealed on his skin. Each of the men glanced at Grishilda but neither spoke. And Ramsay thought they did not really see him at all, as if a servant were beneath any curious notice.

The hall gave upon a wide stairway, beneath that a broader corridor. At the door at the end of that stood two guards whose clothing matched that of those who had been beside the bier. One stepped forward as if to question them. But Grishilda held up her hand imperiously. Grasped in her fingers was a square of silver bearing the outline of a cat's head, this one also with jeweled eyes. The guard drew back, leaving their way open.

The other guard opened the door and Grishilda sailed on, Ramsay in her wake. They were outside in growing dusk now, though still within the confines of whatever building this was. Three of the barriers

surrounding them were formed by five-story struc-
tures; the fourth was merely wall. However, sitting
within a few strides of the door was a vehicle unlike
any in Ramsay's experience. It had a passenger compartment perched on three stilt-like legs, from which
a mounting ladder hung. Grishilda hurried to that,
and Ramsay, in his role of servant, had wit enough to
step out faster, be there in time to assist her up the
steps.

Once inside, they found seats and Grishilda buckled a wide belt around her, Ramsay following her
example. Only a portion of the space apparently was
for passengers, and he deduced that there must be a
separate section which sheltered the pilot or driver.

Then he grabbed at the edge of the seat and gulped,
for the vehicle rose straight up with a lurch that
unsettled his stomach. Grishilda showed no surprise;
in fact, when she eyed him, her preoccupied, worried
look vanished for a second or two, and she smiled.

Leaning forward a little, her ample middle com-
pressed by the belt, she said: "We fly—"

However, this was unlike any plane of his own
world. He had not noted any blades aloft such as a
helicopter possessed, nor were there, to his recollec-
tion, any visible wings. And they had not taxied for a
normal takeoff. There would not have been room
enough for one in that courtyard.

Only they *were* flying, and when he pressed closer
to the window panel at his right, he could see a blaze
of lights spread beneath. There was no doubt that
they had taken off across a city of no mean size.

Without a watch, Ramsay had no way of judging
time, but it was not too long a trip until they set down,
with some of the same speed as they had been airborne. Grishilda freed herself from her seat belt, and,
as the door in the side of the cabin opened automat-

ically, the ladder slipped out. Ramsay descended, set the chest on the pavement, and turned to aid her.

They were only two in a crowd of passengers arriving in such small flyers. The people as they alighted swarmed on toward a large building, and Grishilda set off in the same direction. Ramsay followed, trying not to be noticed as he glanced quickly right and left at those about him. The clothing seemed standard in general, the only differences being in the length of the vest-coats. Those worn by women varied in length from below the knee to level with the ankle, and were all slit up the side to the thigh. The ones worn by the men were as short as his own (and those were the soberest, less ornate kind) or as long as the one he had worn as Kaskar. There was a show of rich embroidery and some gems on the longer tunics. The wearers of these usually had one or two attendants in shorter tunics. Earrings were visible, but the headbands were plain and much narrower than the one he had worn, being fashioned of thread-worked strips of cloth rather than precious metal.

When they came to the building, Grishilda waited for him to draw level with her.

"Go through," she told him. Ready again in her hands was the same silver plate she had shown to the door guard. Now she wove a path through the crowd until they reached a latticed gate. Beyond that were a series of capsule-like objects, strung together bead fashion. Doors in their sides gave access to an interior where four travelers might sit.

Grishilda showed her plaque to the gateman. He studied it, then reached behind him and pulled a length of chain. Within a moment or two a man in a matching uniform came running. He in turn eyed Grishilda's passport, if that was what it was, and then bowed his head, said something in a low voice, and led the way down the line of bullet-shaped carriages to one which he opened with a flourish, waiting only until they were inside to close the door firmly.

Ramsay's companion dropped her cloak with an audible sigh.

"Good. Safe here. Alone—no one else—"

There were four seats, half reclining. She selected one, seated herself, and again adjusted a seat belt, waving him to the one beside her. But Grishilda was not relaxing for any trip. Instead, she was about to fulfill Thecla's command that she teach their tongue to this pseudo-serving man.

And Grishilda had the firmness of one who knew well her duty and had no intention of shirking it. Ramsay found himself already at work before the car in which he sat began to vibrate, and he believed they were on their way. There were no windows to give glimpses of the country and perhaps so distract him from his lessons. And the woman worked hard.

She not only pursued the method of pointing and naming some object, but she produced from the chest a series of pages loosely ringed together at one corner. Whether this passed as a book Ramsay could not tell—but he concentrated on learning with almost the same fervor as she did on teaching. Perhaps if he could learn enough to understand, he could also discover the nature of this strange—dream? Somehow he was not so sure that it was a dream. Though he could not imagine what else held him.

His mouth was dry from repeating words, though his vocabulary had greatly expanded, when Grishilda turned to press a button on the wall near her hand.

"We shall eat," she told him, "drink. This is tiring—to teach one from the beginning."

Within moments, the wall of the compartment before them opened in two narrow slots and covered trays slid forward to rest upon a shelf which then bore them within reach. Ramsay snapped up the cover of his and found, in sections, a square of the yellowish cake bread, something that appeared to be dried fruit (slightly shriveled pears and peaches), and a larger portion of thick stew. In addition, there was a tube from which Grishilda skillfully twisted the top, demonstrating how this was done. Inside that a dark liquid sloshed.

Ramsay spooned up the stew. It had an odd flavor which was not altogether to his liking, but he was hungry and this was food. The drink was tart, he thought perhaps some form of fruit juice. He ate and drank with a will, though Grishilda named all the dishes and made him repeat those after her, shaking her head at times, as she had all through her lessons, at his faltering attempts to give just the right accent to some syllables.

Though he might not be able as yet to please his instructress's ear when it came to accent, Ramsay was learning. He could understand, if she spoke slowly enough, longer and more complicated sentences. They had finished the meal and pushed the tray shelves back into the wall before he took the initiative with a question:

"Where are we going?"

"To Kilsyth, the place of my lady when she wishes to be private, away from all. It is over the border, out of Ulad."

"We are in Ulad?"

"Yes. We go now to Olyroun, which is my lady's own country. Though they plan to take it from her." There was a bitterness in her tone.

"Who does so?"

"Those of Ulad. They wish a hand-fasting with the heir to Ulad. My lady likes it not. But if she goes by her own wishes, then Ulad will seize power and Olyroun will be swallowed up. If she hand-fasts, then perhaps she still can hold rule, see that her people are not just servants to the Empire."

"This heir to whom she must be hand-fasted— who is he?"

"He is—was Kaskar."

"But—" Ramsay digested that. "Kaskar was—is dead."

"I know not the inner plan of this," Grishilda said frankly. "I can tell you only what my lady has said, what I have seen with these two eyes of mine. When we came unwillingly to Lom, where rules the Emperor, my lady went to wait upon the old Empress. Her Splendor Enthroned Quendrida told my lady some secret which lightened her heart. When she came back to me, she said there was naught for us to fear, she would never be forced to accept Kaskar.

"Shortly thereafter came the news that he was dead, quickly through some failure of his heart. Then they bore him into the Resting Place of Kings for a space, before they would set him in the tomb of his House. My lady is not an Enlightened One, for she could not leave her country and go into a Grove, setting aside all things of this world. She had a duty first to her House and her people. But the Way of the Enlightened Ones has already beckoned to her, and a little of their knowledge has been given her.

"Thus, hearing that Kaskar was dead, she went to petition that he not be weighed too harshly at the Final Gate, and that perhaps mercy would temper justice when he stood there. Then she found— you—"

"I am not Kaskar."

"So my lady swore. And because she possesses the Knowledge, I do believe her. Also, there was a great outcry when the bier was found empty and the guards enspelled— But that—" She smiled. "That last was my lady's doing. How else could she have gotten you away? I do not know your secret, but she does. Now she says that you are in danger. Not only does Ochall seek you, but there are others of nearly as great power who wish Kaskar dead as much as Ochall wishes him alive."

"And who is Ochall?"

She stared at him for a long moment before she answered. "Stranger, I do not know what you are, or whence you have come. But my lady has given me assurance concerning you and has said that what you ask of me that I *can* answer I should. But if you know not of Ochall, the Will of Iron, the Heart of Stone, that is hard to believe.

"He is High Chancellor of Ulad and, since the Emperor has ailed in mind and body for some years, he is all-powerful. Kaskar was his thing to be ruled, not his Prince to have rule. All well knew that when the breath at last left the Emperor, then Ochall would command, behind the screen of Kaskar, a will-less prince who was his creature. Now, Ochall believes that the Prince perhaps did not die in truth, but lay drugged and has been taken away by those who have good reason to want him kept from the throne. But the High Chancellor has no proof. And those others, those perhaps who have the most to gain by Kaskar's death—my lady fears that they mean to make his death a true fact—to be able to show a body to the people."

"But I am *not* Kaskar!" Ramsay repeated. "And how did I get here?"

Grishilda shook her head. "I do not know. Though

perhaps my lady does. But such information must be part of that secret that the old Empress entrusted to her. When my lady comes to Kilsyth, she can answer your questions, the ones I do not understand. It is true that you are not Kaskar. For now a different person looks from his eyes, speaks with his tongue. That this is true—it is a thing to marvel at. But because you look like Kaskar, you walk in danger until this matter is righted. That is why my lady sends you to Kilsyth, where you may lie in safety until she comes."

Ramsay shook his head. This was unbelievable—without logic, the deepest sort of hallucination. Yet it was plain Grishilda believed that what she said was the entire truth as she knew it. And he must learn from her all that he might, hoping to stumble on the reality behind this wild experience.

FOUR

THE VIBRATION CEASED as if the train (if that was what one might call their present vehicle) had halted. Grishilda put a hand within one of the slits of her overvest and once more produced the silver plaque with the cat's head.

"We are at the border," she said. "This, my lady's own token, will take us through without question. But"—she turned her head and pointed to one of the seats behind her—"since you play the liege man, play it well, wait humbly on me who am First Companion to my lady."

Ramsay got her point and quickly changed to the seat behind his supposed employer. He hoped no one would ask him any questions that would make his tumbling tongue betray him.

The door through which they had entered slid aside. A man wearing a tight cap that was nearer to a hood, bearing a cat badge on its front, looked in. Grishilda said nothing, merely held up the plaque. The intruder blinked and then bowed his head, and the door slid shut again.

"Good!" That word exploded from Ramsay's companion, as if she had been holding her breath to expel it. Maybe she had not been as confident as she had claimed to be. But Ramsay waited until the train was in motion again before he rejoined her at the front of the car.

"Do we go far?" he asked.

"Not so. Shortly, we shall reach Matering which serves the Hill Province as a station. There will be one waiting for us there. Kilsyth was once a hunting lodge, before my lady came to rule. Those of the Groves do not kill; they maintain life. Thus, there are hunters no longer at Kilsyth, only those who are protecting the life of the Vorst Forest, not draining its strength. Now—" She pursed her lips, and there was a small frown crease between her eyes. "Listen well, man who is not Kaskar. You cannot play the servant at Kilsyth, for those who live at the lodge would speedily know that you were not one of them. Thus my lady has used her wits and thought of yet another role for you. But you must understand and be able to act it well. You are now Arluth, and you come from Tolcarne—which is overseas.

"Those of Tolcarne follow the old ways, and House battles House in deadly feud. It is a wild country, and blood spills easily there. As Arluth, you are of my lady's blood, but four generations separated from her House. And you are the heir remaining, whose life must be protected lest your House die and there be no male left to stand before the Heart of the House on High Days. You lie under blood ban of a mighty feud and so have come into hiding with the welcome of my lady. Do you understand?"

Wilder and wilder, mused Ramsay. Though what Grishilda said was easy enough to grasp.

"Yes. I am Arluth and am in hiding because I have enemies from some feud."

"Thus," Grishilda swept on, "you will be at Kilsyth, and our men there will have excellent reason to beware of any stranger who might come seeking you. They will believe him either a blood enemy from Tolcarne or else a bought killer hired by such. So, if any of Ulad suspect and send after us, their coming will be known. You will have good excuse to keep indoors—in the Red King's chambers to which there is only one door, since Guron the Red had good reason to fear a killer himself. As soon as my lady can, she will come to us with what she has learned."

The plan sounded very neat and logical, if anything in this maze that had caught him could be termed that. He was to lie low in this Kilsyth place, guarded by men who would believe that a hired gun was out to get him, and wait out the coming of some explanation.

What secret had this old Empress confided to Thecla that might even begin to explain what had happened to one Ramsay Kimble? He used to think he had a vivid imagination, but he could not now summon any idea of his own to mind. There was nothing to do but drift with the tide of events until he had some fact he could seize and work from.

It was morning when they alighted from the bullet car. Ramsay could see nothing that might suggest an engine or motive power. And the series of bead-like passenger vehicles ran not on wheels but rather slipped along a groove in the ground, which took the place of the rails of his own world.

The roofs of a town rose beyond. Pulled up to the platform where they had detrained was a small wagon to which was hitched—Ramsay took a closer look. They were not a team of horses, but large wapiti, elks of his own world! There were two in harness side by side, and a third to the fore as a leader. A man sat on the high seat holding the reins of the beasts, which were snorting and tossing their antlered heads as if they had little liking for the proximity of the train. But it was already gliding on.

Ramsay picked up the chest by its woven handle and followed Grishilda, who was heading for the elk-drawn wagon. He helped her aboard onto a padded seat and sat down beside her. The driver, having noted they were in place, loosened the reins, and the elk frisked off at a smart pace.

They did not turn into the road leading to the town, but rather paralleled the groove of the train track on an unpaved lane. Ahead, to the right, Ramsay could see the dark smudge of what was certainly a forest, though there were fenced fields now bordering the way, and ripening crops in the fields.

The train track curved away from them. Now, on the left, was scrub land covered with a thin growth of bushes and brush, with here and there a tree in advance of a distant wood. The wapiti had fallen into a steady trot, but the wagon seemed to have little in the way of springs. Its passengers were jostled back and forth on the bench until they both took firm grip of its edge and tried to hold stiff against each bump and lurch.

The lane itself was growing narrower, assuming the look of a couple of well-worn ruts rather than a real road. They left the last of the fields behind, and came into the fringe of the forest.

Here they trundled over drifts of long-dead leaves, and there was the smell of growing things. Ramsay thought he could identify pine scent, and he was sure he saw maple, oak and birch trees. The wapiti of the team were larger and heavier than any he knew of in his own world, but the trees and vegetation appeared very similar. He could *not* have drawn this all from his imagination, no matter how deeply his so-called subconscious might be mining memories to reinforce any dream.

They were out of the sun into a greenish gloom. At first Ramsay was glad to have drawn away from the heat. Then he became aware of a subtle oppression, a blight upon his spirit, as if the woods about them rejected his kind. Birds called and could be seen in flight among the trees. And there were chattering squirrels giving audible voice to their annoyance of this intrusion. But there was something else—old, formidable—

Ramsay shook his head to deny his own fancy. He had said nothing to Grishilda since they had left the station. In fact, he was less aware of her presence now than he was of his own rising uneasiness.

As the track curved to the right, they penetrated deeper into the green gloom, which he liked less and less. He had had few experiences of any life in the wild, only his logging venture and a couple of camping trips in well-supervised national parks. There he had never sensed this watching—waiting—

Suddenly he caught sight of a monolithic pillar of red stone standing like an upright spear amid the green. He could not believe that that was some freak of nature. As he turned to ask Grishilda about it, he saw her hand loosen hold on the seat, rise quickly breast high, while her fingers and thumb curled into a fist, except her forefinger and little finger which she pointed at the rock. And she was muttering some words he could not catch.

"What is that?"

Her frown grew stronger. "It is of the First Ones—back there—hidden—is one of their Power Places. We do not go there. Nor do we talk of them."

The look she shot him was forbidding.

Obediently he held his tongue. If he was to be Arluth, he had better follow any local customs. And he wondered how much longer they were going to bump through this wilderness. His arm ached from trying to keep his place on the seat, and he was tired—

Yet the journey seemed to be endless. Once or twice the wagon pulled to a stop, allowing the team to blow and paw for a period of rest. But their driver never addressed any words to his passengers, and Grishilda was as silent. Ramsay was afraid to speak, lest his unfamiliarity with the language betray him to the stranger holding the reins.

Finally there was a break in the green wall. The wapiti plunged out into a sunlit space, bellowing as if glad to see the end of their journey.

Here a low house and outbuildings filled at least three-quarters of a glade. The walls were of the same red stone as the pillar Ramsay had seen in the woods, but this was a dwelling with narrow latticed windows and a plank door with huge hinges and latch. The roof was slated, and on the slates around the eaves was a green of velvety growth.

The wagon pulled to a halt before the door, which opened before they had climbed down from the wagon. A woman stood there. The sleeves of her underclothing were rolled well up, and a belt about her overtunic had pulled up those skirts also, as if to free her body for some labor. She was thick of body, short, and her face broad, with a flattened nose, so unlike Thecla in feature that she might have been of another race, though her skin was the same even brown. Her hair was black, but she did not wear it short as did both Thecla and Grishilda. It was braided, and the braid was wound about her head, with a couple of burnished copper pins, their heads carrying small drops of the same metal, that both anchored and ornamented.

She made a low bow to Grishilda and then looked uncertainly at Ramsay. Grishilda spoke a couple of sentences which Ramsay did not understand at all, and now the woman acknowledged him with the same gesture of deference.

"This is Emeka, wife to the head forester, also the keeper of the lodge. And she is a woman of Zagova, so she does not speak our tongue except brokenly. I have said to her that you are my lady's far kin. Later I shall give her the story my lady has arranged."

They entered a long room in which a huge fireplace yawned directly opposite the door. This interior was full of shadows because the narrow windows did not admit much light. The floor was blocked with slate, and the stone walls had hangings of a rather coarse weave on which were painted symbols and designs Ramsay did not recognize.

There were three masks of burnished copper riveted to the wide mantel of the fireplace. And he recognized in them realistic representations of wolf, stag, and wild boar—the curving tusks of the boar giving that mask a wicked, threatening appearance.

The furniture was massive and looked as if it had been there for centuries—the wood darkened by the passing of time. Two high-backed benches flanked the fireplace, and there were several stools, a long table, and some chests and cupboards against the walls.

A few moments later, leaving Grishilda, Ramsay was ushered up a crooked-stepped stairway and through a door into a chamber, where the massive furniture below was echoed by a bed with carved posts, two cupboards, a table, and some stools. The hangings here were painted with various animals as realistically portrayed as the copper masks. And there was a stuffy, musty smell, as if this room had been closed for some time.

Emeka bustled past him to fling open both of the latticed windows, letting in air and a small measure of light. Then she bowed again and was gone. Ramsay explored a little, discovering behind one of the hangings a primitive kind of bathroom—with water running constantly through a stone opening in the wall, as if piped from some spring. It could be caught and held in a basin as large as a small bath by inserting a waiting plug in the floor groove. But any bathing, Ramsay decided, would have to be done quickly before the overflow from the pipe flooded the place.

He was more interested in the bed, for he could not deny that he was sleepy. Sleep—there was always the chance that if he wooed it hard enough, he would awake once more in his own rational world. Now he undressed and crawled into the cavern of the bed. The linen was not musty; in fact, it smelled agreeably of some flower or herb. He settled his head on the pillow with a sigh.

This time he did not lie awake trying to find some answer to what had happened. And if he dreamed during the sleep into which he fell, he had no remembrance of it upon awakening.

Ramsay was aroused by a knocking at the door. There was still the glow of sun outside the narrow windows. As he sat up in bed, he pulled the upper cover about him. For a moment all the words with which Grishilda had pounded his mind during their journey deserted him. He could not recall the simplest of expressions. Then he got control of himself and climbed out of bed, padded across the wooden floor, and lifted the hatch of the single door.

A man waited without, a huge copper jug, held in both hands, giving off steam, while over his shoulder was draped what could only be fresh clothing.

"Your liege man, lord—" The newcomer jerked his head in a rough salute.

His own clothing was brown, with a green vestcoat, the ever-present cat-head badge, this time of copper, fastened near his shoulder. It was apparent that he was ill at ease; perhaps he had never before played the role of body servant. But he dumped the heated water into the waiting basin, and Ramsay, taking the hint of overflow, made haste to use it. The forester had gone back into the bedroom to lay out the garments he had brought. Like his own, they consisted of an undersuit of brown, an overtunic of green, but they were fashioned of somewhat finer material. The cat badge was embroidered in copper thread and had the eyes worked in with glistening green.

"The Lady Grishilda, lord." He spoke slowly, as if he, too, hunted words in a foreign tongue. "She asks your gracious presence. There has come a message—"

Ramsay expressed his thanks and dressed quickly. The man had left him alone in the room where the dying sunlight of late afternoon no longer reached as far. A message? Ramsay thought that could come from only one person—Thecla. And he trusted that he would have a chance soon to ask her all the questions that had been gathering in his mind for what now seemed days.

He found Grishilda seated on a stool by the table

below, over one end of which was stretched a cloth of a deep cream shade. Laid out on it were plates, spoons, a two-tined fork, and a knife with a matching handle.

She arose at his coming and inclined her head, giving the impression, Ramsay thought, that she greeted one who was her superior in rank. But he returned her unspoken greeting with a bow he had copied from that of the forester.

"Lady—"

She smiled. "You are very gracious, my lord. Will you not sit and eat? This is no city feasting. But it has a flavor and appeal of its own."

The stool she indicated stood at the head of the table. Ramsay took his place there while Emeka and a younger girl of much the same cast of features hurried forward to serve them.

He found the food, as Grishilda had promised, both flavorsome and good. There was half of what was clearly some small fowl, steeped in sauce, a dark bread, honey still in the comb, sweet potatoes, beans—both cooked with a flavoring new to him. Again, the food reminded him of his own world, and it was these similarities that really troubled him the most, relatively unimportant though they were.

"You have a message, lady?" He could wait no longer.

Grishilda nodded. "It came by bird wing, as my lady always sends word to the lodge. She is on her way, but since she must go by Irtysh, her own home, she will be delayed. The Ears and Eyes of Ulad watch her—of that she is certain. Though whether they suspect—" Grishilda shrugged. "On suspicion only, they dare not detain her. Since Kaskar is dead, there is no betrothal, so she has every right and need to withdraw to Olyroun. We may expect her in two days—perhaps even less.''

Two days—for Ramsay that time appeared to stretch far too long. And he discovered, as hour followed hour, that impatience could indeed eat at a man. Grishilda warned against any straying from the lodge, even going out from its doors—lest he be marked, though she was also vehement that any intruder would be quickly located and reported by the foresters.

The lodge was kept by Emeka's family—which consisted of her husband, who had driven the wapiti wagon, her eldest daughter, whose husband was acting as Ramsay's rather unhandy servant, and two younger children, a boy and a girl, who peered very shyly at the visitors now and then through a window or from a doorway, apparently much in awe of Grishilda, and perhaps of Ramsay, who had reported kin, if distant, to the ruler of their land.

There was little to do but try to perfect his grasp of the language, in which Grishilda patiently concurred, and to discover from her all he could concerning the situation of this land, of the tangle about Kaskar and how it affected Thecla herself.

He learned that Olyroun was both independent and small. In spite of the greed of Ulad for its wealth of minerals, which the natives mined only frugally, Olyroun's independence had perhaps persisted mainly because it also sheltered a powerful and awesome group of what he guessed were religious leaders—the Enlightened Ones. From Grishilda's comments, Ramsay gathered that they possessed some form of mental power that completely overawed the common people. And had Ulad thrown her might against a country sheltering them, she would

have raised a hornet's nest among her own country-
men.

However, lately the Empress-mother of Ulad had
had as an adviser one of these Enlightened Ones—
Osythes. And the councillors of Olyroun were afraid
that the balance of this unseen power might shift to
their neighbor. In addition, Ochall had recognized
much of the army, letting go the volunteers from the
various steads; in their place, employing mercenaries from beyond the borders, men who fought
not from any inborn loyalty but for the one who paid
them. And from some source, Ochall apparently had
gathered unlimited funds to do exactly that.

With mercenaries under his banner who had apparently no fear of the Englightened Ones, and with
all men knowing that Kaskar was just his creature
and that upon his accession to the throne, Ochall
would be the real ruler—Olyroun was threatened
indeed. So much so that Thecla had had to make the
hard choice of marrying the weak and controlled
heir.

"To the Grove she went," Grishilda said. "And
there she spoke freely with a Listener. The Listener
read the foretelling, and there was only one road—
that she wed with the heir of Ulad. Otherwise there
was destruction to all. For the Enlightened will not
use their power to save any nation, taking sides one
against the other. To do this, they say, will lead only
to their Power fleeing from them. They will advise,
but they will not support any who turn to them.
Every man and woman must make decisions for
himself—herself. Yet, my dear lady must have had
some warning—for she went to Lom as one in
triumph rather than despair."

"But you said," Ramsay pointed out, "that an
Enlightened One now advises the Mother Empress

of Ulad. If they do not take sides—"

"It is so. He can advise. *Advise,* not *act* for the good of Ulad. But we do not know what he advises. For the Enlightened Ones do not see our lives as we do. They follow some greater pattern visible only to those passing through the mysteries. And oftentimes their advice may lead a man to sorrow for himself. Still, they claim that in that sorrow lie the seeds of a greater good to come. So it is not every man or ruler who will ask for a foretelling. My lady did so because she is fearful for Olyroun. I know not what they told her, only that she was shown her choice."

Grishilda was correct in her guess about when her mistress would arrive at Kilsyth. But Thecla came not by the wapiti wagon, but in an airborne flyer, which touched down neatly in front of the lodge just long enough for her to disembark, then rose immediately, to be lost from sight as it shot away over the forest straight toward the setting sun.

Grishilda, with a cry of welcome, ran forward, catching one of her mistress's hands, first kissing it and then holding it tightly to her breast. Tears welled from her eyes. At that moment Ramsay realized that, in spite of her outward calm during the past few days, the woman must have been inwardly racked with uneasiness for the girl she so plainly loved. Thecla kissed her cheek and patted her shoulder with her free hand. But her own eyes glistened, as if tears she did not shed had begun to gather there. Then she looked beyond to where Ramsay stood, and her hand went up in a small salute.

He bowed but did not move toward them. Impatient as he was, he must leave the initiative now to the girl. This was not the time to marshal all his questions.

They did not get to that until after the evening

meal, after Emeka and her eldest daughter had cleared the table and the forester family had all withdrawn to their own quarters at the rear of the house. Thecla watched the door close behind the bowing Emeka and then she swung at once to Ramsay.

"Our forest dress becomes you, cousin," she commented. "But we have little time. I have consulted again with Adise—"

He heard Grishilda draw a whistling breath that made Thecla glance at her.

"Yes, I have been to the foretelling once again, my dear friend. And—" She lifted both her hands, let them fall limply to her lap. "It remains the same, even with Kaskar gone. Olyroun must wed with Ulad, in order that the future be safe for my people. Which means, of course, Berthal, cousin to Prince Kaskar. Well, I have heard naught to his discredit, though little to his credit either. At least he is no creature of Ochall's. But enough of what may be my future—it is yours we must deal with." Again she addressed Ramsay directly.

"Do you know how I came here?" he demanded bluntly.

He did not really expect an affirmative from her, but she was nodding.

"Yes. I was sworn to secrecy before it happened. But I am now absolved of my oath—by Osythes and, indirectly, by the Empress. They were afraid of you—deathly afraid. It is a matter of strange import." She hesitated and then plunged on. "It seems that there are realms of knowledge which even the Enlightened Ones know little about. And in Lom a young expert in such matters, Melkolf, first got the ear of Berthal and then the Councillor Urswic. They took him to the Empress.

"It is proved that there are many bands of worlds which exist side by side, though they are walled from each other by some form of energy. In some, our counterparts live lives different from ours because in those worlds the action of history has moved in another pattern. This the Enlightened Ones have long known, just as they deduced also that, in places, the walls between these worlds grow thin at times, worked upon by some unknown energy. So may a man or a woman fall through, vanish from their own time into this other.

"All this Melkolf also knew, though he is not an Enlightened One, for he works not by mind control, but through certain machines he has been years in building, it being his desire to travel from one world to another. However, he had good reason to fear Ochall, and so he came to Berthal with a plan. It was this: If they could locate in one of these many other worlds the twin to Kaskar, then they could send the personality of the prince into the body of that stranger and arrange his death. Thus would Kaskar—tied to the other—also die—apparently of the failure of his heart—leaving no mark upon him.

"Three times did they do this with criminals condemned to death. But they needed Osythes's aid, for the one on the other plane must be linked in preparation through a series of dreams—"

"Dreams!" Ramsay burst out.

"You dreamed, did you not?"

He nodded, but she continued before he could speak.

"Osythes foretold—he agreed that you could be controlled into a fatal accident, drawing Kaskar with you into death. Melkolf set up the machine. They felt they were justified because of Ochall and what would happen to Ulad if Kaskar came to the throne. But it did not work as they had planned. Kaskar died, and you came to take his body. And Osythes says that this happened because they interfered with your life plan and that you still had a pattern to complete.

"Now, with Kaskar's body gone, Ochall is like a wild man. He believes that the Prince was only drugged and that he is being kept hidden somewhere. For this, Melkolf has no answer. But now Berthal, and Urswic, Melkolf, too—they hunt you eagerly. If they have their will, they will put an end to you—"

"Can I get back—" Ramsay brushed aside her warning. The story was so fantastic that somehow he had to accept its truth, odd though that reasoning might seem. He was here, and he had awakened in a dead man's body.

"That I do not know—" Thecla answered honestly.

"But I must!" And he made of those three words a promise to himself and to those who heard him now.

FIVE

RAMSAY WAS ON his feet, his back to the open cavern of the fireplace, his attention focused on Thecla.

"Can this Melkolf reverse what he has done?" he demanded of the girl

"I do not know. Dream sending—this is of the Enlightened Ones. And I have seen it in action many times among our own people. Foretellings that have come to pass—those, too, are common. But to use a machine—" She shook her head. "There Melkolf has ventured into new ways. I know only that it was his machine, combined with the dreams, that altered the planes so that Kaskar died—and you live. Though that was not what was intended.

"Osythes and the Empress—" She continued slowly. "They want you gone, for you are now a threat to all they would accomplish. But neither will raise hand against you to achieve that desire. For Berthal, Urswic, and Melkolf I cannot promise as much. They might willingly slay to cover their secret. And Ochall—if he could lay hand upon you—" Thecla shivered. "He could make you into such a weapon as would wipe out all who oppose him."

"Do they know that you helped me out of Ulad?"

"Osythes must guess; Ochall certainly knows that the guards were under hallucination that night. But he blames Osythes. Only not even one of his Power can move against an Enlightened One. But naught has been said to me. Nor will it when I fulfill the destiny marked out and hand-fast with Berthal. I am now too precious to their plans—''

Thecla's gaze was level. She was stating a fact that she believed; Ramsay had no doubt of that.

''If I could get to that machine—'' he began again, half to himself, speaking aloud his thoughts.

''I know not what you could do,'' Thecla replied frankly. ''The secret of it lies with Melkolf alone. However, it might well be that, in order to protect their own plan, they would be willing to return you to your world.''

''They have hinted this to you?''

Thecla shook her head. ''I cannot speak for any of them. But if you return to Lom, then you will be within reach of Ochall. And of him I have no doubts. Kaskar was his creature, well controlled. As he made of the Prince his tool, so could he also you.''

Anger was building in Ramsay. Wild as her story was, it carried belief with it. At least, the very fact that Thecla accepted it in entirety was somehow convincing. That he had been used to further an intrigue in another state of existence, callously, without his knowledge or will, chilled hot anger into an icy determination that from now on Ramsay Kimble was not going to be a puppet to be marched about at the whim of these who dared to entrap strangers for their own purposes.

''I want to go back to Lom.'' He did not make that into any question. He stated a determined fact. ''I must get to that machine—''

Thecla stood up. ''It was in my mind that this would be your answer. Though it is the most dangerous act you may choose. However, I shall not speak against it. For, though I am no Enlightened One, I have a feeling that this is the path for you.

"But, since it is one of peril, we must move with caution—"

"We?" he echoed. "I will not depend upon any more help from you." He supposed he should be grateful for all she had already done, giving him this respite, a safe way to hide out for a space from what seemed to be two determined organizations, neither one of which meant him any good. But he chafed at any more limitations being placed on his own action. Unfortunately, at the moment, he had no idea what form that action would take, nothing with which to counter any plan she might have concocted, since she knew the truth. He only felt resentment that he would be in any way bound to a plan that was not of his own devising.

Thecla shrugged. Some of the animation had gone from her face. "Walk openly, to your death, then, stranger. Or worse than death if Ochall's searchers gather you in. Do you know enough of our world to take your place among its people and not betray yourself in a thousand ways, great and small, to the first to observe you closely?"

He rebelled against the logic of that, but he could not deny that she was correct. He spoke the language—after a stumbling fashion—only due to her orders and Grishilda's patient help. But the customs in general usage, even the small ingrained habits of everyday living—she was right; he could make a fatal error at any time.

"So now you understand?" Thecla must have read realization in his expression. "It is only if you understand, and agree to be guided by me, that you can return to Lom. Though that is great unwisdom. It would be better to remain here for a space, then depart overseas, where all strangers have odd habits and so are not greatly remarked if they dwell among the natives, being outlanders—"

"I have no intention of remaining here—nor even in Lom! I *will* get back to my own world!"

"Fair enough. If it can be done. You shall accompany me to Lom as Arluth, within the disguise we have already devised. A Feudman goes masked, by the old custom. And I have no male kinsman, which is of importance in bethrothal, for there is no one of my blood to stand as my champion at that time. This is an ancient form, long a form only. I would have had to choose some one of Berthal's kin for this ceremony. But with a cousin from overseas, that is no longer necessary. You have learned our speech fairly well—now you must learn our customs, what is the role of a Feudman—that you may pass undetected in Lom."

Thecla could not linger at the lodge. She stayed the night and was picked up in the morning by one of the flyers, but before the end of that day, another sky ship dropped a man on their doorstep. He was plainly past middle age, his black hair frosted by strands of gray, a star-shaped scar on his chin below one corner of his mouth.

He saluted Ramsay in an offhand manner, his dark eyes sizing up the younger man as if he must learn all he could by such measurement.

"Yurk," he introduced himself, "Commander of Her Own Guard. Also once out of Tolcarne Overseas."

Yurk became his instructor. Whether or not Thecla had entrusted her Guardsman Officer with the truth, Ramsay was never to know. For Yurk never mentioned his lady after that first moment of their meeting. Instead, he concentrated completely on the task he had been sent to do—making Ramsay into the best imitation of a Tolcarne lordling he could.

The overseas country, Ramsay was told, was in the same chaotic feudal state that Ulad had been in before the rise of the old Emperor and the subjection there of unruly and riotous nobles. There was no central power to bring order into Tolcarne; rather, each House had its own territory. And while House might ally with House for protection, for some more ambitious raid upon a mutual neighbor, or for some temporary benefit to both, such alliances seldom lasted more than a few years, or maybe for a single generation.

The idea of a personal feud was a fearsome part of the general unrest. One branch of a House might assault another in hope of coming into full control. And once a feud was officially proclaimed those caught within it could openly hunt or be hunted. However, when a House was reduced to a single male, that survivor was encouraged to forget honor and retire to some point of safety, while negotiations to settle the dispute were in progress. For the complete stamping out of any of the Houses was, oddly enough, against the highest code which these semibarbarous people bound themselves to follow.

For such a House representative to flee abroad was not uncommon in the least. When he appeared in public, he went masked and unarmed, that state meant to protect him against any paid retaliation.

Neither Tolcarne nor Ulad had always been in such a state of flux, Ramsay discovered, by what he hoped was adroit questioning. There had once been a worldwide civilization with a central government under stable rule. But a sudden and dramatic change in basic trade—brought about by the discovery of a new and far more effective metal—and a bitter dynastic struggle had broken down that concentrated rule.

Countries on both continents turned to war, first over the supplies of ore of what sounded like fissionable materials. There followed the horrors of some kind of atomic conflict, and then a dark age.

Ulad, in the space of three generations, was lifting itself out of this dark past. But the success of its struggle depended upon the defeat of Ochall, who still had the feudal state of mind, and saw only warring conquest as the answer for a strict rule.

Tolcarne had produced no leader as yet who had been able to win any loyalty from more than one or two Houses. Thus, the land remained buried in the morass of petty wars. And since wars defeat trade, few merchants ever ventured now to its shores. In fact, Tolcarne was to Ulad and Olyroun largely legend.

But to Yurk its ways had once been his life, and he recalled old customs and ceremonies, drilling into Ramsay all that he could during the days and nights that followed.

They were not to have too long a time for such study. Ten days after Thecla had returned to her own capital, a flyer dropped in with an urgent message that the party at the lodge move on to Irtysh, where she now held court.

Again Ramsay changed clothing. That which had been a forester's uniform was laid aside for a dull red undersuit, an overvest-tunic of a lighter shade of the same color. The breast badge was that of a broken sword, encircled by a wreath of oak leaves. In addition, there was a mask that hid his face from upper lip to hairline, attached to a tight-fitting cap, which covered his head completely, rather like a skier's helmet.

This had, at the crown of his head, a tuft of upstanding feathers dyed in the same silver as the embroidery of his badge. When he looked at himself in the mirror, Ramsay believed that his present barbaric figure could certainly not be recognized by any who had known Kaskar. At least not as long as he kept the mask firmly over his face, though it was uncomfortable to wear, and he disliked having his vision limited by the eye slits.

With Yurk and Grishilda he embarked, to fly over the long reach of the forest, and then above cultivated fields and several small towns. Unlike the bullet cars of surface transportation, these aircraft had windows, and one could push against them for some glimpses of the land beneath—as the flyer did not soar too high.

Irtysh itself lay at the beginning of the mountain foothills, well into the heart of Olyroun. It was in the mountains that the mines lay. And the only year-long passable road from those mines ran through Thecla's ancient city, which was built more like a fortress than the usual capital. Her palace and headquarters of her government resembled most an eight-sided castle, enough like those of his own world for Ramsay to identify.

The flyer carried them over the clustered buildings of the city to land on the wide roof of one of the sentry towers, where a small guard awaited them. They saluted Yurk, seeming to pay little attention to his companion. Grishilda, her fingers closing on Ramsay's arm, drew him to one side, through a doorway in a nearby turret, where a narrow stairway coiled dizzily down into a not-too-well-lighted interior.

The inner part of the castle was, to Ramsay, a bewildering maze of passages, doorways (nearly always closed so one could not guess the nature of the areas behind them), steps up, stairs down. At last the three emerged into a section where the walls and pavement were no longer dank stone without covering.

Here ran soft carpeting, and wall hangings of painted designs, more stylized than realistic. Not that Ramsay was given any time to survey this art, for Grishilda urged him on as if they were now running some real race with time.

At a door she finally came to a halt, tapping on its closed panel. It was flung open by a man wearing the same servant's garb that had clothed Ramsay on his escape out of Lom. The man bowed, edged out after they entered, and closed the door firmly behind him.

The carpet here was flowered, muted lavenders, golds, roses on a background of spring green. And panels of similar flowers gathered into loose bouquets with silken threads covered the walls, except on the far side, where there were tall windows open to the day.

Thecla sat by the window directly opposite the door, a table before her, its surface crowded by a collection of yellow painted chests, each open, and each full of what seemed separate sheets of paper, though they were thick and coarser in texture than any Ramsay knew.

She had been engaged in stamping one such sheet with her thumb ring, having first impressed that upon a crimson pad shaped in the form of a cat's head and rimmed in silver. At the sight of them, she pushed aside the waiting pile of papers and arose.

"There has been a message." She wasted no moment in any greeting, as if she must let them know immediately of some dramatic happening. "They have found a body that they claim to be Kaskar's. Melkolf and Berthal supplied that. Once more the plans for his funeral are in progress. And I have been summoned for my role therein. Nor will I be allowed to return—that I know—until they have their way of me and I am betrothed to Berthal. But whether or not things will go so smoothly as they desire—that is another matter.

"Ochall has withdrawn into Vidin, officially to gather Kaskar's own liege men to see him to his tomb. Vidin," she said to Ramsay in explanation, "lies under the rule of the Emperor's heir. Though Kaskar spent as little time there as he could. He had no taste for the duties of rule, liking only what he deemed its pleasures and privileges—which he cultivated in excess. However, that Ochall has tamely accepted Kaskar dead and ready to be buried I cannot believe to be true.

"I have had a private message from the Empress Quendrida that the Emperor may depart to the Final Gate at any moment. With Ochall absent, then they will move at once to proclaim Berthal, even if Kaskar be not yet buried. Lom is filled with rumors and counter-rumors. There is much unrest, and the Empress has summoned the Life Guard into field duty order. She had laid it upon me to come at once. The betrothal with Berthal will follow immediately upon his proclamation."

She spoke evenly as if this whole matter had no bearing upon her future; rather, that it was already a matter of the past, sealed into the unchanging wall of history. Ramsay felt a sudden urge to protest. How could Thecla accept as perfectly natural this arrangement of her future, as if she were a thing to be commanded, rather than a person with desires, doubts, wishes of her own? In his own time and world there were few vestiges of royalty. And those rulers remaining were much more free to be themselves, not stiff symbols of history and duty ever walled from ordinary men. Thecla to him now was no symbol of rule; she was a person, a singularly attractive and intelligent person, who had moved on his behalf, though she had had no reason to aid him from the danger devised by those whom she knew much better, those same forces with whom she now proposed to ally herself without any question of their right to demand this of her.

But he could not summon any words to dispute her choice. The very calmness of her speech, her acceptance of things as they were, defeated him before he could even find the words.

"Grishilda, as the Mistress of my body women, you will, of course, once more accompany me to Lom. And you"—she nodded to Ramsay—"for I have told the Empress by message that you have arrived in Olyroun and are kinsman to me through my great-grandfather's daughter who married into the House of Yonec. At this moment you are the only kinsman of my blood, and since Ulad wishes to keep to all the old ceremonies it can resurrect (which is ever the way of a new House), you are acceptable to approve my hand-fasting. You need only remember that you are also a Feudman, not to be seen without that mask. Nor can you lay hand to any weapon. But doubtless Yurk has made this all clear to you?"

"Yes—"

Thecla waited no more than for that single word of assent from him.

"Very well. I am giving you for servant one of my guard who is familiar with the ways of Tolcarne. His uncle is one of the few merchants who still ventures there for trade. He will gossip and his talk will bear out your position among those of Ulad. But since he has not himself been overseas he cannot challenge any small slip of bearing you might make.

"This much I shall do: My party will carry you under their approval into Lom, into the palace. You must thereafter be on your own. If you can influence Melkolf—well and good. But I would adivse you not to move with any haste, and to take very good care."

"My lady, it is folly!" Grishilda burst out. "If he goes to Lom Court as one you vouch for and then is uncovered! My dear lady, this is a matter of too much danger for you!"

"It is by the word of Adise that I do this," Thecla answered quietly.

"Oh, these Enlightened Ones!" Grishilda made a repudiating gesture with both hands. "My lady, I know you will listen to them and obey. But they say frankly that they care not for a single person, only for what they deem the good of all. They would sacrifice even you in some plan of theirs!"

"That could be the Truth," conceded Thecla. "But in this case, Adise gives me bond-word that I shall not lose by supporting the one who moves in Kaskar's place."

"Bond-word?" Grishilda repeated. "Bond-word from an Enlightened One? My lady, seldom have any of our people heard that."

"Just so. And this I will do as I have been advised, and we shall see what comes of it. Now to practical matters of the present. We go by flyer in the morning. This night, cousin, you shall stay in the north tower, better aloof from all save Cyart who is to be your liege man. It is custom anyway that you come not much into open company.''

A short while afterward Ramsay stood by a window, wishing he could shed the confining masked hood, which was overwarm and chafed around his throat. But he knew from Yurk that that was not done unless he was entirely alone. And the man Thecla had assigned to him moved about the room behind. He should be planning what he would do when they reached Lom. Only he knew so little about what he might find there it would be better to wait and see what fate would toss him as a chance.

Oddly enough, in spite of what seemed incredible to the sensible Ramsay Kimble he had been—and would extend every effort once more to be—he was accepting the fact that this *had* happened. He moved through no dream or hallucination. No, he was here in a world perhaps parallel to what he had always known—first tied to it by dreams, and then in a body not his.

That any machine could accomplish what Thecla calmly believed Melkolf's could do— Only he understood from Yurk's comments upon the past state of civilization that this world had once reached a standard undoubtedly in advance of any his own had ever known. There could well be reason to believe that Melkolf had rediscovered some principle those supermen of long ago had once put to use.

There remained only that he must discover whether such a machine would work two ways, whether Melkolf could be confronted and forced to return Ramsay. And since the party of which that scientist was a full member certainly did not want his presence here, they ought to be only too glad to send him back. For their purposes, Kaskar was now dead, Berthal ready to take the throne. Ramsay was a threat; he might even be able to exert a little blackmail on his own behalf, working through either the old Empress or this Osythes. He would just have to wait and see.

Waiting took him into the air again the next morning aboard the largest flyer he had yet seen. Thecla and Grishilda had a cabin to themselves near the fore of the machine. Ramsay sat surrounded by the men of her bodyguard, Yurk to his left. But he did not try to make any conversation as they were carried steadily to the southwest and Ulad.

Ramsay was not even aware that they had crossed the border until suddenly he saw other flyers in the air bracketing them, flying an escort of honor. They ate once and, as evening began to close in, he caught the first flash of the lights of Lom—the spread of the city across the plain beneath.

When they landed, it was outside the walls of Lom Palace, where a saluting guard awaited them, together with an old man in black-and-white, and another in almost as long a robe of yellow; both were bowing to welcome Thecla.

Ramsay started at the sight of the black-and-white robe. That was the man he had seen twice in his dreaming. He could only be Osythes, the one responsible for enmeshing him in this coil. He wanted to be angry at the sight of the other's thin face, the brush of his white hair. Only it was not quite anger Ramsay felt now, rather excitement, the impatience of one who must act. And Osythes could be the key to that action.

SIX

RAMSAY HAD TOSSED aside traveling cloak, unfastened the throat latch of that bonnet with its mask, behind which sweat gathered on his forehead. However, he knew better than to discard that headgear, for Cyart still bustled about the suite of chambers that had been assigned to Thecla's kinsman. Also— Ramsay studied first one wall and then the next with suspicion. Perhaps this civilization had not yet advanced to the refinement of "bugging" a room when those in power wished to check on its inhabitants. But that did not mean that he could not be under some form of surveillance, if only through a secret peephole. This palace was the kind of medieval looking structure that made one think instinctively of secret passages, spy holes, and all the other aids to a court intrigue.

So best to continue to wear his mask, no matter how hot and confining it seemed. If there *was* some spy crouching behind the hanging-covered walls, there was no use in exciting a report that Kaskar had again returned—this time alive.

The chamber was luxurious. One of those long couches, covered with a thick green fabric, balanced piles of wide cushions scattered across a similarly shaded carpet to serve as chairs. And there were small tables, each bearing numerous figurines, bowls, cups, which Ramsay guessed were for display, not use, since they were of precious metals or carved from what looked like semiprecious stones.

Long windows to his left gave not on the outer world but on a narrow balcony above a court. He caught words of command from below. A squad was being put through some drill there.

Somewhere within this pile must lie that lab that he remembered from the last dream in his own place and time. After Cyart had stowed away the baggage Ramsay had brought from Olyroun, Ramsay dismissed the man, wishing he dared take the servant enough into his confidence to ask him to keep his ears open, report anything he heard that might point to the direction in which Ramsay must search. Only he dared not risk any such suggestion.

He sat down on the couch, realizing only too well just how difficult this was going to be. Of course, he could attempt to cultivate Melkolf, but Ramsay doubted his ability to do that without raising any suspicion. Having never before played the part of a detective, he did not have the slightest idea how to begin. Instead, he strove to recall every one of those dreams that had tied him in to this wild venture. Perhaps somewhere hidden in his own memory he could find a possible clue.

The first one— That had been entirely of Osythes, the old man in his full black-and-white robes, seated in a chair with a tall, carved back, his head resting against it so that his chin was pointed up a little, his eyes closed, a certain rigidity and tenseness of his figure suggesting, as Ramsay guessed now, complete concentration. In that dream Ramsay had seemed to watch the Enlightened One through some window, as if between them at that moment there were a pane of clear glass.

Try as he would now, he could bring to mind only Osythes, the chair, that sense of deep involvement in thought that the Shaman had projected. Ramsay had not been in any way an actor in that dream, only an onlooker.

That first contact must have signaled the point when Osythes, searching for Kaskar's "twin" on some other world plane, had at last discovered Ramsay. Then there had been no suggestion of foreboding. He himself had awakened from the dream only curious. So his curiosity had led him to mention it to Greg, mainly because it had been clearer, remained more firmly fixed in his mind, than any dream he had remembered having before.

Now Ramsay saw Osythes in a chair—was the Shaman perhaps dreaming also? Or was the priest forcing his personality to search beyond this plane of existence? What next?

The second dream—Osythes had been in that also, but not passive, seemingly asleep in his chair. Instead he had stood, his eyes open, in his hand a round, glittering object, like a mirror, from which light reflected. The Shaman had held it carefully, moving it back and forth, until the flashes it reflected had struck straight into Ramsay's own eyes. This time there had been no feeling of a protecting wall between them; rather it was as if Ramsay himself, without power of motion, were in the same strange chamber with Osythes.

The chamber? Ramsay closed his eyes now, bent his powers of concentration on trying to recall—not the Shaman with his flashing mirror, but what stood about him as a frame.

Walls—yes—and with hangings on them—much like the hangings of the walls that covered this chamber here and now. What were the designs on those hangings? Not those of animals and birds such as Ramsay would see if he opened his eyes; rather lines of black and white, the same colors as the Shaman's robe. They had formed geometric patterns. But he could not see them except very hazily, and it required a terrific effort of will to recall them at all. The flash of the mirror into his eyes had tended to center his attention only on the Shaman.

Now—the third—

Osythes again, but beside him two others. One was a woman, and she was seated in a chair that had a heavy canopy over her head. That shadowed her figure so much that he could make out but little of it. On the other side of that chair was another man. He was much younger than the Shaman, wearing all gray, both undersuiting and vest-coat—bearing a hawk-eagle on his badge on his shoulder. Osythes had pointed the way; this was Melkolf bringing science to carry on what mental powers had begun.

That suggestion fitted—very well. Ramsay believed that now he could recognize the face of the enemy.

Three dreams. The fourth—?

Osythes no longer occupied the scene here, nor was the woman in the canopied chair visible. Ramsay could see only Melkolf, the scientist, clearly defined against a shadowy background. He was engaged in fitting a box with a rod into the square top of a large apparatus that stood shoulder-high before him. Ramsay drew a quick breath— *That* must be the machine Thecla had spoken of.

He struggled to concentrate on it, but to do so was

like watching an object through a wavering wall of water. One moment it was clear, the next it was hidden by a rippling. It was not the machine, however, he realized quickly, that he must deal with. No, rather the room that held it. What was that like?

Walls—stone, no hangings such as had existed in the first two dream pictures. But the stone was lighter in color, too. And there were other fittings in the room aside from the cube where Melkolf worked. Unfortunately, in some manner, Ramsay's attention had been concentrated mainly during the dream on the scientist. Had he been already so tuned in to whatever had been used to contact him that he had been linked at that moment to the exclusion of all else?

Not quite, for there had been a fifth dream before the final one from which he had been awakened to serve the purposes of Melkolf's companions. In that he had been going down a long hall, before him the black-and-white robe, the Shaman's white head, holding his attention. Osythes approached a section of wall with a large panel that bore the hawk-eagle painted on it in gold.

The Shaman glanced hastily from high to left and back again as if to assure himself that he was alone. Ramsay suddenly wondered about this dream. It was unlike the others in that neither Melkolf nor the Shaman was facing him, or using either the mirror or the box. Rather this was as if Osythes might not have been thinking of his prey at all. Then how had linkage occured? Was it done because once having touched Ramsay through some control he evoked by an Enlightened One's mental range, the Shaman had inadvertently opened a door for Ramsay that could be a two-way one, enabling his victim also to spy upon him?

At any rate, Ramsay watched the Shaman lift old, heavily veined hands to touch the outer tips of the gilded bird's spread wings. He appeared to exert heavy pressure. Then, in answer, the panel split down the center. Osythes stepped through that opening quickly, bundling his robe about him tightly as he went.

He had to move quickly indeed, for the paneling snapped shut again, as if the mechanism that controlled it were on a tight spring. Then had followed a change in the dream, a shifting of background.

Once more Ramsay saw what must be the laboratory, this time from a different angle. Osythes went before him, descending a stairway into what must be, in comparison with the Shaman's slightly stooped figure, a large area. The equipment housed there was in startling contrast to the medieval appearance of the rest of Lom Palace. Ramsay recognized nothing he saw, but it startled him with the feeling that all these installations were centuries in advance of anything he had seen, either in a dream or in reality, in either Ulad's city or his own home.

Centuries ahead? Or aeons behind, Ramsay wondered now. That story Yurk had told him—of a highly technical civilization that had vanished in a chaos of worldwide war. Suppose Melkolf, a man with what passed at present for scientific training, had found some very ancient storage place, or just the knowledge to reproduce such experimental equipment? That could be the answer.

Osythes reached the floor of the lab now, walked across it. Melkolf and Berthal suddenly came into view, as if the Shaman had raised his voice to summon them.

Though the dreams had always been vividly realized as to sight, Ramsay had never heard anything during them. Now he longed to have that second sense added as he saw the three men conferring together. He might not hear their words, but he was able to pick up a sense of excitement, of need for action. As Osythes turned, the other two accompanied him. Then—

Ramsay shook his head, opened his eyes. That had been when he woke up. And there had been only one more dream, that which had been his undoing, after which the compulsion to drive to the mountain and his crash must have been exerted. He remembered Melkolf in that and the man he knew now to be Prince Berthal—cousin to the helpless Kaskar.

That last dream held nothing he could now put to advantage. All he really had was the secret panel that led to the lab. But could he openly tour what might be miles of corridors within this pile, seeking one panel with a gilded bird on it? There could be more than one, since the hawk-eagle was the badge of the ruling house.

What about by night? Were there then sentries on duty along the corridors? How long would he have to hunt? In what direction? Ramsay's frustration sent him pacing reatlessly back and forth, tugging at the throat latchet of his hood. He longed to skin that and the mask off, but he did not quite dare.

Melkolf, Urswic, and Berthal—Thecla had warned him that those three might take matters into their own hands, making sure that Kaskar, or what seemed to be Kaskar, might never rise to trouble them again. Osythes and the old Empress were opposed to such a drastic step. Ramsay began to concentrate on the Shaman.

From what Grishilda had said, these Eniightened Ones did not take much note of the needs of the individual. They dealt with matters of the future, how men and events might be manipulated in the present to bring about the results they had decided were the most beneficial. Apparently Osythes had been of the belief that the removal of Kaskar, which would immobilize Ochall's plans to rule Ulad through a puppet, was of great importance.

But would Osythes support a mock Kaskar in his demand to be sent back to where he really belonged? And if the Shaman was friendly enough to exert himself on Ramsay's behalf, did he have enough control over the Empress's party to enforce such a move?

Thecla was housed in the so-called Yellow Tower, and its position in relation to his own chambers he had discovered easily enough through Cyart. After all, he was Thecla's proclaimed only kinsman. At such, surely he had reason enough to seek her out. Perhaps she could solve a few riddles for him. It would do no harm to see her anyway.

Ramsay rebuckled his hood, surveyed himself in the mirror to be sure that his Kaskar features were truly in eclipse. He thought that he made a rather sinister appearance in this suiting of dull red, the hood and mask concealing most of his face. A picture from a book flashed into his mind, that of a medieval headsman in part so appareled, waiting for the reluctant approach of a victim.

However, he was equally sure that even Kaskar's hostile grandmother could not recognize him at present, and that he dared venture out. In spite of his grim appearance, as a Feudman he was unarmed by the standards of the world, and thus harmless. The customary short sword did not swing from the belt tightened about his vest-coat.

Beneath the feud mask, Ramsay grinned a little. To each world its own arts. He had listened to Yurk carefully, leading the veteran soldier to accounts of his own past campaigns against mountain outlaws. Karate skills were seemingly unknown in either Ulad or Olyroun. Ramsay flexed his hands now. At least he carried a secret protection. For he already knew, from some research at the lodge when he was totally alone, that the skill in his memory could be grafted on to this new body. He was a little slower, a little less tough. But he had been working on that, too.

Now as he stepped into the corridor, he walked with purpose. However, his attention was not only just for the guard who might dispute his way, but also for the wall panels. Here they were designed with arabesques in complicated patterns, no hint of any bird about them. As he turned into another corridor, which should lead directly to the Yellow Tower on a level below Thecla's suite, Ramsay saw that the panels gave way to a series of shallow niches, in each of which was poised the figure of a small, montrous-looking animal. The company of figures were all different and all highly fantastic. Ramsay thought that they, like those pieces on display in his own chamber, had been fashioned from semiprecious stones, quartz and perhaps jasper—but he knew so little of the subject he could not be sure.

There was no door at the end of the hall, only an archway, elaborately trimmed with gilding over a smooth, brown-red surface. This opened upon a stairway. There he met his first guard. But Ramsay did not alter his stride, which was that of a man who knew exactly where he was going and expected no trouble in reaching his goal.

When he had passed and was climbing the stairs, Ramsay gave a sigh of relief. The man had saluted him with raised hand, which Ramsay, after a fraction of a second, had replied to with a flick of his own fingers in what Yurk had impressed upon him was the acknowledgment of Tolcarne between one class and another.

He had to restrain his desire to hurry. Something about roaming these corridors gave him a naked, exposed feeling. He would have to get over that if he was to go hunting his split-bird door panel. Now he wanted most of all to see Thecla.

A second guard stood before her door. Set there to do her honor, Ramsay hoped, and not as a barrier to any meeting with her kinsman from overseas. It seemed that his hopes were sustained, for the man saluted and then himself rapped at the door.

Grishilda opened it. Seeing Ramsay, she gestured a greeting, stood aside to let him in. But her face was expressive, and though he could not quite understand what she was trying to signal, he guessed that wariness on his part was needful.

Thecla stood rather demurely beside that same long divan on which he had had his first language lesson. Facing her was Berthal, the splendor of his person somehow too ostentatious when matched to either Thecla's quiet elegance or the good taste of the room's furnishings.

"Ah, kinsman!" Thecla smiled. Ramsay might have been the one person above all now in Lom whom she was wishful to see. "What fortune that you have come at this moment, Arluth. Prince

Berthal, this is my blood-kin out of Tolcarne, the Master-in-Chief of the House of Olyatt. Arluth, this is Prince Berthal.''

Yurk had schooled Ramsay well. No Master of a House in Tolcarne considered an Imperial Prince, heir or not, more than his equal. He would acknowledge such an introduction with a salute only slightly more deep than he had that of the guardsmen. Ramsay performed exactly as Yurk had taught him.

Berthal frowned. Thecla, in spite of the sober set of her lips, watched them with amused eyes. Ramsay decided that she was enjoying the reaction of the Prince to such offhand familiarity as he seldom met.

"We give you welcome, Master." Berthal's voice was cold. He was already using the royal "we," though he had not been proclaimed, Ramsay noted. "It is indeed fortunate that you have arrived in so timely a fashion that you may serve Lady Duchess Thecla as kin-witness.''

"It is always fitting," Ramsay replied carefully, wanting no slip of word or accent to betray him now, "for kin to stand by kin in any matter.''

"Just so." Berthal was frankly staring at him. "My lady says you are new come out of Tolcarne.''

"Yes." Ramsay kept his assent as curt as he could.

"Then you must have been highly fortunate, Master, to find a ship. Few take the western sea roads these days.''

He was probing, Ramsay knew.

"Few. But some still want the trade in sea-ivory and gold. All merchants are not timid of heart where there is a profit to be reaped. The fewer the ships, the higher the reward in the markets of Olyroun.''

"Yes." Thecla stuck in. "My people bid high on

any such cargo nowadays. Were there less unrest in
Tolcarne, there could be much trade between us,
benefiting both. Perhaps someday a man with the
wisdom and spirit of your own reverend grandfather
will rise there and the turbulence be quenched. But,
Berthal, greatly do I thank you for your pleasant
welcome—'' She waved her hand to indicate a bowl
of deep green in which were arranged a thick cluster
of lilies of the valley which gave off a sweet perfume.
''And assure Her Splendor Enthroned that I shall
indeed be honored to attend her at the fourth hour
after noon.''

This was so evidently a dismissal that Berthal
could not linger now without seeming rudeness. But
he shot Ramsay a glance as he passed which
suggested that he had no desire to leave the Outlander here. Thecla waited until the door closed behind
him. Grishilda came swiftly then from the next room
and stood with her ear against the panel, listening.

Ramsay wasted no time.

''How well do you know this palace, lady?'' he
asked.

''Not as well as that of Irtysh, yet it is not new to
me. When I was small, my mother brought me hither
on visits. The old Empress is her great-aunt. Why?''

''Is there a corridor you remember where the wall
panels are painted with the badge of the Imperial
House—laid on in gold?''

''Yes, such leads to the private apartments of the
Empress. There are ten such panels, five to a side.
What are you seeking?''

''The way to what Melkolf hides. I remember it
from one of the dreams through which they caught
me.''

She bit at her knuckles, her eyes still on him, but as if she did not really see him at all, rather considered some thought.

"And if you find this place? Then what can you do if Melkolf refuses to use his machine to return you?"

Ramsay shrugged. "How do I know? But perhaps there is something to be learned if I can reach there. Lady, do you think Osythes would back me?"

"I do not know. It depends upon what the Enlightened Ones' policy is concerning the future of Ulad. I know that the seeress Adise of my own land has a foretelling that your presence here will make a difference. If it is such a difference as will defeat Osythes's plans, then he may be brought to consider such support."

"And could he in turn influence Melkolf?"

"If he wishes. A true Enlightened One can use his mind as a weapon, to bring about any result he chooses. However, very few are the times they will do so. There must be a very powerful and compelling reason. I do not know what your presence will mean to Osythes. And I warn you about hunting out Melkolf without being sure you do have such backing."

Ramsay shook his head with determination. "I am not going to just sit and wait," he declared. "Let me find this lab, then perhaps I can make terms with Melkolf myself. It is a secret—therefore, he is vulnerable—"

"So are you," Thecla pointed out swiftly. "Inconvenient people, who know more than they should, might—and sometimes do—vanish. Of course, I do not think he would move while my betrothal is not yet carried through. They dare not openly meddle with my avowed kinsman, whose presence is needed to make such a ceremony legal.

Yes, perhaps you are right in your daring. This may be the time that you should discover whatever there is to be found. Perhaps the more you know the more you can impress Osythes."

It seemed she had argued herself from her first hostile position to a reluctant agreement.

"I shall give you reason to go there. Grishilda, bring me the casket of gifts for Her Splendor Enthroned.

"It is customary," Thecla continued, speaking to Ramsay, "for the betrothed-to-be to bring a gift to the eldest woman kin of the House. Since Her Splendor Enthroned holds that position, I shall send you with it. Carry it openly, and all will pass you according to custom. Now—you will descend the stair without to the level of your own chamber, but, where the corridor forks just beyond your room, take the right-hand way and keep straight ahead. This reaches across the length of the castle between the Yellow Tower and the Red, in which Her Splendor Enthroned resides. There you should find your wall."

She handed him the silver box Grishilda had brought, waved away his thanks. However, she followed him to the door of the chamber, and, before he went out, laid her hand upon his arm.

"Take care, Kinsman Arluth," she said softly. "You walk between enemies who are very lightly tethered, and your path is rough."

"That I know. But for your good wishes, lady, I thank you—"

"Perhaps you may have little to thank me for. Wait until you are safe and then speak so. For only then will such return have meaning."

The note in her voice suggested that she was far more uneasy than her words might suggest.

Ramsay found his way easily, holding the casket plain to see in his hands as she had ordered. So it was very little time before, with his heart beating faster, he came into a short length of hall with the panels he remembered from his dream. He strode swiftly along it, delivered the casket to the lady-in-waiting who answered his rap on the Empress's door. She did not ask him to enter and, relieved that he so easily escaped the scrutiny of one of those he had to fear, he hurried back to the panels. Judging by his dream, the one he wanted was the third from the other end of the corridor, on the left-hand side as one approached the Empress's tower. He halted before that, glanced up and down much as Osythes had on that other occasion. There seemed to be no one in sight. And though he listened for several long moments, Ramsay caught nothing but the sound of his own rather fast breathing.

He raised his hands to set his thumbs against the tips of those upheld wings, exerting pressure as he had watched the Shaman do. For a long moment he feared he had counted wrong, or else this way was sealed. Then, with a small, rusty rasp, which sounded as loud as a gunshot in his ears, the panel parted.

Quickly Ramsay forced his way into the space beyond, before the hidden door could snap together again.

SEVEN

HE STOOD ON A small platform above a flight of steep
stairs, but he was not in the dark. At regular intervals
along the wall were blocks that glowed with a bluish-
tinged light he had seen nowhere else in the palace.
Under that radiance Ramsay's own hands took on an
oddly unpleasant look, as if the dark skin were
shriveled and age-touched.

For a long moment he did not move, striving to use
his ears to learn whether he had any guard to fear at
the foot of those stairs. For they turned at a landing
about ten steps down, and he could not get a glimpse
of what lay below.

Not only was Ramsay now enwrapped by silence,
but the feeling grew upon him that he had taken a step
away from the world of the living into one of pre-
served and awesome age. He shivered—not from
any chill, but because the very walls here radiated an
alienness that was counter to all he had met in this
world. All had been strange, yes, but there was also a
human cast to that strangeness. Here he felt as if he
had invaded a place never meant for his species.

Ramsay tried to shrug off his uneasiness. When he
had come into Ulad, he had certainly suspended
logic. But to allow his imagination full rein was to
lead into sheer superstition. Cautiously he began the

descent, one step at a time, wondering, as he planted each foot firm, if he might be so alerting some system of alarms which he himself could not hear. However, he had to take that chance.

He had reached the landing now, made the right-angled turn, and he could see the foot of the stairway. It was lighter down there. The glow was not the blue of these wall lights but that of the normal globes. And certainly no one was in sight. What or who might lurk in hiding he could not guess; no sound reached him at present.

As he went, he flexed his hands, wondering if, when faced by an attack, his Kaskar muscles could respond to his Ramsay mind fast enough to aid him. If he had only had more time to discipline this new body into his service!

From the bottom of the stairs he looked through an open doorway into a room, where there was no sight or sound of any occupant and which his first glimpse told him was what he sought, the lab of his dream visits. Yet as Ramsay edged within, he kept his back to the wall, facing outward into the center of the area, trying to be alert to any sudden rush and yet study the massed machines.

Even in his own time and space, he knew very little of such establishments. How could he judge now whether this was all of Melkolf's own devising, or some legacy from that higher civilization of the past? For the aura of age clung here. What drew most of his attention was that huge metal cube into which his dream self had watched Melkolf fit the rod-on-box equipment. With a darting glance right and left, Ramsay assured himself that he must indeed be alone here. He left his defensive half-crouch by the wall and sought a closer look at that mass of burnished metal.

It was easy enough to find the slit near the top where Melkolf had inserted his hand instrument. That, with its upward-pointing finger of stiff wire (or else another like it), was still within the socket.

Ramsay put out his hands toward it and then drew back. No, he wanted to know more before he tried anything. He began to circle the cube. The top was on a level with his shoulder, and it was about six feet long on a side. The one that had been turned toward him as he entered had only one break in its surface— the gap into which what Ramsay now termed to himself "the finder" had been fitted.

The next side was totally smooth. However, when he reached the one directly opposed to the finder, he discovered a row of dials, below them levers on which one might comfortably rest a fingertip. Two of those, at the far end, were illuminated from within, as if to prove that the apparatus was in working order. Ramsay wondered what would happen if he suddenly pushed down all the levers, but he was not fool enough to try.

All right—so this, according to what information he had been able to gather, was what had transported the personality and memories of one Ramsay Kimble into the waiting body of Prince Kaskar. Only it had not been meant to be used that way—at least Melkolf had not intended to do so.

Suppose the Uladian scientist had been working with some device which he had *discovered*, one which had been built by an entirely different race? What purpose had the thing served for them? Ramsay had a momentary fantastic flash of suspicion— suppose it was intended for some medical use, to transfer a personality from a dying body into a fresh young one? But there was no point in speculating about what it might do—he must concentrate on what it had done, with him as unwilling victim.

He had found this machine, was sure that he had discovered the medium of his exchange. Only that did him little good, unless he could learn how to manipulate it (and he was very doubtful of that), or unless he could force Melkolf himself to reverse the process.

The atmosphere here in the lab was stuffy; there were strange and unpleasant odors that made him cough. Ramsay fumbled with the buckle of his hood and jerked it, and, the mask off, shook his head to enjoy the sudden feeling of freedom that gave him. He continued his trip around the square, finding the fourth side to be as smooth of surface as the second.

Was it the finder that controlled his presence here in this world? Suppose he worked it loose—then what would happen?

"Stand still!"

Ramsay's hand, reaching toward the finder, froze in midair. He had heard no one approach, but he had been criminally reckless in not being alert. The puzzle of the cube had taken him off guard. And he had no doubt that whoever had given him that order and now stood behind him was armed.

"Rabalt, take him!"

A line snaked out of the air, flickered within Ramsay's range of vision, and settled on his outstretched arm, immediately tightening in a painful grip. At the second that one end of it closed upon his flesh and held him prisoner, there was a jerk on its end, a pull sharp as to nearly drag him from his feet to sprawl backward. But he managed to turn and yet keep his balance.

The man who drew the line so taut wore the uniform of a guardsman. Behind him was Melkolf. In the scientist's hand was a glass tube ending in a bulb about which his fingers were curled. That this was a weapon, and a powerful one, Ramsay had no doubt.

Quickly the man who held the line flipped the other end at Ramsay, holding by the center of its length. As if the cord were a living thing with instinct or intelligence, it swung directly through the air to clasp Ramsay's left wrist as effectively as it had already caught his right.

The guardsman might have been more intent upon making the proper throw than he was on the identity of his prisoner. Now when he looked directly at Ramsay's face, his own eyes went wide.

"The—Prince!" He cried out.

"Not so!" Melkolf snapped. "He is a creature of Ochall's under illusion to make us think so. Now he is powerless. You may go, Rabalt. This I shall handle. But tell my Lord Councillor Urswic and the Prince Heir that this one has been found here. That is of utmost importance."

He reached out his hand, and the guardsman, if a little reluctantly, gave the loop of the cord into his grasp, though never did Melkolf allow that other weapon to waver from its aim on Ramsay. Without looking again at the captive, Rabalt disappeared up the stairs in haste, either agog to carry out his orders or because he found the lab itself an intimidating place to be. Melkolf waited, apparently wishing to make sure that the other was gone. Then he spoke again.

"You are very wise to surrender—" With the glass tube he executed a small movement, as if to be sure Ramsay was aware of it. "This will destroy a man far quicker than any steel blade or air bullet. Those who went before us had weapons making ours as clumsy-seeming as stone and wood spears. Kaskar is safely dead. He is not going to rise from the tomb again.''

Ramsay found his tongue. ''You can make sure of that in another way. Send me back!''

Melkolf smiled slightly. ''But that is just it. I would, with every good wish, if I could. But I cannot.''

Ramsay nodded to the machine. ''Then this will work only one way? You cannot reverse it?''

''Oh, it could be reversed easily enough. But the fact remains that Kaskar is dead and buried. Do you not understand, you barbarian fool? Kaskar was in your body when it died, and that body is safely buried!''

Ramsay stared at him. Why had that thought not occured to him? The stupidity of his own simple plan to return struck him speechless. Then he summoned the will not to allow this man to know how that struck home.

''If Kaskar was in my body, then where was I? There must have been some time lapse. I found myself awakening on Kaskar's bier—''

''Yes, that has been our puzzle. Where *were* you during two days between the time when our unesteemed prince had his fatal attack and you came into residence in his carcass? An interesting problem. But of no consequence now. What remains is that of present Kaskar is safely dead, in two time worlds, and he is going to remain that way. There will be no resurrection to delight Ochall, that I assure you. And your foolish return to Lom will avail you nothing at all but—''

''My murder?'' Ramsay somehow found the words, maintained with effort his outward composure. Melkolf indeed had the upper hand, for Ramsay did not doubt that he could easily be put to death here, and no one would ever be the wiser. Nor would his body turn up later to make trouble for his murderers.

"Murder? One cannot slay a dead man." Melkolf laughed. "Had you a single wit in your head, you would have kept away, once you escaped. The Duchess arranged that, did she not? Well, she cannot speak of it, nor will she, knowing that Olyroun is the prize in the end. You will simply disappear. Using that"—he nodded at the cap-mask Ramsay had discarded—"someone will walk away from here and take ship to return to your homeland of Tolcarne. You have made it very simple for us, have you not?"

"No, he has not!"

Another man stood on the stairs, his long black-and-white robe giving bulk to his body. Melkolf shot a quick glance over his shoulder.

"How did you—" he began, then bit his lower lip as if those words had been shaken out of him by surprise and he wished he had never uttered them.

"How did I know, Melkolf? I was on my way to Her Splendor Enthroned apartments and met your messenger on his way. It needed very little persuasion to learn from him what had happened here. And what has been done is not in the least simple, Melkolf."

"How so?" demanded the other defiantly.

"The very fact that Kaskar's body drew this other is a thing we must know more about. Did it happen in the first exchanges you made?"

"No—"

"Then why should it in the most important one? There is always a meaning behind such things. We only follow paths which we choose for good or ill, that is our free choice. But we have not made those paths—do you understand me?"

"That is the talk put about by your Enlightened Ones. He is here because of some misfunction of the machine!" Melkolf scowled.

"But I thought you were certain of the functions of this machine of yours. Have you not shown us in private many wonders you have learned from your discovery of ancient and forbidden knowledge—"

"Forbidden by whom?" Melkolf flared. "By small-brained men who feared what they could not understand!"

"In the past by men who understood very well, well enough to have survived a world gone mad," Osythes returned coldly.

"Legends—"

"All legends lie coiled around a core of truth. But we do not argue history now. This man's fate is something that I do not understand; he is not to be lightly handled!"

"I do not intend to handle him at all," countered the other. "I will use this"—again he indicated his weapon—"and there will be nothing left to handle."

"No? What essence came to inhabit Kaskar's body? You may destroy flesh and blood, bone and sinew, but there remains a part that cannot be destroyed—"

"I do not believe you." Melkolf spoke firmly. "I believe what I see, what I can touch, hear—"

"If you believe what you see—there is Kaskar." Osythes pointed. "Touch him, listen to him. He is what your machine has created. Do you deny that?"

"No—"

"Is he also the Kaskar who was—?" persisted Osythes.

Ramsay listened to this exchange with growing surprise. Just what was the Shaman trying to establish? That if Melkolf disposed of him, he would continue to haunt a lab in Lom? That sounded as impossible as everything else had been since he had had his first dream.

"No! Kaskar's dead!" Melkolf stated that fact now with all the emphasis of one who was determined to hold onto at least one truth in a rapidly shifting play of suggestion.

"I agree. Kaskar is dead. But this man"—Osythes indicated Ramsay—"is someone, something else. And we must know more about him. Since he has flaunted certain laws of existence which were believed to be firmly set—"

"You mean the Enlightened Ones want him?" Melkolf demanded.

"His existence has not been reported to the Grove." For a moment a shade of disturbance showed on Osythes's face.

"Then he need not be."

"Who is Adise?" Ramsay shot that question into their duet. He had no intention of standing there tamely while they decided whether or not he was going to be killed for what might be a second time, if one counted by bodies.

It was as if some potent voice had sounded out of the air, striking both of his opponents dumb. Melkolf stared, but Osythes blinked. Then the Shaman answered his question with a second.

"Where did you hear of Adise?" However, he gave Ramsay no chance to answer; instead, he swept on to reply to himself. "Then the Duchess—"

"What about the Duchess?" demanded Melkolf. "She brought him here—why?"

"If she were not the ruler of Olyroun, she would have entered the Grove. Her testing in the potentials of the true talent were high. Now it seems she has contacted the Enlightened Ones if Adise has been mentioned to this one."

"Well, who is Adise?" Melkolf sounded defiant now.

"She is a Foreteller. I wonder—" Osythes looked more distubed. "But I have no message, no sign from them. No." He pointed to Ramsay. "We must keep him to hand, safe. Do you understand? I must wait for a message. And do not think you can daunt the Enlightened with any tricks." His vocce sharpened and deepened as he spoke. "This man is under protection—"

He raised his hand and pointed his thumb bearing a heavy ring at Ramsay's head, moving that thumb in a small tight circle.

"You can't. This matter comes before the Council—" Melkolf protested.

Osythes simply stared at him, full faced. The scientist's scowl deepened, but he looked sulky also. As if he had been bested at last.

"Keep him in the cells where you had the others," Osythes continued now in a cold, remote tone. "You will be advised when to produce him and where."

With no further word, the Shaman turned to re-climb the stairs. Melkolf watched him go. The sulkiness was akin to hate in his expression. He turned and gave a vicious jerk to the cord about Ramsay's wrists.

"Come on, you!"

There were a couple of tricks Ramsay thought of trying. But the fact that the scientist was very careful to continue to hold the glass weapon on him was an excellent argument against any reckless gesture. He thought he could believe Melkolf's boasts about the efficiency of that arm. Perhaps the scientist would like his prisoner to try something so he could use it and then claim self-defense.

Melkolf rounded back of a tall installation to another open doorway giving on a very short hall. Here two iron-barred cells faced each other. The scientist threw open the door of the one on the left, waved Ramsay in. When he had slammed and locked the door, he gave a sharp snap of his fingers.

To Ramsay's astonishment, the loops about his wrists loosed themselves, fell to the floor, and then the cord wriggled like a living creature out between the bars. Melkolf stooped and caught up the length, which now hung in his hold as limp as any length of ordinary thin rope. He wound it into a few neat loops and went away, with it swinging from his fingers.

Ramsay was left to explore his new quarters. Against one wall there was a shelf that had some coarse coverings tangled upon it. He supposed this served as a bed. And there was a stool and an evil-smelling bucket. As accomodations, these were bleak enough, and he could see little hope of gaining any better in the immediate future.

However, as he settled on the stool, which was so low that he had to sprawl his legs across the floor or perch with his knees nearly up to his chin, Ramsay had enough to occupy his thoughts. He had been near complete extinction. He realized that now, with a sudden onset of mild panic.

That panic he had fought to control when facing Melkolf. Only he was still alive, and that was what counted. Also, there was indeed a sharp division of opinion now over his fate. So far, Osythes had shown himself strong enough to overrule the scientist.

That exchange between the two—Ramsay began to consider every word of it he could recall. They had used the machine earlier, and it had worked as they wished. No untimely return of the safely dead then. So, as Osythes had pointed out, why had it not worked the same way with him?

Ramsay had to force himself to accept Melkolf's flat statement that Kaskar had been buried as Ramsay Kimble, that there was no return. However, at the moment he was more than a little surprised at his reaction; he did not particularly care. Was it because the longer he was Kaskar's tenant the more he became identified with this world? So that the thought of no possible return failed to be a great shock?

Very well. Suppose he had to stay here. Then what sort of future could he expect? Osythes had hinted that he would be of interest to the Enlightened Ones. Not that that sounded too good. Ramsay had no intention of playing the part of some experimental animal while they studied him to see what made him tick, or rather *why* he made Kaskar tick. Ramsay smiled very grimly at that.

Melkolf wanted him dead, to expunge the mistake of his own experiment. Undoubtedly, his revival had sent Melkolf's stock on a sharp downward plunge, as far as the scientist's standing among his associates was concerned.

There was Ochall. How would he like another Kaskar all ready to hand? That talk of the High Chancellor's strange power over the real Prince— how much of that was the truth? Was Kaskar just a weak character under the sway of a man everyone believed was a very strong and malignant personality? Or had Ochall perhaps used drugs, hypnotism, what-have-you, to bring the heir of Ulad under his thumb, unable to operate without Ochall's express permission?

And Ochall had to have Kaskar as a front or he would go under. That was a point to remember.

Thecla—those in the conspiracy to get rid of Kaskar were aware now that she had been the one to help him in his first escape. But her own impression, that she was invulnerable to their counterattack—how true was that? Suppose she married Berthal as they all agreed she must—how much power would that give those of Ulad over her? Ramsay had no way of assessing the customs of this world enough to be able to answer for or against any future danger to the Duchess.

Adise—the mention of that name had plainly disconcerted Osythes. Yet Thecla had had the advice of that person, and the answer had been that he, Ramsay, had some part to play in Olyroun's future. That was why the Duchess had consented to his return.

His own record certainly was not one of glowing success. Though he had located the lab and found the machine, he was now in the hands of one set of the enemy. No matter how Thecla might feel toward Berthal, the old Empress, and her companions in intrigue, Ramsay did not trust them in the least.

All he had won by throwing that name at Osythes was a respite, to face up to his own stupidity. Certainly he had gained no advantage that he was aware of at present. Thecla would know, or guess, where he was when he did not show up again. Did she have influence enough to demand his freedom?

Somehow that thought made Ramsay uncomfortable. Ever since he had fallen into this web, it had been Thecla who had rescued him from one difficulty and then the next. It was about time he did something on his own—something more constructive than walking straight into the first trap they had set for him.

He was angry now. He got to his feet and went over to inspect the door of his cage. Though he thrust his arms through the bars as far as he could and groped about outside to try to locate the lock, his fingers encountered nothing but smooth metal. There was not even a keyhole, and he had not the least idea how Melkolf had locked it.

He squatted down to note how the bars were set into the stone of the flooring, and he could see there was no possible way to break out. Of course, if a jailer showed up, he might play one of the games the invincible hero of spy stories always pulled: gasp that he was dying, and when they opened up to make sure, simply batter his way out. But Ramsay had a grim premonition that if anyone did come, Melkolf would be standing by with his trusty glass squirter. And he had already decided he was not going to gamble a second body on being right or wrong in any showdown with the master of this den.

That left him the unproductive answer of simply sitting and waiting for something to happen. He had never been patient at the best of times, and at present he was even less in favor of allowing the enemy nine-tenths of the advantages. However, there seemed to be nothing else he could do.

If he could manage a little constructive dreaming now—The sudden thought surprised him a little with wry amusement. Then he began to consider it with less amusement and more purpose. Sitting down again on that uncomfortable stool, Ramsay began methodically to recall all he had heard Greg tell about dream telepathy experiments. There were two dreamers and the control. Ramsay had never paid much attention to the apparatus part of the experiment and had absolutely refused to volunteer as one of the subjects. The control waited until the hookup suggested, by way of a brain-wave reading, that the sleeper was receptive (they called that REM—rapid eye movements—because that was the physical signal that dreaming had begun). Once the dreamer was ready for action, the control pulled a picture from a stack waiting, one he selected at ramdom. Then he concentrated on that, and the dreamer, in more than a random number of cases, picked up suggestions of the contents of the picture.

But there was nothing for Ramsay to work with here on that level. Still, his mind played with the idea of dreams. Osythes had dreamed apparently from one alternate world to another to draw him, or else reached through to control Ramsay's dreaming. Could that very act have set up some rapport between them, so that now Ramsay, in turn, could reach the Shaman? He doubted very much that would work. Surely not to the point that he could bring Osythes here, make him open the door.

Melkolf—no. Ramsay did not believe that the scientist could be reached. Greg said it would not work against a closed mind. And Ramsay guessed that Melkolf's mind would be tightly closed, that the scientist believed it was his own ingenious machine that had had the major part in producing Kaskar's demise.

Osythes, however, was a dreamer. The point remained, when did the Shaman sleep—?

Ramsay's head dropped into his hands. He might just as well believe that he could get up now and walk through those bars as that he could accomplish anything by dreaming it.

EIGHT

RAMSAY THREW THE unsavory coverings from the shelf bed to the floor before he stretched out on the hard plank, which he thought was no too unlike the bier on which he had first awakened into this world. He closed his eyes, not to dream but to concentrate on the Shaman, both as he had seen Osythes in his dreams and later in person during Thecla's welcome to Lom.

The Shaman's black-and-white robe was mentally visible. However, Ramsay discovered it was far more difficult to build a face feature by feature. Yes, the hair was white and somewhat longer over the brow, looking thicker, as if fluffed up and out by some wind. Below that the forehead, then brows—also white and thick.

When Ramsay tried to recall the eyes beneath those brows, he nearly met defeat. Dark, a little sunken back into the skull—yes. Still there was a factor missing, a certain expression which Ramsay could not now define. Or was it *lack* of expression? There remained something masklike about the face of his vision—no true life behind it.

He had never tried such a feat of concentration before, not such an intense one. This struggle absorbed him even more than when he had tried earlier to recall the dreams that had led him here. One after another, those dream scenes again crowded in, overlapping, covering his attempted single vision of Osythes. Now those dreams spun a cover for the Shaman. Yet Ramsay persevered.

Then, for one moment, Ramsay singled out the face he wanted, no longer a lifeless mask. Those deep-set eyes were regarding him with a hint of astonishment. That contact lasted hardly more than a breath before it was broken. Again, he "saw" only a black-and-white figure misting away, into nothing.

Ramsay's head, his whole body ached. Muscles must have tensed so much as mind while he had fought for what he had no reason to believe might succeed. Should he try again?"

Black and white—black—and—

Black became gray and scarlet. Someone else—he sensed another presence—yet one, he was certain, who was as yet unaware of him. He cowered mentally away, as a small animal might flatten against the ground seeking to escape the attention of an enemy. That this other personality *was* the enemy—more so even than Osythes—Ramsay believed. But he could assign no name—Ochall? What had they said concerning the High Chancellor gave some credence to that. Greatly daring, Ramsay tried to summon up a face. There was nothing—except that he *knew* there was another there; to meddle further was folly.

Ramsay opened his eyes. Almost he expected that person to be leaning over him, willing to—to what? Ramsay did not know, but a sense of compulsion lingered. He sat up, looked around the cell. No, he was entirely alone. Nor did he catch any sound from the direction of the lab where Melkolf and the guard had discovered him.

If Melkolf was right—and at the moment Ramsay had no reason to doubt that the other believed exactly what he had said—there was no return to the past. He waited for his own reaction to that, perhaps even the rise of panic at being lost from all he knew.

Still—that did not follow. Ramsay looked down at the brown hands resting on his knees. Not his hands. But—they were! He did not feel any different in Kaskar's body than he had in his own. When he looked in the mirror, his features were those of Ramsay Kimble, though his skin might be several shades darker, his scar gone, his hair differently cut. Still, he had seen Ramsay Kimble there as he had all his life.

If there had was any trace of the original Kaskar personality left—well, he had not detected it. Therefore, he was *not* changed, only the world about him. It was like, he thought deliberately, taking a job in a foreign country—Mexico, perhaps, or one of the South American states. There he would have to learn language, customs, which were alien to those of his own land as were the ones of Olyroun, Tolcarne, or Ulad.

There was no one back home to really care if he dropped out of sight. Second cousins— He had been a loner since his parents died in a car accident when he was seventeen. After that, he had been too busy fighting for an education and a living to make any lasting contacts. Greg was perhaps the best friend he had had, although Greg was so wrapped up in the Project that he really cared for little else.

So—he had been free, if one could call it that, to accept a job overseas. This was a little farther than overseas, and much more of an alteration in his life. However, if he could accept it as such, he could push any panic far enough away for it to fade into nothingness.

In fact, though he realized it only now, Ramsay had, in the past days at Kilsyth, begun to adapt. If he accepted the fact that there was no return, then where did he go from that?

Right into the middle of a nasty mess, from everything he had learned. To Melkolf and his aids, the pseudo Kaskar was a danger because he could reveal exactly how they had rid themselves of the real Prince. To Ochall, Ramsay would suggest a possible new game with another pawn—

But he was himself! He was not Kaskar. And it was *his* future they would try to twist and turn—or perhaps erase entirely. Therefore—now he was fighting for himself.

And—

Ramsay started to his feet, facing the cell door. Someone was coming, not that he had heard any scrape of boot across the floor, but he was certain of movement within the lab, headed in his direction. Melkolf again, this time ready to finish him off? Ramsay drew a deep breath. No matter what exotic weapons the other was going to produce, Ramsay would not easily be killed.

Still no sound his ears could catch, just the sure belief that there was someone there, coming for him.

He stooped and caught up the stool, swinging it by one of its legs. How effective a shield that might make, Ramsay had no idea, but it was the only thing he could use. Perhaps he would even be lucky and throw it straight enough to knock Melkolf's tube out of his hands. Always supposing the other did not just stand beyond the bars and ray (if that's what that weapon did) without coming into reach.

A figure stepped into the opening of the short hall where the cells were. Black and white— Only one man Ramsay knew within this pile wore such a robe.

However, he did not put down the stool.

Osythes walked at a slow pace, but from the very moment he came into view, the Shaman tried to catch and hold Ramsay's gaze. There was danger in that! Just as he had sensed the noiseless approach of this Enlightened One, so now some instinct told him not to allow Osythes to meet him eye to eye. Ramsay dropped his own gaze to the other's chin, his wrinkled throat.

The Shaman reached the locked door of the cell.

"It is time that we speak, stranger." His voice sounded rusty, as if he did not use it much.

"Perhaps so," Ramsay returned. "What would you say to me? Since I am your prisoner—I am a captive listener."

"Not my prisoner—" Osythes extended a hand from the folds of a long sleeve, pressed his five finger-tips against the door plate. The gate swung open. "Come forth, stranger—"

Ramsay hesitated. What if he did just that and his action was deemed an escape attempt so they could cut him down easily without question?

"I bear no arms." Osythes sounded weary now. "Nor do I intend you any betrayal."

Ramsay remembered something Thecla had said. "Word-bond for that?" he asked.

"Word-bond," the Enlightened One replied promptly.

Now that was unbreakable, according to Grishilda's comment. Ramsay dropped the stool with a clatter, moved out into the narrow passage.

"Come!" Osythes had already turned away, headed back to the lab. Ramsay stalked warily after him. The Shaman had given his word-bond, but that might not hold for the other conspirators in the Get-Rid-of-Kaskar intrigue.

They were not going toward those stairs down which Ramsay had come, rather toward the opposite end of the crowded room. As they passed one bench, Ramsay saw, lying there, the Feudman's hood. He paused to snatch it up: that disguise might be needed again, especially in Lom, where his present face was a liability.

Here was a second stairway, steeper, narrower. Osythes took the climb slowly, as if such effort taxed his frail body. Ramsay loitered impatiently a few steps behind. He constantly glanced back, expecting to hear or see pursuit at their heels.

The flight went straight up. A thin patch of light at the top suggested an open portal, and perhaps they were expected. Osythes, breathing heavily, reached the opening, Ramsay just behind.

Here was another richly appointed chamber. However, Ramsay was given little time to survey his surroundings, for Osythes had advanced to stand by the side of a tall chair from which extended a canopy of carved and gilded wood overshadowing its occupant.

She seemed very small in that thronelike seat, yet such was her aura of presence that she was not in the least dwarfed or belittled by it. Instead, the throne provided the perfect setting for her.

A fur cloak was drawn about her shoulders, although, to Ramsay, the room felt warm. And all but her face was concealed by a scarf of golden tissue held in place by a begemmed circlet. Her hands, as thin as bird claws, rested quietly in her lap. On her right thumb was a seal ring such as Thecla wore, a band so heavy and thick it overpowered the flesh and bone the metal encircled. And she wore other rings, too, all richly jeweled.

Her small feet, covered by soft boots, were

planted firmly together on a footstool. All added to
make her stance one of complete authority. That this
was the old Empress Ramsay had no doubt. And he
studied her face curiously. What was she like, this
woman who had rid herself of a grandson in the name
of duty to her country?

Age had sharpened her features. If she had ever
possessed any beauty, it was now withered away.
Only she did not need beauty. She would draw all
eyes in any company wherein she chose to move.
Ramsay was impressed as he had never been before
in his life. But he determined not to show that. As far
as he was concerned, at this moment she represented
the enemy.

They were alone. A quick glance about the room
told him that just Osythes and Quendrida were united
in full power. What had Thecla said—these two
found him a menace, but they would not agree to his
killing. That left the other three: Berthal, the new
heir; Urswic, the Councillor; and Melkolf. Where
were those now? Did the absence of the junior three
mean that there had been a split in the party? If
so—how could that be put to Ramsay's own advantage?

At this moment he was well aware of the very
searching stare the Empress had turned on him. He
met her gaze calmly, with none of that instinctive
withdrawal that had warned him against Osythes.
The silence in the chamber grew, but Ramsay determined to let one of the others break it first.

"What manner of man are you?" It was the Empress who spoke. She asked her question sharply, as
if to gain some quick, perhaps too revealing retort
from him.

"I am a very ordinary man—" Ramsay hesitated,

and then gave her the term of respect he had heard was used when speaking directly to one of the last reigning queens of his own world—"Madam."

She raised her hand to sketch an impatient gesture.

"In some manner," she retorted, "you have importance. Or you would not be here."

"You mean, ma'am"—Ramsay schooled to such indifference as he could summon—"I would be more use to you were I dead?"

Beneath her hook of nose, her mouth quivered. It was Osythes who replied to that challenge.

"You are bold—" There was rebuke in his tone.

"What else have you left me?" Ramsay was amazed that he could find these words; stilted they might be, but only such were appropriate in this company. "I am told that I am a dead man. In two different worlds, it would seem. Therefore, as a dead man, who can deny me plain speaking?"

To Ramsay's surprise, the Empress suddenly gave a cackle of laughter.

"That was indeed aptly expressed, stranger. You have a quick tongue and a mind"—she hesitated—"a mind that differs from those we know. Now what must we do with you?"

"What shall *I* do?" he corrected her. "The choice is mine now, ma'am."

Again the Empress was silent, studying him. Then she asked, as if she might be inquiring politely, not really caring, concerning the intentions of any mere acquaintance: "What is in your mind to do, boy?"

Ramsay shrugged. "As yet, I have not been given any chance to choose, ma'am. Melkolf has told me there is no return to my own world. If I can believe him, then it is here I must make a place for myself."

She shook her coroneted head slowly. "Not here,

not in Lom, not in Ulad, while you wear *that* face.''

"And who presented me with it, ma'am?" Ramsay challenged again.

"We had no choice." Any momentary lightness vanished from her voice. Her tone was again that of cold authority. "You must know the situation—Kaskar's rule would have produced disasters our country could not endure.''

"So—now you must accept me." Ramsay refused to be intimidated.

"I have said—we cannot." Again, authority in her voice.

"Your answer, then, is Melkolf's—kill?" he demanded.

Her ringed hands moved; the thin fingers tightened about the edge of the fur cloak, making the jewels in her rings catch and reflect light as rainbow sparkles. Osythes moved a step forward from beside the throne chair, as might someone guarding his companion. A faint shade of indignation crossed his face, breaking that masklike serenity he had worn since he had released Ramsay from the cell.

"You make too free!" Now the sharpness was in the Shaman's voice, but the Empress interrupted him.

"Who has a better right to question us so, Reverend One? No stranger, we will not kill. But there is another—perhaps others—who will not be so forbearing, because they fear. When men fear, then they act, wisely or rashly, but still they act. If you would live—I say this again with all truth, if you will live—then not in Lom, in Ulad, even on this side of the ocean. You have taken the guise of one out of Tolcarne—very well—live by it!''

"And why should I be governed by any desire of

yours, ma'am?" Ramsay did not ask that with insolence but hoped that these two would get his meaning, that he was no man of theirs to be commanded.

"Such an *answer* is not my desire," the Empress replied. "It is only good reasoning. I can restrain Melkolf; my orders will be obeyed in that direction, as long as my son, the present Emperor—though failing fast—still lives. When he dies, I have still a place in Lom, but I cannot command such power. I can only suggest then, not order.

"In the meantime, you have been told of Ochall—of what he desires. One of his creatures, those Eyes and Ears that serve about this court, need only glimpse you unmasked and he will speedily hear of it. And I promise you, if Ochall comes to hunt you down, not death, but death-in-life will then be your portion.

"Do not believe that Kaskar was always a weakling, an easy tool in the hands of a stronger will. Once he was as you stand now, a youth proud in his strength, quick of wit, able as to mind. This I do not declare because he was blood of my blood, flesh of my flesh, heir to my House—no, this I say because it was true.

"What evil means Ochall used to make Kaskar his we have not discovered. It may even be that he perverted some of the Old Knowledge, that which we believed only the Enlightened Ones retained, to achieve the fashioning of the Kaskar he would have. And, having done this once, can it not be that he will be able to do so again? Do you wish to be only a shadow of what you now, are, stranger?"

She was not trying to frighten him, Ramsay guessed that. This Quendrida who ruled in Ulad meant exactly what she said. Drugs—hypnotism—

it must be such as these she hinted at. And he could
also imagine what might happen *if* Ochall could lay
hands on him. Suppose they were entirely right, that
he had no future in this land? A quick retreat at
present began to sound like the best move he could
make. Still, it did not follow that he could not, at
some future time, return. If they won their battle with
Ochall—But it was the immediate present that mattered most, not the future.

"Can I accept," he asked of them both, "that
Melkolf did speak the truth—that I have no return to
my own place?"

The Empress left the replying to Osythes.

"It is true. I have sent the dream probe once more
into your world. It met with nothing. There the man
you were has passed the Final Gate, alone with him
who was Kaskar. May the abiding pace of all time
gather about him now!" The Shaman made a small
gesture, tracing some symbol in the air. For a moment the Empress inclined her head.

"All right. Then if I go out of Ulad—say, to Tolcarne? How may that be arranged?"

"It is arranged. We needed only your consent,"
the Shaman replied. "Though the merchants trading
overseas are in these times very few in number, there
is one venturer whose ship lies now at anchor in the
west harbor. He is willing to take a passenger. Clothing, weapons, credit with this merchant, all will be
waiting for you on board. You will leave within the
hour—"

"You make such a decision with speed," commented Ramsay wryly.

"It must be done so," Osythes answered. "For
the sooner you are out of Lom, ocean-borne, the less
either you or we have to fear. Ochall may have al-

ready heard rumors of your existence. There is no reason to believe he has not. And we do not understate your danger if he searches with all his resources."

Ramsay shrugged. "It seems I have no alternative."

That you have not!" the Empress affirmed. "That you have been caught up in this matter we must deplore, but the reason for it was of such importance—we cannot deny that, if faced again with the same choices, we would make the same decision. One man weighs very little against the safety of a whole land."

Ramsay looked to Osythes. "I am told that is also the belief of the Enlightened Ones, why they will advise but do no more. Yet it seems that here you have done more—"

"On my head and heart that action will lie. Which is none of your concern, stranger! But since you have said yes—then we only waste time with our chatter here. You must be on your way at once!"

"I would see the Lady Thecla first."

The Empress leaned forward a little in her thronelike chair, her old eyes turned searchingly upon him once more.

"Why so? Such a meeting has no reason. She knows well all we have just said to you and agreed to what we would offer. The child has done very well in every way. Now she will do even better, joining peacefully our two lands, for the greater safety and progress of both. Berthal is not, as Pyran, my dying son—a great ruler. But he is one who will listen to good counsel, and he hates Ochall bitterly. We need not fear that that son of evil will much longer send his shadow out across our land!" Her voice deepened, was filled with emotion as she continued. "No—you go now—Osythes will accompany you to the gate. Beyond, there will be one to play your guide to the ship. And—wear that mask—put it on now! Would you allow a dead man to walk so all can see?" She pointed to the cap-mask swinging in his hand.

He could demand again to see Thecla, but he thought it useless. Anyway, the Empress had made it very clear that the girl knew all they had planned for him. Still, as Ramsay adjusted the hood and mask, fastening firmly the throat latch, it was with a sense of disappointment. Of course he, as a person, would not matter to Thecla. She had been working from the first not to save Ramsay Kimble but to salvage the plans of the two now fronting him, agreeing that the good of any nation came before that of one man, though she had refused to leave him prey to either Ochall or the hotheads on this side of the intrigue. For that much he must thank her. She would now marry Berthal. Ochall would lose his power. And history would continue along the path this old woman, this man, saw fit to set it.

The Empress gave Ramsay no formal farewell, nor did he offer her any. She had leaned her head back against her chair, her face now much in the shadow of the canopy, but not so much that he could not see her closed eyes. Perhaps she had already dismissed him from her mind now that the problem he had presented was neatly solved.

But Quendrida of Ulad could not foresee *all* the future, much as he had heard talk of the Enlightened Ones' foretelling. Perhaps she would have a surprise or two. Ramsay was already beginning to wonder if he was not the one to deliver such a surprise. He had made up his mind while in the cell below that he was no man's puppet. Nor did he intend to be any woman's. His own man, that was what he was going to be—even if he had to plan and fight for it.

They traversed corridors, descended stairs, came out at last in a courtyard like the one which Grishilda had led him to on his first escape from Lom Palace. Again one of the flyers waited and, by its steps, a man wearing the uniform of the guard. He saluted Osythes and then Ramsay, waiting for the latter to climb into the vehicle before he himself entered.

The flyer soared aloft in such a leap as had startled Ramsay on his first ride, but now they were skyborne for a much shorter time. They set down on a square of pavement that was lapped by the water of what must be the sea. A wharf ran on out, and berthed alone it were ships, though they had no sign of spars or sails, only a stubby post in the center. The guardsman waited for Ramsay to join him.

"Not far—" He gestured down the wharf. "It is the—" He had been facing Ramsay. Now his gaze centered over Ramsay's shoulder. There was startled surprise in his eyes; his mouth dropped open.

Ramsay acted half on instinct, dropping to the ground, rolling. A man with a drawn "sword of state" in one hand plunged past. The attacker was slightly off balance, mainly because he meant that sword to have gone well into Ramsay's back.

That his treacherous attack had failed in the first blow did not appear to defeat him. The stranger whirled, to leap again. As he did so, he shouted: "Feud vengeance!"

Ramsay did not try to regain his feet. Instead, he rolled onto his back and waited, seemingly an easy prey. This fellow also wore a mask, only it was bright yellow. Through its slits his eyes glistened avidly as he leaped again. Ramsay's back muscles tightened as he kicked out smoothly, felt his boots thud punishingly against the other's body.

NINE

THE ATTACKER, unprepared for such a countermove, sprawled backward. With another roll, an upward push, Ramsay regained his feet. Falling, the other had lost his sword. Ramsay planted one booted foot on the bared blade. As the man lunged at him for the third time, Ramsay brought the edge of his hand into precise alignment, not to kill, but to stun. For the last time Yellow Mask wilted, face down on the pavement of the wharf, now to remain there. Ramsay, breathing hard, stooped, picked up the sword, wheeled with it bare and ready in his hand.

He discovered they had gathered a circle of spectators. However, if Lom had a police force of any kind, no such officer was present. Nor had any of the watchers moved to interfere. Among them Ramsay did not see the palace guard who had been supposed to see him safely to the waiting ship.

"A clever toss, that—" remarked one man, moving out a step or two from the rest.

He was lean, tall, his dark hair almost completely covered by a crested cap, not unlike the one Ramsay now wore, except that it lacked a face mask. His vest-coat was as short as that of a servingman, but he wore a wide belt that supported both a short sword of ceremony and a holstered weapon of some kind.

Also, there was no badge on his breast. Rather, a diagonal stripe of violet slashed dramatically across the uniform gray of the rest of his clothing.

As he addressed Ramsay, he raised one hand in a casual salute, as if in passing courtesy only.

"Dedan, out of Kental," he introduced himself. "Free Captain."

"Arluth of Tolcarne," Ramsay replied. He was thinking furiously. The prompt disappearance of the palace guard from the scene led him to only one conclusion. He had been set up for murder! Someone had taken neat advantage of Ramsay's cover as Feudman to do this. And he believed he need not have to search very far for the one, or ones, who had arranged the attack. All the Empress and Osythes had told him that had been meant to lead him tamely here, to his death. Perhaps the plan reached further back than their interview; perhaps even Thecla, in arranging such a disguise, had had this eventual end in mind.

His anger shimmered within him. They had played games with him. Very well—he owed them nothing from this moment on. He was his own man. And now there would not be any retreat to Tolcarne. Ramsay at this moment doubted very much that any ship bound there was really docked at Lom.

The Free Captain dropped on one knee beside the flaccid body of Ramsay's attacker, rolled the man over on his back to strip off the yellow mask. He gave a low whistle and glanced up, appraisingly, at Ramsay.

"Someone wishes you very dead, stranger. Do you know him?" He jerked a beringed thumb at the inert fighter.

"No."

"This is Odinal, a hired killer. And his pay comes high. Those whom you feud with must be willing to empty their pockets." He brushed his hands together as he rose. He might have been wishing to rid himself of any lingering trace of the touch of the mask.

"I would suggest," Dedan continued, "that you now cease to be the center of attention." His fleeting glance right to left indicated the gathering crowd. "It may well be that Odinal had a shoulder man to back him."

At that moment Ramsay felt lost. If what this fellow said was true, he might expect another attack. And, having surveyed Ramsay in action, any prudent back-up man would do his killing from a distance. He could see no one who looked suspicious among the crowd, but this life of constant peril was totally new to him, and confusing.

Dedan's hand fell lightly upon his arm. "I believe prudence indicates a swift withdrawal. Retreat is often the right arm of valor, or so we are told."

Ramsay nearly jerked away from that light touch. Why should he trust this Free Captain (whatever *that* meant!) any more than any other in the crowd? But the man was right! Ramsay had to get out of sight, hide until he could make some coherent plan.

"We are but a matter of strides from the Cask and Bowl—" Dedan waved down a street leading to the wharf. "Their fare is rough enough, but passable for a dock tavern. Shall we go?"

"Why—" Ramsay began.

"Why do I take a hand in this matter?" Dedan finished for him. "On two counts, stranger. First, I have a constitutional dislike of seeing an unaware man stabbed in the back. Secondly, I am very much interested in the strange ways you use your hands

and feet. In my own profession every new defense
adds to one's capability, and eventually to one's
worth as a hired fighting man. No." He shook his
head as if he read Ramsay's sudden thought. "I am
not of Odinal's cult brothers. I am a soldier for hire,
not an assassin against one private enemy."

No one moved to dispute their going. And Ramsay
went, mainly because at the moment he could not
think of anything else to do. The betrayal had been so
sudden, had so completely altered the scene for him,
that he was nearly at as big a loss of understanding as
he had been on his first awakening as Kaskar.

Dedan waved him through the door of the tavern,
where a strong mixture of odors suggested stale and
ancient meals, and not much use of water and soap
thereafter. The Free Captain continued across the
large room where there were benches and tables,
massive, much stained and rubbed smooth at the
edges, as if generations had eaten and drunk there.
There was a buzz of conversation, for the tavern had
patrons in plenty. However, Dedan skirted even
vacant benches, proceeding into an inner room
where there was a measure of quiet, though the
smells were stronger.

He kicked a stool out from under a small table,
waved Ramsay to another opposite him. A girl, her
upper tunic slit so extravagantly that one could see
well up the plump swell of her thigh, her hair caught
tight to her head by a tarnished gilt ribbon, pattered
in.

"Isa, my beauty, two cups of the White, and whatever you have now stewing on the right-hand stove."

She giggled and nodded, scuttling out as if Dedan
were not one to be kept waiting.

"I will not ask who could have set Odinal on you."

Dedan eyed Ramsay. "Tolcarne you have claimed for a homeland, and you wear a Feudman's hood. But it is not like the Houses of the West to reach overseas to pull an enemy down. And if you are a proclaimed Feudman, you should have been secure. Now, I wonder, whose boot toes have you bruised *here!*"

The Free Captain spoke lightly. Whether he expected a quick answer or not, he gave no sign. Ramsay placed the sword he had taken from Odinal on the top of the table between them. Now Dedan leaned forward a little to study the weapon.

"Good workmanship, and a double threat, too—"

"Double threat?" Ramsay was surprised into asking.

"Yes. Behold!" The Free Captain touched the hilt, pressing his thumb firmly on one of the ornamental bead bosses. From the point of the blade oozed two large drops of a liquid.

"I would advise you not to touch that," Dedan warned. "It is not meant to nourish a man; quite the opposite. This is a sword out of Zagova, where they have some very peculiar customs. I am a little surprised at Odinal under the circumstances. Even a hired sword does not usually choose such tricks."

Ramsay stared at those dark drops. He did not doubt in the least that Dedan was perfectly truthful. Perhaps the yellow-masked assassin need only have scratched his opponent. At the thought of what might have happened, Ramsay's hand clenched on the edge of the table.

"Just so. You were far more fortunate than you guessed, stranger, when you escaped that. However, it is how you escaped that interests me most. I could judge your actions well enough to believe that you have trained in a new form of fighting."

Though he did not make a question out of that, Ramsay nodded.

The girl Isa returned, balancing a tray on which were cups and bowls. Suddenly Ramsay was very hungry. She was about to set the tray on the table when she sighted the sword, those ominous dark drops.

She cried out, jerking away so sharply that the liquid in the cups slopped over. Dedan threw out an arm to steady her.

"Isa, my beautiful one, do you now find one of those foul rags Bavar keeps to wipe down those outside tables of his. I promise then all shall be well. Put your tray here—"

She did as he bade, then was gone and back again so quickly, a grimy rag flapping from her hand, that Ramsay could only believe unusual fear had driven her. However, she would not come near the table. Instead she tossed the rag to Dedan. Carefully the Free Captain mopped up the spilled liquid. Then, holding the cloth folded together, he went to the fireplace, tossed the wad into the charred ends of wood lying there. Going down on one knee, he brought a small box from an inner pocket of his tunic, spun a wheel on its side with his thumb. The resulting spark fell on the material, which flared angrily, giving off a puff of evil-smelling smoke.

Isa voiced a deep sigh of relief. Still she did not return to gather up the tray or serve them. It appeared she believed that the sooner she was out of the room the better.

Ramsay ate steadily; nor did his companion break the silence that filled the room now. While he ate, Ramsay's mind was busy. He wanted to know more about this Dedan who had appeared so fortuitously on the wharf and had knowledge of unusual weapons. However, as a man of this world, how much would Dedan presume Ramsay already knew? And if Ramsay dared ask any questions at all, would he not then reveal that he was more than a simple stranger? He had a very complicated problem.

Dedan finished what was in his bowl. Now he nursed his cup between both hands, watching Ramsay across its brim. There was a lazy, engaging quirk on his lips that was not quite a smile but implied something amusing in this situation, though Ramsay gained no indication that such amusement was aimed at him.

"I have an offer for you, Arluth—" For the first time the Free Captain used Ramsay's Tolcarnean alias. "If you teach me that trick with the feet, I'll give you safe passage out of Lom and guarantee you won't have to face another Odinal, or the same one recovered. You have hurt his professional prestige badly by that trick of yours. He will be prepared now to make your disposal a personal matter, you understand. I am not a merchant to bargain; my offer is a simple one. Teach me that trick, and leave Lom as one of my Free Company. We are due to sail up the coast tonight, land at Yasnaby, then proceed inland along the border there. If Odinal tries to follow, he will be as noticable as a rashawk in the open-sky, always provided he can find the means to travel. In addition, if you are oath-bound to the Company, your quarrel becomes our quarrel. And the world knows well that the Free Companies protect their own. What think you of my offer? I do not believe that you shall have a better one, at least not here in Lom."

Ramsay, remembering the sudden and doubtless

well-rehearsed disappearance of the guardsman, could readily accept that.

"Your Company—for whom does it fight now?" He made a guess that these might be among those rootless mercenaries whom Ochall was gathering. That being so, he had no intention of leaping from a fire set by the Empress and Osythes into another stirred up by the apparently universally detested Chancellor.

"Not for Ochall. Is that your problem, Artluth?" Dedan studied him shrewdly. "Be that so, you have a right to look over your shoulder night and day. No, we have been hired by the Thantant of Dreghorn. He holds the Western Marches for Olyroun, and they have been invaded twice by the Lynarkian pirates. Those raiders grow bolder. This time they managed to sack Razolg and hold it for a full week, standing off a seige by the largest force Thantant could put against them. Olyrounians will fight attackers, but they are not trained to the field. Thus we are to join them. The pay is good, and there are bonuses added for each skirmish that puts those of Lynark underground or back to sea, licking wounds. Now, what say you—your knowledge for a safe passage out of Lom?"

Ramsay emptied his cup. As he set it down on the table, he said slowly: "I am no soldier. I do not even know how to handle such a weapon as this." He touched the hilt of the short sword. He knew such frankness betrayed him, for how could a Feudman be so ignorant? But Ramsay saw no other way. He did not believe he could bluff a trained fighting man. Now he continued, raising a finger to touch his mask.

"Neither am I a Feudman from Tolcarne. Though, as you have seen, there are those who want me dead.

I believe now that this very disguise they wished upon me was to provide an easier target for Odinal, or one like him. I cannot tell you who—or what I am. But Lom—Ulad—means death—''

For a long moment Dedan regarded him. Then the Free Captain said: ''Truth may be a harsh lady to her liege men, Arluth, but when a man is frank, he deserves the same openness in answer. Do you flee some crime?''

''If you count the fact that I exist at all as a crime, yes. For no other reason am I a menace to others.''

''Ochall?''

''Among others, yes,'' Ramsay returned. ''I have inadvertently spoiled a plan in which he had a prominent interest.''

Now the Free Captain showed once more a faint quirk of smile. ''That would fit well with what I have heard of that very unworthy Chancellor. So you are no soldier? Well, there is no lacking the means of making you one. And your own skill—that I wish to learn in turn. Hunted man or Feudman—what matters it? To me, the cases are more than a little equal. I owe no liege service to any within Ulad. Have you reason to believe that Olyroun would also close doors to you?''

Could Ramsay be sure that Thecla was not one of the prime movers in this intrigue? He longed to believe that she had been unaware of this last small refinement of plan someone had set in action to wipe him permanently from the playing board. But, Ramsay decided, he was going to take this chance.

''I do not think so,'' he guessed. ''Though if certain powers in Ulad pushed—''

Dedan raised his eyebrows. ''Now you interest me even more, Arluth, who is *not* of Tolcarne. But will they seek you among a Free Company?"

"Perhaps not."

"Well enough. Now—take off that mask. We shall make good use of the window yonder." He indicated the grimy pane, cross-latched with strips of metal. Then he counted some small coins on the table top. "It is better not to risk passing through the outer room again. Who knows who may sit there snuffling into his cup?"

Ramsay hesitated only a moment before he tugged off the masking hood. Dedan was already at the window, using his strength to force up a latch which plainly had been long set in place. A moment later they slipped, one after the other, over the sill into a noisome side alley.

The hour was past sundown, and there were enough shadows to furnish some kind of cover. Dedan's shoulder brushed against Ramsay's.

"To the wharf. Our coaster sails with the night tide."

Ramsay was very conscious of his unmasked face. The warnings, beginning with Thecla, that his features might mark him down to any spy, had deeply set in his mind. Still, he was not, he thought, even glanced at by the few men they passed. However, he gave a sigh of relief when he boarded the ship and passed down into the hold quarters of Dedan's company.

Three days later, in midmorning, Ramsay grinned as he lightheartedly surveyed, with mock criticism, Dedan, who sprawled on the deck.

"You merely use a man's own action and strength against him," Ramsay repeated for about the tenth time within the hour.

Dedan gritted his teeth. "Well enough, when you do it! However, my turn will come. Your hand is not as sure on sword hilt as it is against my aching neck!"

Ramsay had a half-dozen pupils out of the company of thirty, which was Dedan's command. The rest shied off from this new method of fighting, being content to watch, and jeer at those taking ungainly tumbles across the planking. Dedan was also right in his statement, for Ramsay remained certainly far from mastering the sword. He could use to better effect the odd handgun that was the other close-combat weapon of the company.

That impelled darts of glass, nasty when they broke upon impact, slivering to enlarge the wound. He saw nothing akin to the glass tube with which Melkolf had threatened him. There were also larger, long-barreled weapons, meant to fire globes, which burst in the air, loosing upon the heads of the enemy a burning liquid. Though these arms were faintly akin to a rifle, the military of this world appeared to have nothing that shot a solid bullet.

In addition to personal arms, Dedan showed Ramsay several field weapons mounted on planes, which, properly controlled, floated a foot or so above the surface of the ground. Weighing far less than their bulk suggested, these could be towed into place, and, once aimed, they broadcast, fanning wide in a way damaging to enemies, waves of vibration which tormented all not equipped with ear plugs.

The mixture of weapons—the reliatively primitive sword with the strange and much more sophisticated "rifles" and "vibrators"—puzzled Ramsay. He learned that side arms, rifles, and floating vibrators were very costly. Dedan's company hire price went two-thirds into buying and maintaining these—while replacements could be found only at a metal market in the far north where another nation had redis-covered, and then copied, certain weapons from the Older Days.

These northern arms merchants were jealous of their monopoly, and the weapons they produced possessed built-in-destruct mechanisms. Thus any-one striving to decode their construction did not survive his curiosity. Or, if he did, he was not in such a state to enjoy life greatly thereafter. So far, no one had managed to circumvent this particular safeguard on a profitable trade monopoly.

One had to be sparing of ammunition, using it only when it would be to the overwhelming advantage for either attack or defense. Dedan considered the cases of ammunition his main treasure. In an attack the mercenaries relied first on the swords. Thus all of the men Ramsay watched in practice were, he admitted, deadly foemen with what was in his own world an archaic weapon.

Without the use of sails or other visible aids, the coaster headed steadily north. At intervals the vessel seemed close to complete submergence. Ramsay speculated as to whether that stub of pillar in the midst of the ship was not the source of the mysterious energy that kept them going. Another vestige of the earlier and vanished civilization?

Ramsay had to be careful about questions. To dis-play too much ignorance would be dangerous. He listened as men talked, attempted from scraps and pieces to build up for himself a more concrete idea of this world.

Descriptions of certain portions of the land, espe-cially to the northeast bordering on Tolcarne, suggested that an atomic disaster had occurred during the ancient conflict. These man-made deserts were deadly, though some strange mutant races were reported to be living along the sea coast even within the fringe of that avoided area. Similar deserts existed to the east and had taken a large portion of the continent which now held Ulad, Olyroun, and two other nations. The people now living in these "clean" sections had a recorded history of having moved up slowly from the south.

Their ancestors had been wandering tribal barbarians when they had re-peopled the land. However, contact with the Enlightened Ones had brought about a radical change in their nomadic lives. They had settled and started to build anew, but their legacy of tribal custom led them to develop as feudal states often at war with one another.

Within three generations, Ulad had united some twenty of such small antagonistic kingdoms, duchies, and lordships, and now ambitiously proclaimed itself an empire. To the north Olyroun remained free. Along the coast, still farther north, buffers between the culturally advancing south and the awesome merchants who dealt in bits and pieces of forgotten technical lord, were the islands of Lynark, which were the present seat of a loose confederation of dedicated pirates. Nearby, on the mainland, was Zagova, whose people were adept workers in metal and allied with the merchants of arms.

Mentally, Ramsay tried to draw a rough map of this world; he had yet to *see* one. He knew that what he learned in this way was far from accurate. The one thing that all his informants agreed upon was that the Enlightened Ones had certain gifts or powers that no ordinary man could counter with any known weapon or tool. The Shaman-born might originally have been of another race; speculation on this subject seemed divided. However, it was now well known that they did draw recruits, both men and women, from all the "civilized" nations.

Simply a wish to be an Enlightened One had no force. One had to possess qualities of mind which were recognized by those already gathered into that fellowship of power. It was necessary, after being selected, that the untested recruit retire for a number of years to one of the Groves, which were scattered headquarters. Rumor said that the lifetime of one of the Fellowship far outlasted that of ordinary mortals. The Shaman brood was held in awe, and also, perhaps, a measure of dislike, mainly because of their policy of selecting some goal of their own, thus refusing help at times, even if the cause was good.

Advisers entered courts as Chief Shamans (as Osythes was in Lom), but they could only advise as to certain actions. Oftentimes they remained stubbornly dumb, refusing any words at all. They even had been known to desert a ruler at a time of extremity, simply because the course they foresaw as paramount demanded that this man or woman fall from power, a decision issuing from impending action.

"They are unchancy," Dedan stated frankly. "He who seeks out a Foreseer does so at his peril. I believe they can weave such a man into serving them, seldom to his own good."

"Foreseeing—" Ramsay said musingly. "Have you ever seen this done for another?" He wanted to ask *how* it was done but knew that he must approach the question obliquely.

Dedan frowned. He did not reply at once. Instead he shot a glance sidewise at Ramsay.

"Once," he replied shortly, "and no good came of it. It was—" He hesitated, again eyeing Ramsay. The Free Captain might have been trying to make up his mind whether the other could be trusted with confidence. "It was in the matter of the assault on Vidin. I was Second then—Tasum comanded the company. He, poor fool, thought that perhaps he could gain a high seat—the Rule of the Outer Reef Land. So he sought a Seeress and pressed me to go with him. Though I did not give assent to any reading, mind you. No ill luck from that would I have touch me.

"She threw Twenties and drew. I can see them yet, all lying out on the handboard of her table. There they were —Hopes, Fears, Fates, Dreams. Tasum got the King of Fate. He thought it meant victory. Only he died the next day screaming, with Hot Rain flooding over him. No, I have no wish to see that again!"

Ramsay was no clearer in his mind after an explanation. He sensed that Dedan had no wish to continue his story either. And he was hoping furiously to find some way of learning more, when the signal was given from above the deck that they were nearing their chosen harbor.

Here was no wharf or easy landing. They had to lower their equipment and baggage into small boats, then be rowed through surf and lashing spray toward a rocky spit of land which projected into the tameless waves.

All of them were well soaked by the time they assembled far enough above the water to escape the dash of foam. Ramsay was not blind to the tension among them. There was more unease here than just a rough disembarkation would cause.

Ramsay had shouldered his own backpack and made sure his side arms, sword, and all were fast in place. Dedan climbed to the highest point of the rock, his head turned toward the shore, his eyes shielded from wind and spray by cupped hands. Ramsay thought that the Free Captain was seeking something he expected to see but that was not there.

The boats were all on their way back to the ship. Thus the wild rocky coast, the constant beating of the water, gave an impression of loneliness, which increased the unrest of those among the rocks.

Dedan signaled three scouts, who fanned out as best they could, moving inland across the rocks. But the Free Captain held the rest of the company where they were until those he had dispatched reached the distant beach and climbed to the highest dunes there. Finally they turned to wave all clear.

Ramsay wondered what danger the Free Company expected. There had been no hint on shipboard of this lonely landing. He knew they were to meet, shortly after disembarking, men sent by the Thantant. Perhaps it was because that force was not already camped in sight that Dedan had turned so cautious.

However, the Free Captain now ordered them on, and Ramsay picked the easiest road he could discover across and among the spray-wet, weed-bedecked rocks.

TEN

THE ROCKY RIDGE slowly gave way to shifting dunes. Then they saw, flowing toward them across the ground, a mist—or a fog? Though this ground-based cloud appeared to move more swiftly than any normal fog, Ramsay thought.

Dedan's alarm whistle raised a shrill, ear-piercing call, echoing over the beach. The company closed in tighter formation. Now they began to take on the appearance of a beleaguered host. Still Ramsay could see nothing ahead but the gathering of that thick yellowish mist. Again, more furiously, Dedan blew. Ramsay realized that already the scouts had vanished, curtained off by the fog. A glance back over his shoulder to the sea confirmed the fact that the ship was rapidly dwindling toward the horizon. Retreat in that direction was impossible.

"To the ridge—" Dedan's arm waved them right.

That tumble of stone that had formed a very rough wharf for their landing was here rooted in a rise of rock, pitted and crannied, but, even so, providing a more solid surface than the sand through which they had started to plough.

To that ridge they made their way at the best speed they could manage, the fog rolling inexorably behind them, rising not from the sea but, oddly enough, from an inner point of land. Ramsay was scrambling up the first of the stones when he heard, even through the now continuous pipe of Dedan's whistle, a scream of such agony that he clutched convulsively at the rock in instant reaction. Out of that mist had that cry come. He could believe it a death shriek. Friend? Or still unseen foe?

They fought their way higher among the water-worn rocks. Here was no spray to lash at them, but the footing was so treacherous, because of the many hollows and crannies in the stone themselves, that they had to give strict heed to their going. At last they reached the crest, men fitting into hollows, dodging behind any rise of rock, dropping field packs, unslinging weapons. Those in charge of the two vibrations machines dragged off protecting coverings, swung fan-shaped antennae back and forth in search of the foe.

Ramsay squatted beside Dedan. None of the scouts had yet returned. Now the dirty yellow of the fog, washed around the foot of the ridge on which they were perched, was rising higher and higher.

He looked to the Free Captain. "What is it?"

Dedan shrugged impatiently. "Your guess will equal mine. I have not seen the likes of it before. But to my mind the fog is not natural."

"Pirate magic!" A man behind them spat. "Some trickery of Northerners. Perhaps the sea devils bought such with their loot from Razlog."

"A gas—something noxious in the air?" Ramsay felt his throat tighten, his breathing grow faster, shallower, even as he asked.

Dedan shook his head. "With the sea wind rising, they could not control such an attack well enough."

"They might have masks to breathe through, to purify," Ramsay pointed out from the knowledge of his own time and space.

The Free Captain looked unconvinced. "I think this is to provide attack cover." He turned to the man who had suggested pirate magic. "Give me the message bird, Rahman."

From his shoulder the other slipped a thong supporting a small cage in which sat, silent, yet watching them with its black beads of eyes, a gray-winged bird, slightly smaller in size than the pigeons Ramsay knew.

To Ramsay's surprise, Dedan made no move to fasten any message clip to either slender red leg. Instead he lifted the bird, now lying calmly content between his palms, to eye level. Staring straight at the winged messenger, Dedan repeated slowly: "Besieged—Yasnaby—fog—foe unknown—"

The bird's long, pointed bill opened, then closed with a sharp click. From its throat there croaked a somewhat garbled but still understandable imitation of his speech: "Beesiege—Yassby—fog—foe—unnnknownn—"

"Right!" Dedan tossed the bird upward. Aloft, it spread wing, to circle the rocks of their natural fortress twice heading inland, flying well above the curtain of the fog at a swift rate of speed.

"Let that speaker reach the frontier post—" Dedan did not continue.

Rahman laughed. "The Marchers will then come thudding, perhaps in time to bury us, Captain. It is a long ride from the nearest post, though they may have a flyer or two." Maybe hope made him add that.

Dedan whistled imperatively. All heads turned in his direction. By now the first wisps of fog had already curled between those men in lower positions on the ridge.

"Stay set," their Captain ordered. "Let them come to you no matter what ruse they may employ to shake us loose. With the stones of our walls we shall not prove the easy prey they expect—"

His answer was a low growl of assent spreading from hollow to hollow. Already some of the company farther away were half hidden from sight. Mist, damp and cold, puffed into Ramsay's face. At least his worst fear was not realized. However this fog had been engendered, it was not a gas—

"Captain—"

A rattling sound rose from below. Someone was climbing toward them. Ramsay's hand tensed on the butt of his hand weapon. However, the man who climbed was no enemy, rather one of the missing scouts.

He fought gaspingly for breath, as if he had outraced death. Then, as he spilled forward beside Dedan and Ramsay, he mouthed rough sounds before he could find meaningful words.

"Pirates—out there—" He gestured wildly at the mist as he drew himself up to his knees. "They were waiting for us."

"How many?" Dedan wanted to know.

"I saw only two. They arose out of the very sand to cut down Hoel. You must have heard his death scream. Ury? Ryales?" He repeated the names of his two other comrades not accounted for.

"Have not reported in," Dedan returned.

"Then—count them as dead." The man spoke dully. "I could hear men moving through the dunes everywhere. It was only because I was closest to this ridge that I made it.''

"Pirates?" It was not as if Dedan protested the report of the scout—rather that he was astonished at some other factor Ramsay did not understand. "You saw nothing of the beginning rise of this fog?"

The scout shook his head. His chest was still rising and falling swiftly as might that of a hunted runner. "Only that it spread first from a point north and inland. There the mist arose into the sky as might the smoke of a fire growing ever stronger and thicker. I was on the crest of a dune when first I sighted it. But I swear by the Four Fangs of Itol it is not of nature.''

"So we had guessed. You saw no trace of any of the Thantant's force?"

''This only.'' The scout opened his clenched hand, let fall a small object which hit the rock with a metallic clang. By now the ominous mist crawled up, to settle about them, so thickly that even Dedan and the scout, close as they were to Ramsay now, were enwreathed nearly to the point of invisibility.

There was just enough vision left for Ramsay to see Dedan pick up what the scout had dropped.

"A belt badge of the March forces. Such might have been dropped and lost any time.''

"Uneaten by salt wind and with blood on the edge, Captain?"

Dedan held the badge closer to his eyes. He might not have been studying what he held but sniffing at it.

''You are right, that clot is fresh. Perhaps this explains the ambush awaiting us.'' If pirate scouts had witnessed the coming of the Marchers and wiped out those sent to meet the Company, there was little hope they could entertain for any help within perhaps hours—or days.

The yellow of the fog already lapped about the base of the ridge, rising about pockets where part of the Company had gone to ground. Dedan gave a quick glance right, then left, before he wheeled to face the crew of the vibrators that had been brought into position on the very crest of the ridge. His Second, standing by the vibrators, nodded. Dedan raised his whistle and once more blew a thin, shrill blast. Insert ear plugs—that was the order for his own small force. The Free Captain was going to bring into action his most potent weapons at once.

Ramsay fumbled for the plugs issued him, got them into his ears. The rest of the orders would come now in dumb show. He watched the vibrators lower their wide amplifiers to the farthest notch, so that the effect of their unseen assault would strike as close to the now-hidden dunes as possible. The Second himself stepped from one machine to the other to make certain of their aim. At his nod Dedan brought down his hand in a sweeping motion of command.

What happened then Ramsay was never able to find any explanation for. Out of the fog came a spear of light rising high, darting in. There followed a vast concussion that sent him sprawling, brought him up with punishing force against rocks, driving the breath momentarily from his lungs. But he lay in such a position as to see the site where the vibrators had been.

Had been! For only twisted masses of red-hot, smoking metal remained where, moments before, the two trim, highly prized weapons had been positioned for use.

Ramsay clawed at his ears, freeing them from the plugs. Now he could hear. Screams—shouts filled the air. Out of what had been an inferno of explosion crawled a single seared shape, inching painfully across the ground. It was plain that these pirates had come with an effective answer to Dedan's most cherished arms.

Somehow Ramsay got to his feet, unable as yet to take in the magnitude of that quick stroke from below. The heat still radiating from the wreckage of the vibrators made him cringe away. But a small yammering cry from the thing which crawled brought him to his feet, sent him wavering into that blasting heat almost against his will.

Much of the clothing had been charred from the body. Ramsay had no time to be gentle. He stooped and hooked fingers under the armpits of the wounded man, heaved him up and away from that fierce furnace. Back—he must get back into some kind of shelter. At the moment, confused as he was, Ramsay guessed that the worst of the battle had just begun. Wedging the man he had rescued into a hollow behind him, Ramsay drew his needle weapon and crouched, waiting for the enemy to loom close enough in the fog to provide a target.

A glance around was enough to make plain the disaster. There had been eight men near the vibrators when those blew. Crews of two each serving those weapons, Dedan, Rahman, himself, and the scout. Ramsay saw at once those of the crews could be written off. And there was another blackened bundle where fire fanned sideways over the rock.

Half missing—out of that first count. He hesitated to leave the hollow in search of men already dead. Was the mist at last beginning to clear? Ramsay thought those evil billows more ragged—showing holes—downslope.

Through that now tattered cover came a wave of

fire—but not such as had ruined the vibrators. No, this soared in banners upward from the hidden sand. Ramsay had never seen flamethrowers of his own world in action, but what he sighted now along the ridge sickened him. He fought the bile rising in his throat and mouth. These attackers were not trying to capture, to accept any surrender. They were simply killing as they came, and those of the Company had no shield against this new and fearsome weapon.

Ramsay squatted beside the man who was now moving feebly, moaning. He knew it would be only a matter of time before the pirates reached the crest of the ridge. Then he and this other, in turn, would be roasted before they could even strike back. To wait for a useless and horrible death made no sense.

Half dazed, he tried to see any other survivors. As the mist cleared further, Ramsay bent over the one man he had found. Dedan lay there, his scorched clothing also stained with blood. Around the officer's neck still hung the command whistle.

If the others had sense enough to take out their ear plugs— But had they after the vibrators blew? Ramsay could only hope that a few had done so. He snatched off the chain, brought the tube to his lips, though he knew none of the coded calls. Perhaps just this familiar sound would lead any survivors to fight their way in his direction. Ramsay blew lustily. The discordant note he made must have carried through the inferno raging up the walls of the ridge.

No use waiting any longer in this exposed position. He had no idea if he might outpace the flamers with Dedan as a burden. But he could try. He lifted the Captain and began to move in and out, retreating toward the land end of this crest of jumbled rock.

As a figure loomed out of the mist, Ramsay,

steadying his needle gun, ready to fire, just in time
became aware of the other's crested hood. One of the
Company. The man stumbled slowly along, and behind him wavered three others. Ramsay raised his
arms, beckoned.

A moment later Dedan was being carried between
two of them, Ramsay and the others playing rear
guard. No one else came out of that hell below.
Under their feet the ridge arose as they advanced.
There was better cover, larger blocks of reddish
stone that could stand between them and the flames.
Also the fog was fast dissipating, so they could better
choose their path ahead.

The man by Ramsay was Rahman. One arm hung
limp, and there was the scarlet print of a burn on his
cheek. He muttered as he came, his eyes fixed, as if
he did not really see Ramsay, instinct only keeping
him moving toward an improbable safety.

Those ahead, supporting Dedan, halted. Ramsay
impatiently waved them on. In reply one shook his
head determinedly. Ramsay drew nearer to Rahman,
touched his shoulder. The man winced, showing a
drawn face with empty eyes. He just stood there,
staring, when Ramsay signaled him to cover. Finally
the mercenary had to be pushed into a hollow so
Ramsay could join those ahead. The third man in
their pitiful rear guard stepped with more alertness
behind the same rock that sheltered Rahman.

"What is the matter?"

"They've got someone stationed upslope there.
He just took a look down to see the fun," one of the
men answered bitterly. "If he can get at us, we'll be
fried like all the rest!"

Ramsay followed the pointing finger of his infor-
mant. Yes! He caught sight of a sleeved arm. The

enemy must be very confident that they had little to fear from any of their victims who might possibly try to escape in this direction.

One man with a flamer? Or a whole guard here? Ramsay rubbed the back of his hand across his eyes. He was no real soldier. That seemingly easy victory over the assassin had been a fluke. Then he had had no time to think out any move; he had merely reacted, and fast, to an attack. This was different. His mind had already closed to what lay behind. To think about that did no good. However, there was in him a stubborn determination to escape with this handful of men, to live as long as he could in order to make someone pay for the ghastly death of men who had welcomed him as a comrade.

"Have you sighted more than one?" he demanded, his own eyes searching for any hint of a possible second sniper.

"No, but he does have one of those flamers—I saw the mouth of it when he hitched it up."

"If there is only one, and they might believe one was enough to keep us bottled up here—" Ramsay was thinking aloud. "All right. You stay right where you are. There is only one way to handle this if he has a flamer."

None of them still carried the rifles that shot the exploding bullets. Ramsay had lost his own when the explosion hit. However, if he could move up close enough to get at that sentry—

He stripped off his overtunic and belt, nothing left to catch on any rocks. Clad in the tight-fitting gray undergarment, he hoped to match the mottled surface hue of the ridge. Ramsay moved out, flitting to the left and up the ridge.

From one outcrop to another he raced as fast as he

could, his palms sweating, his mouth dry, expecting any moment to be swept with flesh-crisping flame. So far he had escaped notice. Now—over the highest point of the ridge and down. If he had judged his distance rightly, he must, at this point, be behind the sentry. Perhaps overconfidence in this disastrous effect of the new weapons would make the enemy less alert.

Ramsay was almost certain there was only one man. At least, though he stopped his advance several times and studied the landscape carefully, he could pick up no sight of another. And that one opponent was now revealed fully to him.

Crouching between two rocks, Ramsay drew off his boots. He must take no chance of making any sound. Moving as lightly forward as his bruised and aching body would allow, he leaped.

Ramsay's hand chopped so expertly at his throat that the sentry did not even cry out. He dropped, a dead man; perhaps he was not even aware that any attack had come. Ramsay caught the flamer, then arose, cautiously, to his full height, so that those in hiding out there would see and know the way was clear.

Ramsay remained where he was, alert for any sign of movement, ready to cover his comrades' advance with the flamer should a challenge arise. He could hear a ragged shouting, still see the flames wasting the lower ridge. There, however, some of the fog clung, enough to make him heartily glad, for it hid what must be the horrors there.

"The Captain—he can't go on much longer," panted the same man who had pointed out the sentry to Ramsay as they drew level with his guard post. "Nor us either—"

"Do any of you know this country?" Ramsay asked.

His only answers were shaken heads.

"Arluth—" Rahman, his eyes no longer blank, but his face twisted with pain, wedged the hand of his limp arm in to the front of his belt. "If the Marchers got out message, they'll come riding right in—to that!" He indicated the battlefield behind without looking directly. None of them had, and Ramsay believed that the sight of it sickened them beyond endurance, hardened mercenaries though they were.

"Is there any kind of road inland, one the Marchers will take? I know you said this is country you are not familiar with, but do you know anything about it at all?" He appealed to them. Dedan lay at his feet, eyes closed, moaning a little now and then.

Again shaken heads answered him. They could not go on much farther; that was the truth. Not one of them lacked burns or other wounds. Rahman was not the only one kept on his feet by sheer willpower. Also, sooner or later someone was going to come hunting the sentry left here. And when he did, the chase would be up.

A sudden thought came to Ramsay as he glanced down at the body. A broken neck among these rocks might seem an accident. However, to stage such a scene would mean abandoning the weapon. He surveyed the ground about them. It could be set up—and success might be their only chance. Catching the body under the arms, he dragged the dead man a little to the left. Then he took the flamer, to drop it a pace or two farther on, as if it had fallen so from the enemy's hands.

"What are you doing that for?" Rahman lurched closer.

"He has a broken neck. There's no wound on him." Ramsay nodded at his victim. "Suppose he fell when he came up here? See, he is wearing clumsy boots, not footwear made for climbing around rocks."

"But the flamer," protested one of the other men. "With that we'd have a better chance to fight ourselves."

"Without it we may well have a better one," Ramsay pointed out. "If that was missing, its loss would be a sure sign that someone escaped from back there."

He could see by their change of expression that they understood what he aimed to do. And he wondered if they would agree. After all, he had no official command among them. The Second was dead. He had been standing within touching distance of the vibrators when they were blasted. Any one of these men might challenge his assumption of leadership at the moment.

However, Rahman had a tight grin. "You think fast, Arluth. I'd say this gives us a shadow of a chance. We are lucky." He looked about. "You can't leave any prints on such ground, at least none that sort can read. But we'd better watch as we go. And the sooner we do that the better."

As they started on, Ramsay lingered to give a last searching survey to his carefully arranged "accident." He found himself rubbing his hands up and down the tunic one of the men had brought along, as if he must wipe from his flesh the feel of that death blow. Resolutely he pushed that out of memory. He had struck to save his own life, and the lives of those stumbling ahead of him. He had never slain a man before. But somehow this killing held no meaning for him—not after the flaming death among the rocks.

Their small party had to move very slowly. And they took turns, except for Rahman, who could not use his left arm, in carrying Dedan. However they were now well above the dangerous level of the beach, crossing a cliff top. Ahead a strip of green seemed to offer promise. Ramsay thought of water when he saw that, and moved his stick-dry tongue about in a mouth that seemed filled with salt.

All this shifting about might well kill Dedan, but they had no choice. It was necessary to get as far as they might from the scene of the massacre before any search for possible survivors began.

With much time and effort they got Dedan down the steep side of another rocky drop and then pulled into a green pocket where trees provided cover. Rahman fell rather than lowered himself to the ground. His face was a greenish shade under the dark hue of his skin. But the others took first-aid kits from their belts, while Ramsay struggled on under the trees seeking water, until he discovered a small spring-fed pool.

At the sight he flung himself forward, buried his whole face in the water. The raw burns on his face stung as he gulped several mouthfuls. Then he rinsed out his belt canteen, refilled it to the brim, and lurched back to their small and beaten company.

That they had lived through the massacre seemed now something hardly to be believed. He had a curious feeling that, having done just that, they were in some way immune to further disaster. Though, he reminded himself of that fatal carelessness of the enemy sentry, they dared not relax any vigilance.

ELEVEN

RAHMAN'S ARM was broken. Ramsay set the bone as best he could between splints whittled from one of the saplings that gave them cover in this pocket. But Dedan's burns were too serious for him to treat. It was Melvas who went hunting through the grass until he found a flesh-leafed plant which he jerked triumphantly out of the soil. After washing the leaves in the pool, he crushed them into a thick mass between two strips of bandage from the field kits.

This was, he stated, a native rememdy for burns known to his own province. At least it would reduce the inflammation and pain. They spread-eagled Dedan on his stomach, and, with infinite care, Ramsay and Arjun worked to strip off the charred remains of the officer's tunic and undergarment. Ramsay had to fight rising nausea. Surely Dedan could not be still alive! Yet he was, and moaned feebly as they worked.

When the burns were as bare as they could lay them, Melvas, the mass in the bandage between both his hands, squatted to squeeze carefully from what he held in a thin green jelly, spreading that as evenly as he could over the tortured flesh. The shoulders and backs of the upper arms were the worst, but in the end Melvas had them covered with the stuff, which dried quickly, leaving a glazed surface.

Dedan's moans ceased. At first Ramsay feared that the young officer had died under their clumsy treatment. But he was still breathing slowly, as if now under the influence of some strong narcotic. Melvas studied the Captain's face, raised an eyelid to see the eye.

"He sleeps," the soldier announced. "Now, for the rest of you—"

They all had burns, but none as bad as those Dedan had suffered. Ramsay found that the stuff Melvas applied to his own burns brought a release from pain which he would have not thought possible.

Having tended their hurts, they sat back, Dedan lying at their feet, and glanced at each other. At last their attention centered on Ramsay. And, for the first time, except when he had grunted under their treatment, the last man spoke.

"I served in Renguld under Nidud—before I joined with this company. Your face, stranger, suggests to me an odd thought."

"My face?" Ramsay repeated. Perhaps it was some action of the herb on his burns, but he felt slow of wit, drugged with fatigue.

"Your face. There is one—was one—who is like enough to you to look back from any mirror," the soldier continued.

With effort Ramsay recalled the man's name: Sydow. He had been a Leader of Ten, but not one who had shown interest in the unarmed combat lessons. An older man, he judged, and more conservative.

"That other is reported dead—and is now buried," Sydow continued. "Then who are you who wears his face? Prince Kaskar—"

They watched him now, as hounds might center upon a fox unfortunate enough to have approached their kennel.

"I am not Kaskar." Ramsay made his voice as emphatic as he could. "However, there are those who would set me in Kaskar's place," he improvised. "That is why I wore a Feudman's mask and left Lom—"

"Ochall would pay much for you—" Rahman commented. "To have a Kaskar, whether or not he was the real one—. The High Chancellor wants nothing more in this life at present."

"I begin to wonder"—Melvas now took up in question—"whether it was your presence among us that brought an end to our company."

Their concentrated stares grew hard, menacing. Ramsay wondered if they would turn upon him now to relieve their own misery. A suggestion such as Melvas made could set them at his throat!

"There are Eyes and Ears all over Lom," Arjun added. "You need only to have been seen in our company for a message to be sent to Lynark. Yes, it is possible, very possible!"

Ramsay did not like the expressions that were beginning to show on their drawn faces. At the moment they sought a scapegoat on whom to unload the bitterness of their defeat, all that fury blazing in them as they thought of the ridge and those left there. He could understand that, but he had no mind to be such a sacrifice.

''Your Captain''—he spoke again with such force as he could summon—''told me that any wanted man, once he took troop oath, was one of you. I am not Kaskar, and if I am one who had to flee Lom because I wear a face like unto his, is that any fault of mine? Save your wrath for those who caught us with their fog and fire. Ask yourselves''—his mind began now to awake from the daze of that sudden accusation—''did pirates ever have flamethrowers or this obedient fog before? Are you sure they *were* pirates?''

Sydow blinked. There was a murmur from Rahman.

''The scout—he reported—pirates''

''Or perhaps men dressed as pirates,'' Ramsay supplied promptly. ''In the tales I have heard of battles with Lynark raiders, no man has mentioned fog or flame—''

Sydow nodded. ''That is the truth. Unless their chiefs have made some new deal with the Merchants of Norn, they would not have such weapons. I have never heard tell of these before. So—'' Again his gaze narrowed as he stared straight at Ramsay. ''If they were not pirates, then who are they?''

''I do not know. But think you—I met with your Captain only a short time before sailing. Could any message concerning me have brought this enemy into the field, so well equipped, in as short a time as the length of our voyage, with the additional information as to just where we would land?''

Ramsay was taking a chance now; he did not know what methods of quick communication this world might have. Sydow stirred, there was a reluctance in his expression, as if he had been made to face a fact he did not care to acknowledge.

"Such weapons," he answered slowly, "must have been brought secretly from Norn. Had they been used before by any force, the news of it would have reached the Council in Ulad. These must be of the banned—only those risking outlawry would handle them. While to transport such in secret—" He shook his head. "No, I cannot say, Arluth, that they were turned on us because of you, when I consider the matter."

Ramsay noticed that he was no longer "stranger," that Sydow now used the name by which he passed, a step toward closer understanding.

"Why would anyone wish to keep you from your engagement with the Thantant?" Ramsay persisted.

"Now that is a good question." Rahman shifted his shoulders where they rested against a boulder, as if his arm pained him. "Our commitment with the Thantant was simple enough. We all voted on it before signing. We are—were—to reinforce the sea beach patrol against raiders. It is—was—an ordinary enough engagement. The Thantant needed experienced men to patrol; his are used only for seasonal field service. They are not professionals, but are called up for six months or a year, and then returned to their homes and their work. It is ever so in Olyroun. The only real enemy they ever have to face is the pirates. But those have been growing bolder and stronger of late. Instead of one or two ships slipping in to strike and be away with what loot they can garner by a surprise attack, they have appeared twice in sizable fleets—"

"Yes," Sydow interrupted. "And *that* is unlike those of Lynark. Their commanders seldom serve together except in a very loose confederacy. They are too independent to yield much authority to any one man. I wonder—''

"Wonder what?" Ramsay prompted as Sydow did not continue.

"Wonder whether Ochall has not stirred the pot in that direction. It is common knowledge that he must have the mines of Olyroun in order to exchange the ores for the products out of Norn which he wants. There is the prospect of marriage between the Duchess and the Heir, true enough. But Ochall would rather have Olyroun under his thumb entirely, not through the agency of any woman, especially one whom it is well known he mistrusts. Suppose he put into practice arming those of Lynark and urging on them such raids as they would be only too willing to try, with the proper weapons, thus draining the forces of Olyroun. Then, in the end, he need have no fear of any rising, should he proceed against that land—''

Melvas gave a short, approving bark of half laughter. "Well argued, comrade. You have put forth thus a good reason for preventing any reinforcements to reach Thantant. But"—he arose suddenly—"we forget now that those whom we have sworn aid-bond may come rising in answer to our message, and go down in turn before that hellfire!"

"So what do you propose to do?" Sydow asked gruffly. "We know nothing of the way inland, we have not a second message bird. And night is coming—''

Melvas dropped a hand on the other's shoulder, gripped it tight.

"Remember the Isle of Kerge and what we did there?"

Rahman arose also, turned his head slowly, surveying those heights down which they had recently come.

"Were it between Company and Company," he said, "it might be done. But these halftime soldiers of Olyroun, what do they know of such matters? They would see a fire, that is all—"

"You forget they have already been warned of an attack." Melvas pushed the matter. "Also I do not speak of just any fire. I would have one laid out in the Fate symbol."

"The Fate symbol—" Rahman repeated. "Yes—a powerful warning. But do you think that those who have mauled us nearly to extinction will not be expecting some such move?" He shook his head.

"Not altogether." Melvas's eyes were fiercely alight. "We are on the opposite side of the sea cliff, remember. If we are able to find up there a spot whence the light can only be seen in this direction— then we are able to hope. Also there is a trick a man can use— Give me, each of you, what you can tear from your tunics and I will show you!"

Using their swords to hack at the stout cloth, they tore free strips, which Melvas began typing together until he had a clumsy knotted rope. Under a late-afternoon sun already dipping to the west, he strode back and forth among the trees and bushes of their hiding place until he found a stand of thick canes, brown and shiny, with leaves growing at sparse intervals from the knots along the surfaces. These he hacked through with his sword and cut them into pieces about the length of his forearm.

When he returned with his load, Sydom looked surprised. "Gasserwood—I had forgotten!"

Melvas laughed. "I thought I saw it earlier. Yes,

here we have that which will help." He dropped
cross-legged on the ground and began to tie the
pieces of cane together to form a crude latticework.

Meanwhile they ate sparingly of the rations they
carried in their belt pouches. Dedan still slept heavily. At least he no longer moaned with every breath.
His own burns, Ramsay realized, did not hurt enough
to make him conscious of them. Whatever remedy
Melvas had applied appeared to have an element of
magic in it as far as the ease of pain was concerned.

Melvas had produced a firm lattice. Now, into
that, he began to weave the cloth strip they had
earlier knotted together, not to fill all the spaces of
the cane work, but rather in a circle first and then two
lines which crossed that, dividing it into quarters.
When he had finished, he faced the frame around for
their approval.

Now with the sun gone, twilight was well upon
them. But Melvas did not hurry. He opened a small
flask taken from an inner pocket of his much shor-
tened tunic. From that he dribbled, using extreme
care, a dark liquid, spreading it back and forth across
the cloth he had woven so carefully into place. When
the last drop had been used, he rubbed fingertips
gently along the lines he had soaked with the liquid.

"For once"—Arjun spoke up—"I am willing to
admit that your taste in seasonings is worth much,
comrade. I never thought I would see the day, or
evening, when I might say that—having had to endure watching you spread that slime over your ration
bread for years!"

Ramsay sniffed a rather sickening fishly smell
spreading from Melvas's work. The latter laughed.

"Comrade, I am from Pyraprad. There we eat sea's

fodder like men. The Oil of Shark is a fighting man's seasoning, as I have so often told you.

"Now—" He stood up, holding the frame of oiled cloth a little away from him. "Here we have Fate, and we had better get it in place before night is utterly upon us."

Ramsay pulled off his boots, as he had done before when he made the attack on the sentry. He got to his feet to join Melvas.

"Where do we plant it?" he asked.

The last thing he wanted to do was reclimb that slope down which they had had such a hard time making their way earlier. He moved stiffly, all the bruises he had taken when the vibrators had blown giving him notice of their existence. However, he was, he was sure, in better shape, in spite of them, than any of the squad except Melvas.

For a moment it appeared that Melvas and Sydow might refuse his aid, then the latter said, "You did prove you know your way around rocks, Arluth, when you cleared the path for us back there. But if you would go, it must be now, before the dark comes."

They angled farther back, not down the slope whence they had earlier come, but along the edge of the cliff that enclosed this pocket of a valley, until they were as far west as they might go. Here the cliffs pinched together again to present a wall.

Luckily the twilight lingered and that wall was a rough one with holes easily found for hands and feet. Melvas had slung the lattice on his back, and, though the frame was unwieldy, it was light enough not to cause him undue strain as he climbed.

They reached the top of the wall and went on,

farther north, for Melvas was firm that any road from
the March fortress must lie in that direction. At last,
as the twilight was deepening so that they could no
longer move safely across this broken terrain, he
chose a site to wedge the lattice into place with
stones, facing it toward the heart of Olyroun.

Both Melvas and Ramsay made very sure, as they
piled loose rocks about the frame, that no chance
wind could topple it. In fact the cliff wall at this place,
rounded out a little over it—not hiding it from the
ground, but providing something of a sheltering roof.

"Will they understand?" Ramsay asked. He did
not mention the more important point—would any
inland see it at all?

"That symbol? No one can mistake it for aught but
a warning. They might believe that the enemy set it,
of course. But then they would deploy scouts and
take all precautions." Melvas was busy with his
wheel lighter. He spun it vigorously so the spark fell
on the oiled cloth.

As Ramsay and he drew away, that line of fire ran
quickly along the dampened strips until the pattern
was aflame. It could certainly be seen, Ramsay believed, for some distance.

"We go." Melvas jerked at his arm. "If any scouts
of those sea devils sight it, they will come hunting.
And this is no land to travel hastily in the dark."

As they both speedily discovered, moving from
one hold to the next by feel now rather than sight.
The circle of rags still flared out above them. Perhaps
the oil Melvas had used was not so easily consumed,
instead protected the material for a longer burning.
Yet Ramsay realized that the other's warning was the
truth. Their whole party would be better away from

the small sanctuary they had discovered.

When they half tumbled down the last of the climb, landing in what was now a pocket of darkness, a low voice hailed them.

"Come on—we're moving west—"

"The Captain—" Ramsay was sure Dedan could not have recovered to the point that he was on his feet, no matter what miracle Melvas's herbs wrought.

"They've started on, carrying him," Rahman half-whispered. "We made a litter after you left, lashed him in. Only way we could hope to move him now—"

The other end of the valley, where a stream ran from the pool until it disappeared underground, took a curve to the left. Luckily there was not a second wall beyond, rather a wider range of land covered mainly with scrub, but this caught at their already tattered clothing and raked their hands and arms viciously.

Their blundering ahead could not be made without sound, and Ramsay feared that here they were nearly helpless. To keep going minute after minute was all they dared hope to accomplish. Then, just when he felt if he stumbled once more over some exposed root he could not rise, but would lie waiting for some doom, they were again in the clear.

Here was a sweep of bush grass little more than ankle high, through which they swished. They were far too visible in this open.

Ramsay stopped short, brought both hands to his head, swayed back and forth. His mouth opened to cry out, closed again without giving utterance to that protest.

This sensation was unlike Osythes's dreams, yet

instinct told him there was an underlying kinship to those in it. He only knew that he was— "summoned" was the only word he could find to describe that feeling. And in such a way that he had no hope of defying the power that claimed him.

Nor was he alone in his reaction. All of them staggered a little to the right, began to trudge forward as if they obeyed the jerk of a leash held in some strange and alien hand. None spoke, they only moved, the Captain borne between Sydow and Arjun, Rahman, Melvas, and Ramsay behind—six survivors, perhaps now fatally entrapped.

Ramsay had never experienced anything to equal this compulsion before. Even the aches and pains of his tired body appeared suddenly to belong to someone else. It was necessary only to obey, to reach a goal ahead. Though what the goal might be—?

Ramsay, locked in a struggle between his innermost self and that compulsion, became dimly aware of a light. Their cliff-top signal? By rights they would have had their backs to that. Some dwelling in this debatable land? Even a campfire of the enemy, astute enough to move this far inland in order to cut off the escape of any who survived the ridge attack?

The beam was too steady to be fire, he thought confusedly. More like a steady beacon, such as were familiar in his own world. Toward it his party marched as single-mindedly as if they were on some ordained maneuver. They all made a quick right-angle turn that brought them onto a road of sorts. Not paved, but smooth enough underfoot to suggest that it was well traveled. Perhaps they had found their way to the frontier post—but why then this— *drawing?*

The light grew no stronger as they approached it—it remained very much the same. Yet Ramsay was sure that its source was not retreating in the same measure as they were advancing. That beacon was fixed, and someone there reeled them in, as easily as if they were hooked fish on a line too strong to fight.

Now the light touched on stones—erect, slender— Some half-buried memory moved in Ramsay's mind. Yes, that red rock pillar he had seen near the hunting lodge, the one Grishilda had described as part of a very ancient, shunned ruin. Were they indeed approaching the lodge? But even in the dark he could not see the forest, which should have been wide enough across the horizon to make itself clear now.

Also there were more than one of those pillars— six, to be exact, three flanking the source of light on either side, while their party was drawn away from the smooth surface of the road, which had curved again, as if to avoid any close touch with those very ancient monoliths. Now Ramsay picked out a figure moving deliberately into the path of the light, one which threw a shadow like a long warning finger pointing in their direction.

Those left of the company were very close, close enough to see the light, a rod slender enough for Ramsay to span with his two hands, planted in the earth. The one awaiting them by it wore a black-and-white robe. Osythes? But the face was now turned half to the light, and these features were not of the Shaman who advised the old Empress. This was a younger man, though he had the same detached look about him. A second figure glided forward to join him, and this, in spite of the identical black-and-white and cut of her robe, was a woman, slender, delicate of feature. Impassive, the two stood waiting for the six fugitives to come to them.

As the men advanced into the light, Ramsay felt a tingling throughout his body. His nostrils expanded to take in a queer, unidentifiable odor. Sydom and Arjun put down the litter holding their commander almost at the feet of those who awaited them. Then, panting, they half collapsed, to sit beside it. Ramsay felt his strength ebbing also. He managed to push forward another step of two and then subsided, his hands braced against the ground on either side of him, fighting to keep both his mind control and what little strength remained in him.

The woman stooped above Dedan, who was lying face down, his back covered with the hardened crust formed from the herb. A hand came out of hiding in her voluminous sleeve as she touched the First Captain's cheek lightly. She spoke to her companion, but she did not use that language Ramsay had fought to learn. Then she turned to face the rest of them. From face to face she glanced, lingering on each set of features for the space of a breath of two as she studied them in turn.

It was her companion who spoke, and now in a language Ramsay could understand.

"Whom do you follow, beaten men?"

Ramsay watched the others stiffen, and knew a swift jab of anger at what he thought might be contempt coloring that question.

Sydow replied. "We are of the Company of Dedan. He, our First Captain, lies before you, Enlightened Ones."

"Mercenaries," the man returned.

It was Ramsay who flashed a swift, hot reply. "Men who give their lives to keep their oaths—and this time were betrayed." He did not know that for a fact, but he had no qualms against throwing the charge into the calm, expressionless face. "Men who were coming to serve this land and were—were—finished before they could raise hand in their own defense."

"Ah." The Enlightened One now looked directly at him and him alone. "Of you there has been knowledge sent us—You are the Knave of Dreams—"

"The what?" Ramsay was mystified.

"The Knave of Dreams, he who enters to disturb a pattern of foretelling, the one changing and changeable factor that cannot be controlled and whose advent completely alters all. You have already held two names, now you are granted this one—which is truer than the rest. That you and your comrades have won free so far means that there is still a use for all of you. It remains to understand what that use can be—"

"We are men!" Ramsay fought an insidious lethargy which threatened him—the him who was a man, who was Ramsay. "We are not used, we move of our free will—"

"No man moves of free will, he is pushed here, drawn there, by events from his past, needs of the future, perhaps even the will of a stronger man or woman. No one is free of the chances life itself lays heavily upon him from the moment of his birth. But this is not the time to speak of freedom, of choice, of belief or unbelief. It is apparent that the game is not complete, or you would not be here. Therefore, we agree that you shall be under the protection of the

Grove until such a time as we know what is meant for you."

The Shaman raised his hand with a quirk of the wrist, tossing back the full sleeve. In the light, his hand appeared to possess an extra radiance of its own. The lifted forefinger pointed directly to Ramsay's head.

Ramsay felt himself slumping forward. A few moments of panic and fear were swallowed by soft, welcoming darkness.

TWELVE

DID HE SLEEP and dream? Or had he come to this place unknowing and just now was beginning to see, hear, understand? So much had happened to Ramsay in so short a time that he wondered if he dared ever again depend upon the evidence presented by his own senses. He only knew that here and now he was seated by a narrow table that glowed with a wan light, as if it were no real board, rather a slab that was in itself a lamp.

Yet the wan radiance so given forth did not spread far. Ramsay could see only what lay upon the length, two hands which moved deftly over that. Very slender were those hands, bare of the massive rings that were the common fashion of the people in this world. Their delicate grace made him believe that they must belong to a woman Yet when Ramsay tried to see beyond, to make out even a shadowy outline of her who might be seated opposite him, nothing but a wall of dark faced him.

Thus, fascinated against his will, he watched the hands at work. Against his will, because, deep within him, an ancient warning awoke hints of enslavement of his senses in a way he had not ever believed possible. Ramsay was only sure at that moment that, even if he drew upon all his forces and attempted to stand, to move away from the table, leave behind those hands with their quick, purposeful movements, he would not be able to do so. Whether he would or not, he must sit and watch.

His own hands lay clasped together powerlessly in his lap. He could not loose a single finger from that enforced intertwining. Fear was his immediate reaction to this complete helplessness. Then anger followed, and, with the swell of that, his will strengthened, hardened, as metal worked by the smith's knowledge and skill takes on a keener cutting edge, a greater power for use.

Still in spite of the anger that strove to arm him, Ramsay discovered that he must watch the hands.

The fingers had deftly dealt out slips of what might be some light metal, for, as each was placed firmly into position, it produced from the board a small ringing sound. On the slip's length there then blazed a symbol that might have been the direct result of meeting with the table surface.

The symbols were complicated. Now, as Ramsay continued to watch, he discovered he could pick out a meaning from some of the lesser ones used to border each slip. How *did* he know that those curling tendrils—which were not unlike those full-bellied clouds one might see in an old Chinese drawing of his own time and world—stood for Dream? And that the small heart from the center cleft of which sprang a five-petaled flower was Hope? A jagged lightning strip that took on a dusty, threatening purplish color upon meeting the board—that was Fear. Last of all came a small figure completely hidden in robe and cowl—pointing a too long-fingered hand to either right or left—that was Fate.

These identifying borders were only the least of

the pictures on the strips. For each had also a larger central design, very intricate. Those flashed boldly alive as they were put down, only to blur again, so that he could not distinguish them with any accuracy.

That there was a purpose—a pattern—the hands before him sought—of that Ramsay was sure. He did not understand the method of the dealing. Some strips were allowed to lie in place for a moment. Then the fingers, expressing impatience in the very abruptness of their movement, would sweep them into discard, to deal again. At last only five cards remained in place between Ramsay and this unknown who played the game, if game it really was. For the first time since Ramsay had come to consciousness of where he was, the hands were quiet, fingertips resting below that line of cards.

Though they were at rest, there was a subtle emanation of impatience about them. In a moment the index finger of the right hand tapped the board beneath the middle card.

"Did I not say it—" The voice was low, a whisper that echoed eerily through the dark. "Always the Knave—the Knave of Dreams! That Knave who comes to destroy all proper patterns and realign the Fates—" Now the finger tapped emphatically under that card farthest to Ramsay's right, where the cowled figure forming the border wavered, appeared to grow stronger, even threatening, as Ramsay's eyes followed that pointer of flesh and bone, centered on the card.

"Fate—Fear—" The finger pointed again. Now it passed the center card, indicated the first to the left, which also showed the lightning flash that threatened. "But then the Queen!—The Queen who rules the House of Hope. Dream, Fate, Fear—and at

the end of Fear—Hope. Knave are you yourself
bound to, and your way is the dark one which dreamers own. You have dreamed, you are dreaming—you
shall dream! Fate and Fear linked together are a
mighty enemy to face, Dreamer. But this is the truth
of foretelling—you must rely upon your dreams before you depend upon the strength of arm, your
quickness of wit. Dream—and ask—and then face
Fate and Fear—and—'' The hand hovered over that
last card of Heart and Flower and a glaze of design
his eyes saw only as a radiant blur. "No, there is no
telling, even for me, of the end of this. For even the
Grove must bow to a dreamer. Too often he dreams
true!''

The hand swept in a flowing motion across the
board. Light vanished. For an instant Ramsay had a
sensation of loneliness, as if he had been abandoned
in some place of utter darkness.

Then—did he dream to the order of the owner of
the hands? Or to his own whim?

He only knew that just as the dreams woven by
Osythes to tie him to Kaskar had had this same vivid
life to them, what he looked upon as if through a
window must have a real existence somewhere.

A man dominated the scene. He had none of the
calm and measured authority of the Shaman, none of
the unquestioned inherited rulership of the old Empress. No, he radiated a kind of raw power. He was,
Ramsay thought, of a little more than middle age, but
passing years had not dimmed either the bull physical
strength of his barrel-chested body nor the determination and will that were expressed by every curve of
his heavy-jawed face, every turn of his eyes and lips.

He was seated in a chair that aped in general the
canopied one that had made a throne for the old

Empress. But, whereas her mere presence within its
shadow had turned it into a seat of state, this usurpa-
tion was unnatural, carried a shadow of menace. His
left elbow rested upon the arm of that chair, his jowly
chin was set firmly in the upraised palm of that hand,
as he glared in Ramsay's direction with such concentration that, for a moment, the Dreamer could believe that he was now visible to the other.

Yet there was no sign of any astonishment on that
broad and lowering countenance. In a second Ramsay guessed the stranger's glare was a cover for the
fact that the other was intent upon his own thoughts.
That they were disturbing could be readily believed.

In the stranger's right hand was grasped a ragged
bit of cloth, the color of which seemed familiar. That
was like the hood Ramsay himself had worn when
playing his role of Feudman, that pretended disguise
that had nearly been a key to his death—for him—a
second time.

Ochall! Ramsay's mind produced a name for the
enemy he had never seen but of whom he had heard
so much. So this was the High Chancellor who as-
pired to rule the empire. Ochall might have lost his
main piece in the game, yet there was nothing about
this brooding man to suggest that he saw defeat now
for all his plans. No, much to the contrary, his expression was one that suggested a search, hunted a
new way. And his fierce grip upon that rag of cloth
meant that perhaps he believed he had begun to
understand the inner meaning of a problem.

The Empress and the Shaman—Ramsay had believed in their offer—and as a result nearly lost his
life. As he watched Ochall, now he began to wonder
what sort of reception he might expect from the
Chancellor were he to provide him with a second and

perhaps more durable Kaskar.

What had they said of this man—those who were his enemies? That he had mastered and perhaps even hypnotized a weakling prince into a puppet. However, all that Ramsay had been told about Ochall had come from those who had good reason to be his bitter enemies. And it had not been through Ochall that he himself had been paired with Kaskar—killed—to be reanimated in a world where those representing law and order once again wanted him safely dead.

Ramsay could not say that he was in any way attracted to the man brooding in his dream. Ochall should be a nasty enemy—but perhaps an open one, apart from the uses of intrigue such as had led Ramsay out of Lom Palace to a waiting assassin. Somewhere in his own mind a plan as nebulous as one of the clouds marking dream cards began to take on more weight and substance.

Ramsay's sight of Ochall vanished as completely as if a window had been clapped shut between them. Just as he had awakened from such ordeals in his own world, Ramsay found himself, sweating and shaking, sitting up on a narrow bed in the cold gray of a predawn. He gasped, then his heart settled into a more regular beat. This reaction appeared merely physical. He experienced no residue of any fear or unease at this time. Perhaps because he had been led to accept in a new twist of logic that what he experienced was normal, at least for the new Ramsay who had been Kaskar.

Kaskar—what if he were to *be* Kaskar again?

The plan that had been born at the far back of his mind as he watched the brooding Ochall was growing stronger, bringing in more details. The last thing that the Empress and the Shaman would want was Kaskar's return. They had set him up for death while masked, had warned him over and over against the folly of showing his face in Lom, even in Ulad. One of the company had known him, or thought the resemblance to the dead Heir very close indeed.

If—just suppose—if the people—not the intriguers of the Palace, the nobles who made up either the party of the Empress or that of Ochall, but the common people of the Empire—were presented with a true heir who had escaped both the control of the High Chancellor and the domination of the Empress, what would they do? Suppose a *third* party could so rise to challenge both? If he only knew more about Kaskar himself!

Though he might wear the Prince's body, no fraction of the other's identity remained to give Ramsay a single clue as to what had been done or undone. He only was quite sure that he was now entangled in a game played by others, and he resented that bitterly indeed.

The Enlightened Ones—what had been the reason for that dream of vision of the foreteller? Or had that actually occured? Fate and Fear—those symbols to flank the Knave of Dreams. And the strange mistress of prevision had made very sure Ramsay understood that he was the Knave, that variable which could overthrow the regular patterns by which they wove their own designs of the future. But beyond had stood Hope—and as a Queen—which meant a sign of greater power.

"You must rely upon your dreams before you depend upon your strength of arm, your quickness of wit—"

Very well. He had dreamed of Ochall, and to him had come a meaning from that dream. He would—

Ramsay tensed. There was a curdling of shadow within shadow in the far corner of the small chamber in which he lay. He was not alone. And—such had been his experiences in this world—he was very glad that he now had a wall to his back through which nothing—or no one—could come upon him unawares. Carefully he arose to face that form that had a misty outline, and he spoke first.

"What do you want?" There was truculence in his demand.

The other did not reply, only moved into the best light the small chamber had to offer, a gray shaft from a single window on Ramsay's left. A hand—and that hand he thought he knew—appeared to sweep aside a drooping veil. Here stood the woman who had come earlier to meet their broken band. When? Hours—days—earlier?

Her features were regular but lacked expression. Ramsay might be fronting a statue given the power of movement. Even her eyelids were half-closed, as if to conceal any betraying gleam of life within.

Yet her hands stroked her veil, smoothing that length across the shoulder of her dark robe sleekly, as if she absentmindedly caressed some pet animal, not woven fabric. Ramsay was very sure of those hands. Those long fingers had dealt out the strips of Fate, Fear; Dream—

"Yes." The single word did not trouble the lips between which it issued. "I am Adise, the Foreteller."

Adise? He had heard that name— Adise! This was that Enlightened One upon whose advice Thecla relied. Ramsay had no reason now to believe that Thecla was any real friend of his—

"You are the Knave—your path is of your own

choosing,'' she continued. Never did those heavy-lidded eyes open to meet his probing gaze squarely. There was a kind of indifference in the way she stood, stroking her veil, which he would not allow to irk him.

''I have been told that the Enlightened Ones sometimes give advice which the unwary would do well not to follow, that their foretellings can mean either victory or defeat and are not to be depended upon.'' He did not know why she had come, what message she was attempting to convey.

The light within the chamber was growing steadily clearer. Somehow the window rays centered upon those ever-moving stroking hands. Ramsay resolutely looked away, centered his attention upon her statue-calm face.

''We only foretell what *may* be.'' She accented that ''may'' as she spoke. ''From any action, no matter how trifling, there spreads a circle of consequences. Each may alter again a variable future. Then there are those without the pattern—for such there can be no measuring of choice. Such as you, who are not seed or root of this World.''

''Why do you come?'' He was impatient with her failure to be plain. ''Do you instruct—or warn?''

''Neither. If you have dreamed, then you already know what is to be done.'' Her tone was as remote as the sense of her words.

''Very well.'' Ramsay tried shock tactics. ''Can you at least give me direction? Where do I find High Chancellor Ochall?''

If he expected to strike some vital spark from her with that sharp demand, he was disappointed.

''Three days ago,'' she replied, her serenity unruffled, ''he was reported at Vidin—that Vidin which owes ancient allegiance only to the Heir of Ulad.''

Ramsay digested that information and did not in the least doubt that Adise was speaking the truth. But if Ochall was at this Vidin—what was he trying to do? Did he still believe that Kaskar might live, or only hope that he could lay Kaskar's death upon his own enemies and so draw to him those who owed the dead Heir traditional allegiance?

"And where lies Vidin?" Even as he asked that, Ramsay knew that he had made up his own mind. He must seek out Ochall, know the man as he really was and not as rumor and his enemies reported him to be.

"A morning's flight southward. There is a flyer waiting to your order."

They appeared eager enough to get rid of him, Ramsay thought. He wondered if his being this "variable," which they so insisted upon, was in some manner an upsetting factor in their own private concerns. Or were they urging him into this action for purposes such as they had been accused of in the past—to bring about some change in the chain of events to favor their own far-reaching plans?

Adise raised her eyelids completely for the first time. Her eyes were odd; they seemed to have, in place of the pupils normal to mankind, small dots of flame. Only for an instant did he perceive that, if he did at all; then she was like any woman again.

"Do not doubt your place in the great game." For the first time a trace of emotion troubled her level, monotonous voice. "No one controls the Knave of Dreams—Remember that, for your own protection—*no one*!" The accent she put upon the repetition of those last two words might have been a warning.

It appeared clear that the Enlightened Ones

wanted him away. Ramsay smiled. There was a certain satisfaction in being a nuisance to the All-Powerful, which, at the moment, he was inclined to relish. However he was also willing to opt for any aid he could wring out of the aloof Foretellers, Shamans, and Masters of Dreaming Extraordinary.

"Those of the Company," he asked. "How is it with then?"

He owed his life to Dedan. Even in his preoccupation with his own affairs, he remembered that.

"They mend. The Thantant has been warned." Was there again a faint irritation in Adise's answer? She could be urging him to immediate action. And that impression became a certainty as she added, using the prosaic words of any ordinary housewife: "Food, clothing—all you need"—she made a small gesture with one of her ever-moving hands—"shall be brought."

Without adding anything to that, she turned away, back into a corner which was no longer a cave of shadows, disappearing behind a curtain she swept aside for her passing.

As if her exit had been a signal, a man wearing a shorter version of the black-and-white Shaman's garb entered, carrying a tray of covered dishes which he put upon the table. He did not speak—perhaps a servitor of the Enlightened Ones, he was under some vow of silence—but his eloquent gestures brought Ramsay to a bath, to fresh clothing, to a meal of fruit, sweet bread formed as small, puffy rolls, and a tart drink which was cool on the tongue and pleasingly warm in the throat.

The belt he had worn as a member of the Company had been laid with the new dress of gray over black underclothing. But that gray was not drab. The tunic bore on the breast that Eagle emblem that had been widely in evidence in Lom Palace. Also, there were scrolls and lacings of silver thread to suggest rank.

After Ramsay had buckled on the belt with its ceremonial sword-knife, plus the other, more potent weapon Dedan had supplied to him, the silent servitor ushered him along several passages and then through a grove of trees. These grew in so maze-like a planting that Ramsay believed that, without the other's guidance, he would have been completely lost while still not more than perhaps six feet away from the building itself, so ensconsed by growth as to seem a mere lump of greenery.

That this concealment was meant, Ramsay guessed. But against whom or what had it been intended? By all the accounts he had heard, the Enlightened Ones had no active enemies. Yet they chose hideaways of this type.

As they twisted and turned to follow a way which was no vestige of a path as far as Ramsay could recognize, he saw that here and there among the trees were standing stones of the type associated with the half-fabled fallen civilization, which had left such a mixed heritage to the present time. Had this site, in those unnumbered years past, marked some ancient temple or sacred place?

The standing stones became thicker, drew closer together, until they formed a wall on either hand. Now Ramsay's guide led the way between those barriers, to come out from the shadow of both stone and tree into a cloudy open. Here stood one of the flyers, and his guide waved Ramsay toward it.

For a moment he hesitated. Was he truly making this choice in freedom? And if so—what might he have chosen? Follow the dream—to Ochall—Then what? The future depended mainly on what he found in Ochall himself. At least he would not be betrayed again by trusting in any word or promise.

His hand shifted along the belt until his fingers touched the grip of the hand arm. There was something reassuring in it, though his first taste of soldiering had been short and disastrous. Yet to have it fit now into his grasp gave a last urge forward, and he climbed into the flyer.

There was no sign of the pilot because of the closed-off cockpit. Ramsay must assume that he had already been given orders as to where to deposit his passenger. As soon as Ramsay was buckled into his seat, the craft arose in one of those unsettling leaps, and they were circling well above the ground.

Or he supposed they were, for there were no windows in this cabin. Thus Ramsay had nothing to occupy his interest except his own thoughts, which, he began to realize ruefully, were not so well sorted as to prove very useful.

He retraced in detail all that had happened to him since he had awakened on the bier of the dead Prince, to be given temporary safety by Thecla. Now, weighing one memory against another, he could not be sure that she had meant to save him, after all. That her allegiance was to the Empress Quendrida he had never doubted, though he gave her credit for joining in Quendrida's scheming for the sake of Olyroun.

He found he could now give mind-room to one excuse after another as far as the young duchess was concerned. Even her ultimate betrayal of himself could well be because she believed that was necessary for her duty.

In his own world, during these past years, duty, service, self-abnegation for the sake of an ideal, had all been sneered at by many of his peers. Not to "get involved" was the goal of their own twists and turns of action and thought. Now he was involved in as wild a piece of action as any dream could raise. Yet he stood alone with only his own personal desires, no ideals or "duty" to back him.

Ramsay shifted on the padded seat of the flyer. Loneliness. He had always been a loner. Why should he suddenly now feel the burden of it? With the Company—once more Ramsay's hand sought the weapon at his belt, the symbol of the only really carefree time, or so now it seemed—that he had known since he came here. His choice—*why* had he decided to go to Vidin—to confront Ochall?

It would have been better, easier, far more natural for him to throw away the past, to keep his oath with the Company, become one of them. Yet in turn his mind shuddered away from the slaughter along the ridge. Anger roused at that memory.

If he discovered that Ochall was indeed at the back of that massacre— Was it not now his "duty" to discover just what game the High Chancellor was attempting to play in the border countries? He could not believe that even the death of his chief pawn could stop Ochall from seeking power.

Well, the choice had been his, and he had made it. He was not going to slink out like some beggar. He was Kaskar—perhaps not Ochall's puppet prince— but nevertheless Kaskar now returned to his own holding as the ship settled down.

As firmly as if Dedan and the whole of a resuscitated Company played bodyguard behind him, Ramsay descended the ladder and stood looking about him.

He was on a rooftop, some private landing place

situated on a building of impressive size and height. Beyond he could see the rise of several towers; perhaps this was even within the heart of a city. But he was given little time to survey his surroundings. Moving swiftly toward him across the landing space came a squad of men.

This was it—his first trial in his role of Kaskar. Ramsay hoped that he showed no hint of uncertainty as he took only a stride or two forward and then stood, waiting for them to come to him, guessing that might be so by custom.

Though the men wore the crested hoods common to the Company, their faces were bare. Now Ramsay could clearly see the play of expression across the features of the officer in command. Utter and complete surprise!

The advance faltered. Not only their leader had been struck by astonishment, there were others as open-mouthed, wide-eyed as he among that guard.

Ramsay raised his hand in the half salute of superior to inferior. The officer snapped out of his daze. He barked a command Ramsay could not understand. The others moved into line, their weapons pointed barrels to the sky, plainly offering Ramsay the official welcome due Kaskar, the Prince of Vidin.

THIRTEEN

THERE WAS SO much that could go wrong in this masquerade, as Ramsay well knew. His presence here committed him, and with his first order to the Vidinian guards he sealed the commitment.

"His Worthiness, the High Chancellor—?"

"Will be summoned at once, Your Presence." A turn of the officer's head sent one of his command from the stiff line, trotting across the landing platform.

Behind him Ramsay heard the beat of the flyer's motor. He turned his head a fraction, just in time to see that craft leap into the sky, his last chance of withdrawal gone.

"Your Presence"—the officer moved a step or two closer—"may I express for all of Vidin recognition of the honor you pay us in coming to this, your own city, for the proclamation. That rumor spoke false and you are not dead—that is a matter for thanksgiving—"

Yes, thought Ramsay—just how *had* he excaped death? He hoped that the rumors of intrigue and counterintrigue at court would be his cover for any vagueness on that score.

"When one has enemies," he began, "subterfuges are necessary. In Vidin, among my liege men, I need not fear that I go without shield for my back."

The officer's sword of ceremony whipped from its sheath.

"Your Presence commands—Vidin answers! By blood right and liege right has this always been so!"

"As well I know," Ramsay acknowledged the formal words of the other. "You are—?"

"I am First of the Inner Guard, Your Presence, Matrus of the House of Lycus. It is now your will, Your Presence, to proceed to your Chamber of State? Since the High Chancellor arrived among us, we have been prepared. For we did not accept the dark tales out of Lom."

So much, Ramsay thought, for that surrogate body Melkolf had produced to be buried with state among Kaskar's forefathers. He supposed that Ochall's suspicions had carefully fostered this unbelief in the one principality within Ulad that would be most fertile soil for the growth of a possible rebellion.

"That you did not believe," he returned aloud, "is heartening. To most of Ulad, Kaskar lies now entombed. There may be reason, for the present, that he not arise again too soon nor lustily—" Ramsay smiled, an expression which he had but seldom used since he entered into the dream world—so seldom in fact that the very stretch of lips came now with difficulty.

An honor guard formed—at least Ramsay trusted that their movements signaled an honor guard and not a possible prisoner's escort, for his suspicions were not completely allayed by the response of the

First Officer Matrus, who could be—probably was—Ochall's man. So surrounded, he reached a lift which descended from the rooftop landing strip, passed several floors, and came to a stop. More guards snapped to attention, and Ramsay was conscious, as he stepped out briskly, of a ripple of surprise that spread outward as those in sight caught a glimpse of Kaskar's features.

Though all he had heard of Kaskar in the past had not led Ramsay to believe his double (would he term the Imperial Prince his "alter ego?") had any great merit, it appeared that in Vidin at least his rule and importance were undimished. The guard, the servants they now passed, were too well disciplined to break the silence of the corridors. Still Ramsay sensed the spread of excitement. He never turned his head to see, but he was sure that the tramp of the boots of their party was fast doubling in sound, as if he now led a procession that grew larger with every passing moment.

More saluting guards. One hurried to throw open a door. Ramsay passed into a long room, one wall broken by a series of wide windows, each of which was bordered about its embrasure with red and gold. Opposite these, mirrors, with heavily gilded and carved frames, were set into the wall. The floor, on which the boots of those who entered rang so sharply, was of marble, the ceiling and as much of the walls as could be seen between individual windows and mirrors were of a burnished red lacquer interset with enameled plaques.

Silver candlesticks standing as tall as Ramsay's head formed two columns between which he was ushered. Flanking both mirrors and windows there were as many wall brackets made in the form of queer heads wreathed in flowers and ferns, all gilded, each bearing figures which glinted with enamel or gemstones.

The mirrors reflected and re-reflected all this magnificence, until it seemed that this was not just one chamber but a series of fabulous halls echoing on into infinity.

At the edge of a two-step dais the column of candlesticks ended. And on the dais was a chair almost as wide as a small sofa. This lacked the canopy of presence which Ramsay had seen in the palace at Lom. But it was equally impressive with its gold back and arms, cushioned crimson seat. As First Officer Matrus drew to one side, Ramsay gathered that this state throne was now his proper place.

He trod purposefully up the steps, seated himself on the chair, with, he hoped, the appearance of ease of one who was in the right place at the proper time. For the first time he could see now that he had indeed gathered more followers along his route from the landing stage.

Guardsmen stood at impassive, statue-still attention flanking the candlesticks. The others, wearing heavily embroidered overtunics, could only be civilian officials of this miniature court, or the nobility of Vidin.

Ramsay hoped desperately that court etiquette might be such that he would not be required to single out for special attention any former acquaintance of Kaskar's. To play this role when so ill-prepared was dangerous, yet it was all that was left him.

"The High Chancellor!" From the now distant doorway (the hall somehow appeared not only to have been widened by the use of the mirrors but also to have lengthened, as Ramsay looked back down the way he had come) that voice carried well.

A man, wearing a servant's shorter tunic, but that so emblazoned with stitchery as to emphasize his importance in this Household, stood forward. His right hand curled about a staff of silver. This he raised solemnly, thudding it down with a metallic beat against the floor three times.

Having so gained the full attention of the assembly, he took a step aside, giving way to the man Ramsay sought. This was the Ochall of his dream, except now that the raw aura of power held, power desired, power sought, was not so apparent. Were the dreams able to heighten emotions so that the inner motives of those who moved within them could be read better?

Ochall had plenty of presence still, but he was not the overwhelming, dominating character either rumor or dream had made him. There was even a trace of deference in his manner as he faced Ramsay.

This was not the confrontation Ramsay had hoped for. If he could only have met Ochall immediately after landing, been able to read the first reaction of the High Chancellor to Kaskar's dramatic second return from the dead, that would have given him some small clue as to Ochall's position. But by this time the High Chancelor had had good time to assume any role he wished.

Now he advanced down the lane of the candlesticks, his longer overtunic nearly touching the floor. There was no sword of ceremony at his belt, rather around his bull neck lay a long, elaborately wrought collar of gold and gems. From that, resting against his burly chest, dangled an outsize golden key, probably his badge of office.

The slight hum that had hung in the chamber when Ramsay had taken the throne died away. There was not even the whisper of fabric against fabric as some of that company changed position slightly, not the scrape of a boot, not even the sound of breathing. The arrival of Ochall might have suspended all life in the court; those gathered there would not exist again until he chose.

Ramsay suspected this effect was deliberately produced by Ochall, that it fed his sense of power. But if he expected that it would also bring to heel a new puppet princeling—no! Ramsay's instinctive reaction was to prepare to fight the other's overpowering personality.

"I give you greeting, High Chancellor." He attempted to make his voice bland, though to his own ears it sounded odd. However, he must take the initiative in this meeting. "That you have so faithfully awaited me in this, my own court, I take as indicative of your ever-loyal service to the Crown—"

He did not know where he found the pompous words. Perhaps the very air of this room could produce such a change in one's speech. Only the most rigid of formal phrases seemed appropriate to echo through such surroundings. What he wanted most of all was some small hint from Ochall as to what the High Chancellor was thinking. Yet Ramsay knew that Ochall would never reveal anything that was not coldly calculated and aimed directly toward his own advantage. If Ochall had been astounded at Ramsay's arrival, no one would ever know it.

Ochall bowed his bull's head in slight inclination.

"His Presence knows that Vidin is his liege state. Where else would his friends gather in a time when strange matters happen in Ulad and there is much to make those of the deepest loyalty uneasy? That Your Presence would be safe has been our constant prayer. That Your Presence now sits in our sight, unchanged, unharmed,"—Ochall's hand arose to his breast, touched the glitter of the key—"is our reward for trusting Providence during all the hours, days, of dark story and threat, now happily past."

Ramsay saw that, under Ochall's touch, the large key was moving slightly, back and forth. His attention was thus being drawn from the High Chancellor's jowled countenance to the key—its movements—slight as those were.

Back and forth—back—and—

Ramsay blinked, jerked his eyes up and away. Was his suspicion correct? Was the High Chancellor's play with that badge of office more than just an absentminded mannerism? What had they said of Ochall?—that he had held Kaskar in some spell. Hypnotism? Perhaps the Heir had been carefully conditioned to react to just such a supposedly innocent personal fidgeting as the movement of the key. That his own attention had been so quickly riveted by a gesture was a warning, Ramsay firmly believed.

"Your concern for the welfare of the crown," Ramsay returned, wondering if Ochall would read into that a double meaning, "has always been recognized. Those of the Imperial line are aware of the depth of your loyalty, that high sense of duty which always is an example to all."

Once more Ochall's head inclined that inch or so of acknowledgment. But, Ramsay made sure with a single glance, he no longer fingered the key. If he had attempted to test the suggestibility of this revived Kaskar, the experiment had been a failure.

Ramsay believed that of all this miniature, atten-ive court, the High Chancellor might probably be he only one with courage enough to ask questions, hose pertinent questions concerning the immediate ast of an Imperial Prince who had been publicly uried with every pomp of ceremony, yet now lropped from the sky into his own domain very much live. However, that Ochall would ask such ques-ions openly Ramsay very much doubted. And this vas his own chance to get widely circulated the very ketchy explanation he had worried together during is flight to Vidin.

"These are days of stress." He smiled at Ochall. 'Sometimes it is difficult to tell friend from foe. That here are those who would willingly see me laid to est with the elders of my House is a fact all within earing must know. It is because of you, High Chan-ellor, that such a fate has not overtaken me. Your lan worked well—"

He was watching with the concentration of a unter Ochall's impassive, heavy face. At this mo-nent Ramsay knew of no other way to achieve even a nodicum of understanding with the High Chancellor han to provoke a response from him. Surely the nan, praised publicly for the salvation of his puppet rince, would seek to know what had happened. Iow it was that Kaskar lived, breathed, and declared hese facts to be of Ochall's doing.

"I serve—" Ochall returned with no change of eature Ramsay could read. "That I am able so to erve is my pride, Your Presence."

"Your pride," Ramsay continued, "but Ulad's ain. Now, my lords." He looked away from Ochall. There was no prying open the High Chancellor's shell y such efforts. He would have to devise a much more vigorous attack. "My lords, my faith in your liege-oaths, in those of Vidin, have sustained me through much these past days. Within these walls I find that which will regain my inheritance in truth. For a man's strength is not solely of his own hand upon any weapon, or his own wit, but rather in the faith which others hold in him. Now—" Ramsay leaned forward a fraction on the wide seat of the throne. "There may come a day when our mutual faith shall be put to hard testing—for I shall keep no secrets from you in the name of needed security and possible safety. You may hear that Kaskar is indeed dead and buried. In fact, doubtless some of you were in attendance in Lom when this occured."

Ramsay allowed his glance to sweep from face to face along the lines of the nobles. That he had their full attention there was no denying. There *were* troubled frowns, as well as startled surprise and the soberness of those who awaited enlightenment, to be seen there.

"Look upon me!" He stood up, moved one step downward from the throne. The glitter of the mirrors, the brightness of the sunlight from the windows, fully revealed him in a light that could conceal nothing. He held his head high, challenging silently by his very attitude any who might now dare to raise a cry of "imposter."

"They wished me dead, they employed certain stratagems to achieve that wish. But they failed. I have been hunted from Lom—secretly—lest the fact that I lived be known. Because I could not name friend from pretend-friend-secret-enemy I knew not where to turn.

"Until—" Now he undertook to advance his

strongest attack. "I came by chance to the Enlightened Ones—"

For the first time there was a faint, a very faint, change in Ochall's set of lips. However, those about the Chancellor were more open in showing their astonishment. There was a faint murmur, indrawn breaths.

"There was a foretelling given me," Ramsay continued deliberately. "And so I came to Vidin."

The murmur of those listening grew stronger. Ochall had his countenance once more under conrol, but open excitement spread through the rest of the company.

"Your Presence." An older man, one wearing a gemmed collar of state only a little less elaborate than that which encircled Ochall's neck, moved out a little from his fellows. "This foretelling—" He hesitated. Ramsay believed he could guess what lay behind that momentary check. The notoriously undependable advice of the Enlightened Ones must be mistrusted by any who were prudent.

Ramsay nodded. "Yes—the foretelling. As is well known, the Reverend Enlightened Ones are far more intent upon a future that may run so far ahead out of our present years that the results of actions taken now will not be to the advantage of any living. So we must shift and choose, and hope that we have chosen right. Believe it that I would and will walk warily and not pledge any liege man of mine to a dubious course. I am young in statecraft, but in this chamber stand men who can speak their minds from experience, and those shall be harkened to. Have we not at hand the High Chancellor himself? Any future plans we shall discuss in council. I have only this to say to you, that it is by the aid of the Enlightened Ones alone that I have come to Vidin. In that measure, at least, I think they have done me only good.

"Now my lords and liege men, I give you leave to withdraw until such a time as we must take council and—"

He was so eager to get Ochall alone that his impatience at this playing Prince in high ceremony grew. How *did* one dismiss a court, get some privacy—? He was sure that reference to the Enlightened Ones had given Ochall a jolt, and he needed to push any small advantage before the High Chancellor was again assured enough to lift his barrier.

Apparently Ramsay had hit upon the right formula, for there was a ripple of bowing toward him, men were backing away from the line of candlesticks. All was proceeding smoothly—

Then came an eddy by the door. Men were pushed to one side or the other, last being he with the silver staff, who was thrust impatiently and protestingly from where he had tried to bar the way to a man wearing a military hood. Hands tried to grasp the newcomer's shoulders. He shrugged these off, strode forward, while the court froze in position, quickly sensing that this interruption to the formalities was important.

The officer tramped to the foot of the dais. Judging by his badges of rank, one would say he was the First of some regiment, and he was fairly young. His dark features were a mask of excitement, and he was breathing fast, as if he had indeed raced to be where he now stood.

Raising his hand, he gave the salute to a commander, which Ramsay had wit enough to acknowledge. Then the man spoke.

"Supreme Mightiness! Our great Emperor Pyran has departed through the Final Gate. Trumpets have sounded his farewell from the towers of Lom. Now they call the summons to the Heir-of-Blood. Supreme Mightiness, may your rule be long of day and unshadowed!"

So the dying Emperor was at last dead! But certainly they were not proclaiming Kaskar in Lom!

Ramsay schooled himself as he noted Ochall had taken two steps forward, almost as if he would grasp the messenger, drag him aside for some private word. There was no time left now for any bargaining. The Empress's party would have Berthal standing ready, perhaps near to crowning at this very minute. Ramsay's own small chance for any safety in this world had lessened—halved, been made a third, even a fourth, by the messenger's report.

"I think they do not hail Prince Kaskar—" For the first time Ochall took the initiative.

The officer showed his teeth in a grimace.

"No, Your Dignity. They have brought forth Prince Berthal and stood him high upon the Place of Flags. However, as yet he has not taken oath."

Now there was a rising mutter, exclamations from the court. Again Ochall asked a question that had already risen in Ramsay's mind.

"Yet, Jasum, you have come to Vidin, to see one proclaimed dead. What knowledge existed in Lom to bring you here?"

"There was word from the Enlightened Ones, Your Dignity. One came by night to my chamber with this news: that our Prince had truly not been dead, but hidden away, and that he had won to Vidin. Thus, knowing that he must be told—Supreme Mightiness!" Now Jasum addressed himself directly to Ramsay. "They will swear allegiance to this usurper. Already they plan his enthronement in the Hall of Light, his quick wedding thereafter to the Duchess of Olyroun. Let him be sworn and wed, and there shall be many who would otherwise raise standards in the name of Kaskar who then will be persuaded not to make trouble lest such split Ulad!"

Ochall caressed his jaw with his wide-palmed hand.

"An astute observation, Jasum. I wonder now why this message was brought only by your voice, why the wire talkers of Vidin have not carried it. Unless, of course, those in Lom would do just as you have said before any loyal Vidinian has had time to object. Supreme Mightiness"—now he spoke to Ramsay—"let word now be sent throughout Vidin and the trumpets sounded at once—thus assuring that the usurper shall not be seated upon the throne with no voice raised against him. With protest raised, this becomes a matter of public knowledge, of confrontation with those who have named Berthal— maybe even of a Last Challenge!"

Ramsay had no idea what Ochall might mean by the letter, but Ochall spoke the words with such emphasis that Ramsay guessed it was some extreme of serious opposition.

"Let us take council as you have urged, Supreme Mightiness—first let it be known to the Lords of Thousands—yes, and even the Lords of Hundreds—that they must gather to show true allegiance."

"So be it," Ramsay agreed readily, though he had a feeling he had lost all control of the situation and that authority had slid smoothly into Ochall's grasp, exactly as the High Chancellor had always intended it should at this long-awaited hour. So it was with a small warning chill inside that Ramsay again dismissed the court, watched the nobles of Vidin drain from the chamber until only he and Ochall remained there.

Much as Ramsay had earlier wished for this personal private meeting, he willingly would have foregone it at this particular moment. Yet he felt he must wait for Ochall to take the lead, in that way perhaps learning what would move the High Chancellor.

"Time—" Ochall's fingers had ceased to caress his chin; instead with thumb and forefinger he plucked at the thickness of his lower lip. "What time may we have? Did the foretelling of the Enlightened Ones in turn enlighten you, my lord, to any answer on the subject? Time we must buy somehow—" The last sentence was uttered as if he were thinking aloud.

However, Ramsay had a shrewd idea that the High Chancellor never so forgot himself as to utter *any* words of which he was not entirely conscious, both of the subject and of the person to whom any random-seeming remarks might be made.

"I was told," Ramsay answered deliberately with part of the truth, "that my own person was of significance in events to come, also that any choices I would make would in turn lead to changes in the foreseen future to an extent the Enlightened Ones were not yet able to assess."

"Kaskar—" Ochall eyed him from head to foot and back again with a detached measurement. "Life—or rather death—has been your portion in ways unknown to us who are but mortal men. First you die and lie in your last sleep in the Hall of Lords Gone Before.

"Then it is discovered, with the coming of the day, that four guards, plainly bemused, their recollections tampered with, corner an empty bier. Kaskar has risen say the ignorant. There is talk of a miracle, such as those of the very ancient of days were supposed to effect. Yet if Kaskar has arisen and walks his land, none has seen him.

"Once more a body is discovered, this time in such a state that only the clothing, certain well-known peculiarities of size and being, can identify it as the strangely lost prince. For it would seem that Kaskar perhaps *did* rise from the dead, perhaps mindlessly, and wandered from his royal bed, to crash from a convenient window. Perhaps his brush with death made him believe the tales of legends, that those of exemplary character, when they pass the Final Gate, are no longer bound by the limitations of this world but can ascend by their own desire into the skies about. Believing this, our half-dead prince strove mightily to prove legend fact, but merely learned that he had not yet discarded his mortal body.

"Thus we have a body which is buried with pomp and much outward grief, much inward satisfaction. Ochall," he smiled grimly, "has been outwitted, outplayed. So cleverly done, and if any have suspicions they are keen-witted enough to keep them shut tightly behind their teeth, not stupidly voicing them aloud. Yet in this hour Kaskar the lost, the—as you might say—'oft-buried,' stands here in his very loyal holding of Vidin about to lead a loyal march against a usurper."

He shot a glance at Ramsay. "You speak of the Enlightened Ones. I will not doubt one word of what you have said of your relationship with them. Their games are well known to be devious, beyond the unraveling of those who have not their peculiar gifts. They say you are Kaskar. Thus it is for us to accept a second miracle. Only, perhaps even the Enlightened Ones are not above the side effects of miracles. That we shall in time come to see.

"Time"—he came back to his first statement—"is what we must have. No man can push wind, water, a flyer, a ship, a rail runner, faster than it is designed to go. I have not been idle, Supreme Mightiness. Given time, I can prove Ochall is not a piece to be easily swept from any playing board. Even that of the Enlightened Ones."

FOURTEEN

"BUT IT NOW seems," Ramsay pointed out, "that such time may not be granted us, High Chancellor. You state my appearance in Vidin is a miracle. Well enough, but the news of that miracle must spread beyond Vidin if we do not wish to find Berthal enthroned lawfully." He was probing now. That something lay behind Ochall's preoccupation with time was very apparent. "How much time must *your* plan be given to bear the fruit desired?"

For a long moment the High Chancellor did not answer. Once more he kneaded at his lower lip with thumb and forefinger.

"It would seem that, momentarily, you have the favor of the Enlightened Ones. Or, if not their favor, their desire to cast a very large stone into the pool of Ulad, disturbing affairs—working now for you. As to time—perhaps five days—"

Once more he played with that glittering key, and Ramsay averted his eyes. Then Ochall spoke again.

"Who are you?" He asked his question bluntly, as if such simplicity might well invite full truth in return.

Ramsay found a second smile less difficult than the first. "Kaskar, come out of great danger to claim his rights again."

Ochall uttered a strange sound. Though there was little that was jovial in it, it might have been a bark of laughter.

"Well answered, Supreme Mightiness. Kaskar you have claimed to be, Kaskar you shall be. But I wonder if you realize that you have put out your hand perhaps too willingly to grasp at a very unsteady crown. If you have fallen for the trickery of the Enlightened Ones, a man could find himself ready to pity you—"

"A warning, High Chancellor?" queried Ramsay. "I take it kindly of you to show concern. I only know that there are those in Lom with whom I have certain scores to settle. If claiming my rights will bring me closer to that settlement, then I shall outshout any of your trumpets of the tower. Be assured of that. And what"—he struck back for truth, if truth could ever be gained from such as Ochall—"will your needful five days bring?"

"Weapons, out of the North," the High Chancellor returned as frankly as Ramsay had asked. "There are certain new ones, as yet unused in any large combat, but well proven, as my own Ears and Eyes report. The merchants of Norn promised their efficiency, and all that they said is true—"

"Tested in action?" Ramsay schooled himself to what he hoped was only a small show of interest. What action? That in which the Company had been ruthlessly done to death? Had that only been a show, put on to impress such a buyer as Ochall of the worth of his projected purchase?

"Tested in action," agreed Ochall. "Proven. I

know not what new secrets those of Norn have now chanced upon, but such arms have not been seen upon these shores since perhaps the last days of the Great Era."

"And those last-used arms," Ramsay pointed out, "are reputed to have left this world half dead. Even to rule in Ulad an ambitious man would be a fool to lay hands on such as those!"

"Oh, these are not the Ultimate Forbidden. No, these are still but as pebbles flung from a boy's sling in comparison with them. To use these would not break the Everlasting Covenant of the People Alive. In fact they are merely superior modifications of two already known." However, Ochall went into no details.

"And where were those new weapons demonstrated—upon whom?" Ramsay pressed.

Ochall shrugged. "In a small skirmish of no importance, between pirates and a relatively inefficient mercenary company which had been hired by the Thantant of the Marches in Olyroun. It is to our interest, of course, that those of Olyroun be kept occupied by nuisance raids for the present. That the duchy should continue free is not to be supported. But to move outwardly against it, no."

The High Chancellor was watching Ramsay with a measuring stare as he spoke.

"With the Duchess Thecla united to Ulad in marriage," Ramsay returned, "such matters in the future can be quietly and carefully arranged without any need for outright invasion."

"Just so. Still it is well that Olyroun be kept occupied with internal difficulties until that auspicious date. Any encouragement on the part of such as the Thantant, his hiring of mercenaries and the like, must be prevented. To try the weapons so thus accomplished two needful results. I do not think that the Thantant will find another Free Company to accept his offered employment, and the pirates of Lynark are invited to make themselves successfully busy—''

''The pirates!'' Ramsay repeated. ''Those were so armed? Is there not danger in that?'' Inwardly he marveled at the calm he was able to maintain. The realization that that hell along the ridge had been in the nature of a planned experiment awoke a rage which perhaps earlier in time he could never have kept under the control he now exerted. To discuss the death of those men who had accepted him as a comrade as the end product of a demonstration—! He seethed and fought his own emotions. The Empress and the Shaman—they could condemn one man to exile, and then to an assassin's sword under the pious cloaking of that conscience they labeled ''duty.'' While Ochall could accept the horrible death of nearly a full company of men because it gave him another lever for his ambition—

''You plan to march then on Lom,'' Ramsay said as evenly as he could, ''with such weapons in hand, given your five days?''

He had been so overwrought behind the facade he fought to maintain that he had not been this time as careful of his choice of words.

''I, Supreme Mightiness?'' Ochall shook his head. ''My power rests only as a shadow of that you lawfully wield. Nor do I give any commands, except in your name—''

Ramsay did not need to close his eyes. There seemed to him now to be a weaving veil of illusion between him and Ochall. He did not see clearly this stocky man who was an embodiment of power, rather than a yellow fog torn through with flames in which men twisted and died screaming. This was no dream vision, yet the sight was as deeply engraved on his mind at that moment as any of those Osythes had turned upon him to begin this nightmare.

Work with or through Ochall? He had been supremely foolish in believing he might do that. In this world he had no touch with any man except Dedan. And the First Captain lay far away—his wounds keeping him from any immediate summoning. An awful loneliness shook Ramsay during that second or two of true realization.

He was not aware that he wavered as he stood, that he reached behind him for support and laid hand upon the arm of the massive throne. Then that mind-wrenching memory thinned as he saw Ochall's eyes, avid, greedy, fixed on him. What knowledge the High Chancellor had gained from those few seconds of loss of control Ramsay dared not speculate upon. But surely the High Chancellor believed that he dealt with another weakling prince, and Ramsay knew that, whatever move he made from this moment forth, he could not follow, even outwardly, any suggestion from Ochall.

To send that fog, those flames into Lom—that was unthinkable! Could the Enlightened Ones have known what Ochall planned? If so—then they were rightly the treacherous menace many thought them. He owed nothing to the Empress and her party. To go to Lom was to invite another attack from some hidden assassin. Still—where else might he now move? Even if he were somehow to disappear from Vidin as quickly and strangely as he had come, his very appearance here, his recognition of Ochall before the court, would give the High Chancellor the power to act in his name. No one would question any order given him in his supposed master's behalf.

"Five days—" Ramsay seized upon the first excuse he could summon. "Five days' wait may be too long. Let Berthal be proclaimed, then there will be, as has been pointed out, those who hesitate to support my dear cousin, but who would close ranks against me should there arise a hint of war between two factions in Ulad."

"Your answer then—?" Ochall asked.

"That you, High Chancellor, and I, and such dignitaries from Vidin as can best back us in a righteous cause, go to Lom. Not in threat, but as we should to support a claim that no man can question."

He wondered if Ochall would dare refuse. However, the High Chancellor seemed prepared for such a challenge.

"You go directly into a nest of enemies, Supreme Mightiness. Yet, too, courage is rightfully the virtue of any emperor, and with a guard of liege men, they cannot come at you secretly. Just as they dare not question openly the one who is so plainly Kaskar. When would you go?"

"Now, as soon as it may be readied." Ramsay did not doubt that Ochall had his own loyal followers, who would carry out to the letter any orders their master left. But he himself would gain some time to—to what—warn? He did not know. The only small satisfaction he had was that Ochall would be with him, and that half vision of the High Chancellor advancing upon an undefended and helpless city behind a cloud of fog and flame would not now come to pass.

The flyer that took them from Kaskar's holding

was far larger and more luxurious (being divided into several cabins of varying degrees of appointment) than Ramsay had heretofore seen. He noted before he boarded that there had been some hasty painting of insignia on the side, a reproduction of that fierce bird which he had seen on the hall paneling in the palace. It would appear that his liege men were determined that he make his entrance properly, with the bearings of a rightful ruler in full display.

"The Place of Proclaiming?" Ochall had not seated himself too near the well-padded and gilded seat Ramsay had chosen as properly being his. He had to lean forward now from his more lowly position in order to ask that.

And Ramsay, in relief at the solving of one of his problems, nodded. To enter the Palace of Lom without his presence being known to the city at large had worried him. This "Place of Proclaiming" sounded open enough to satisfy the most demanding of publicity seekers.

Having agreed with Ochall, he was apparently to be left to his own thoughts, for the High Chancellor settled back with a wriggle of his broad shoulders, closed his eyes, and gave every appearance of desiring a discreet withdrawal from any further conversation. Ramsay closed his own eyes. What had they told him—those unfathomable Enlightened Ones? To dream? But there was no way he knew of summoning dreams at will.

Instead he recalled in detail again those cards and the fluttering hand of Adise as she dealt and fingered the final ones that foretold his fate. Fate—yes, and Fear—Dreams—with only the promise of Hope at the end of it all.

Events were moving too fast, and he knew far too

little. This was like being pitched blindfolded into some battle where everyone else he blundered against had both sight and purpose. Ramsay had had just one purpose—to save the skin of one Ramsay Kimble. Now he had moved by emotion to try to save a city—perhaps a nation. His mouth twisted bitterly. What allowed him to yield to the anger Ochall's matter-of-fact explanation had evoked?

Though he knew little of air distances from one city to another, he was a little startled at the short duration of their flight. Perhaps Ochall had given orders that their craft be pushed to the utmost. For Ramsay was still trying to marshal his chaotic thoughts into order when the signal flashed as the flyer spiraled downward.

The richly paneled walls of the cabin had no windows. Ramsay sat tense and stiff. They could be alighting in the midst of enemies waiting to ring them in. Ochall seemed to read his mind then; perhaps Ramsay's own posture gave him away. For the High Chancellor said: "Though it would seem that the talk-wires could not carry a message into Vidin"— his tone was sardonic—"our own clearance call has been openly broadcast, Supreme Mightiness. Be very sure that Lom knows *who* arrives—openly, with only his suite about him—coming as a rightful lord and no invader."

That that was any great condolence at the moment Ramsay doubted. But he had chosen to play this role, and he would not allow the High Chancellor to see him flinching from it.

"Rightfully done," was his comment.

"We set down," Ochall continued, "in the Four Square of Heros. There is no landing stage, but our forecast will have cleared the necessary space. Then you have only to mount to the Place of the Soverign Flags and show yourself—"

Ramsay thought he caught a flicker of a glance in his direction. Did the High Chancellor hint that so showing himself might well make him a target, providing some action that would totally settle once and for all who would be Emperor in Ulad?

The flyer touched earth, the vibration of the flight ended. Ramsay unbuckled his safety belt with hands he was glad to see did remain steady. After all, he had been through a similiar experience before, when he had emerged from that other flyer on the roof in Vidin.

He arose as those of his following filed through to the narrow exit. The guard, now under command of Jasum, was first. The guardsman snapped to attention on the pavement below, forming an aisle through which Ramsay could walk.

Deliberately he descended. They had indeed set down well within Lom. Buildings arose about them as thickly as those trees that embowered the Grove dwelling of the Enlightened Ones. The natural rusty red or dull gray stone walls were veiled and draped with brightly colored banners and swatches of cloth. Streamers, ribbonlike in their length and light weight, stirred in breezes that swirled them outward thorugh the air.

Immediately before him was a pyramid of the red stone he had come to associate with the remains of that legendary Great World which had been. This structure was truncated, so that its top was like a triangular platform. About its rim were six sturdy poles from which billowed, in that same movement of air, five flags. The sixth pole was bare. Leading up to this was a flight of steps, hollowed and worn, as if the Place of Flags had stood there for more centuries than perhaps Lom itself had had existence. Among these other bannered buildings, this did have a curious barren look.

Deliberately Ramsay set foot on the hollow curve of the first step. Though he looked neither to left nor right, possessed by his own sense of what Kaskar, Emperor of Ulad, must do at that moment, Ramsay was aware that Lom's streets were not deserted. There was a multitude gathering closer. None of those who had come with him from Vidin were following. Perhaps only his Supreme Mightinesss (what cumbersome titles they chose) dared make this climb.

From below the sound of voices grew from a gabble into nearly a roar. Ramsay climbed on. He planted each foot precisely and unhurriedly, refusing to allow himself to look right or left. That gathering below might be getting ready to mob him. A bead of sweat loosened from the line of his black hair on the forehead, trickled slowly down his cheek. He kept his face impassive and climbed.

Now he reached the top. To his right, before he turned, was the pole of a yellow banner, one centered with a geometrically lined criss-cross of a violently vivid green. To his left was the pole that bore no banner at all.

As deliberately as he had climbed, Ramsay now turned, to gaze over that city Kaskar had meant to rule. His head was bare except for a silver circlet tight across his forehead. There was no hood, no mask, to hide him now. And he stood, his feet a little apart, one hand resting lightly on the hilt of his sword of ceremony, looking out and down.

What he saw was a massing of faces, all turned in

his direction. Even the windows of the neighboring buildings were packed with people crowding each other to look upon him. The effect was like a blow, yet he knew he must stand impassively under it.

They were shouting now, and from the din of sound rolling about the four-cornered Place of Heroes, seeming to echo from the buildings, he could pick out his borrowed name:

"Kaskar, Kaskar!"

It took him a second or two to realize that there was no threat in that recognition. Amazement, yes. Even if Kaskar had been so disliked by the court and those of his own blood, this city seemed not to have shared those sentiments. When he raised his hand in acknowledgment it appeared that his liege men were not limited to Vidin—for there was a roar of cheering that must have reached even to the walls of the somewhat distant palace.

Someone else now moved up the worn steps. Ramsay saw a man wearing a brilliant short tunic, fashioned so the fierce bird of Ulad's crest hovered over the upper half of his body. He carried a horn of such length that he needed to balance it over his shoulder carefully as he made the ascent. Behind him a second similarly attired and burdened trumpeter emerged through the thin line of guardsmen to climb in turn.

Ramsay stepped back a little when those two reached the summit of the pyramid. They bowed to him, then swung around, resting the bell mouths of their trumpets against the ancient stone, putting the mouthpieces to their lips.

Above the roar of the crowd sounded deep grumbling notes. They might have issued from clouds as thunder, except that there were no clouds; Ramsay stood in full light of a brilliant sun. Three times those notes were repeated. The cheering faded away, a silence fell. Still all the faces were raised to Ramsay. They were waiting, and he did not know for what! His hand twitched with a touch of panic—this was all part of an old ceremony. Courts and kings were enveloped, made secure in part, by the uses of ceremony. But he did not know what to do now—

To his vast relief, and in that moment he forgot his distrust of the High Chancellor, Ochall had climbed behind the trumpeters, though he did not join Ramsay at the summit of the pyramid. Instead he swung about, not too easy a maneuver on that narrow, worn step, to speak.

"Hear you, all liege men! In this, the Square of Heroes, on the summit of the Place of Flags, which point lies in the very heart of Ulad, is now proclaimed our lord paramount and reigning—under whose rule shall we be as fruitful land well watered, warmed by a sun of glory. By the right of the House of Jostern, bearing the true blood of that same Jostern of old, comes now Kaskar—his birthright unquestioned. Pyran who was his passed through the Final Gate—may all the Watchers, the Comforters"— Ochall bowed his head and paused for an instant, his gesture of conventional reverence echoed by all in that throng—"bear him forth quickly to eternal life, joy, and blessing. In life he acknowledged Kaskar, Prince of Vidin, as his true heir of body and line. Therefore now this same Kaskar stands before you, as Supreme Mightiness, Guardian of Ulad, Watcher and Comforter this side of the Gate, for all his people. The Emperor is gone, the Emperor has come again!"

Four times the thunder of the trumpers sounded in nearly deafening blasts. Then the cheering broke out anew.

A shiver ran up Ramsay's back. He had heretofore looked upon this as a dangerous piece of playacting. But this—it was real! Far too real! He was not Kaskar; he wanted to run and run from those cheers. What new net was he caught in now? He swallowed. The cheers were lessening—They must expect something from him.

Almost against his will his hand went up. In answer to that nearly involuntary gesture quiet fell even as it had before the proclamation made by Ochall.

He *had* to say something— But nothing in his past had prepared him for such a moment. The real Kaskar would have been carefully trained for this hour, so any fumbling on his part might now be remarked upon. Once more the weight of his masquerade pressed upon him. Liege men—the term had a definite meaning in this world—it was a bond of honor. If he accepted their offering, then he must give something in return to keep the balance. He had begun all this thinking only of himself, his safety, of a private struggle against those who had used him. If he accepted what these now offered him—then he was tied. Already he had gone too far, there was no going back unless he denied he was what his appearance labeled him. And that he could not do.

"Liege man also is your Emperor." Ramsay tried not to fumble for words as he searched to express emotions he had not had time enough to label or even fully understand. "Liege to Ulad. No more than that can any of the House of Jostern swear. For the safety of Ulad and those within its borders is the first duty of him who is proclaimed."

A short speech, perhaps an awkward one. But at that moment Ramsay meant it as he had never meant anything before in his life. There was a moment of silence. Ramsay began to wonder if that abrupt speech had been the wrong thing, after all. Then the cheering began—

But also noted a flurry in the mass of crowd below. A party of guardsmen pushed forward, urging a path through the throng. Men and women were giving way to the determination of that group. And within the ring of guardsmen Ramsay thought he saw the elaborate clothing of courtiers. At last the Palace must be on the move. Though Ramsay could not believe that the intriguers would attempt any counterstroke in this open and very public place.

At the foot of the stair his men from Vidin closed ranks a little. But Ramsay sensed some uneasiness in their stance. The purposeful approach of the other party began to make itself more strongly felt. Already the crowd drew farther apart, letting them through. When they reached a point where they faced the guard from Vidin, they drew up in a similiar line, as if prepared to go into combat. Ramsay took a step forward, knowing that by all possible means he must prevent such a confrontation. Then almost instantly he realized there was no need for intervention, at least not on the level of the opposing guardsmen.

From their group the civilians whom they had escorted across the square now advanced. Berthal— and Osythes. The Prince wore scarlet and gold, bright enough to issue challenge by color alone, while the Shaman was almost a shadow of ill omen in his black-and-white, which, next to Berthal's ostentatious magnificence, was more black than white.

The Shaman's old face was as impassive as ever, but Berthal's was flushed to a degree that nearly matched the scarlet of his trappings. Though Osythes put out a hand as if to dissuade him from any imprudent move, the Prince avoided the Shaman with a twist of the shoulder, and sprang for the steps that led to the Place of Flags.

The noise of the crowd had faded to a murmur. It was plain that they expected drama to come and were not to be denied any of the action they could witness between the rivals to the Throne of Ulad.

Ramsay remained where he was. Berthal was the embodiment of rage. They might even meet in physical combat, certainly an edifying sight for Lom. Ramsay was sure he could handle the irate Prince without any interference from the guard. But he hardly wanted to be so publicly entangled in an undignified scuffle.

Berthal fairly leaped up those age-worn steps. Osythes, in spite of his years and the hindering long skirts of his robe, was only a little behind the Prince. Berthal, his eyes blazing, his mouth a crooked grimace of hate, had barely reached Ramsay's level when the Shaman joined them.

"Imposter!" Berthal was breathing so heavily that he gasped rather than shouted his accusation as perhaps he wished to do. "You thing of dreams! Think you to rule here? I say no! And with my body shall I make it so!"

He whirled out his sword of ceremony. Ramsay made no move to draw his own weapon. With narrow eyes he watched the Prince, now foaming spittle at the corner of his lips. If Berthal was wild enough to rush him at that moment, the Prince would have to take the consequences.

But that knife was not pointed toward Ramsay's body. Berthal had grasped the point instead of the haft of his weapon and flipped it through the air. Not at Ramsay, but rather so that the blade crashed to the stone of the pavement and slithered across, until it lay, point foremost, at Ramsay's feet.

FIFTEEN

THE SOUND NOW—not the cheering of moments earlier—rather a sighing that might be produced by the indrawn breath of hundreds. This was surely some kind of formal challenge, but Ramsay, again caught in the net of his own defeating ignorance, was at a loss. Yet, if he hesitated, the Shaman did not.

His robes swirling about him, Osythes pushed between the two, planted his booted foot directly on the sword blade.

"No." A single word to erect a barrier, but it did. Berthal's color heightened, if that was possible; his hands twitched. To Ramsay's eyes the Prince was fast losing self-control. He looked as if he were about to elbow past Osythes in order to leap directly for Ramsay's throat.

"It is my right!" choked out Berthal.

Osythes nodded. "Your right, by the code set by Jostern at the birth of your House. But this is not the time or the place." His hand closed about the Prince's right wrist and, though his thin fingers did not look to have such strength, Ramsay saw that Berthal could not break that hold.

However, it was to Ramsay that the Shaman now looked as if Berthal were no longer of consequence.

"You have returned." Osythes stated the obvious. "For what gain, dreamer?"

So simple was his question that Ramsay suspected some hidden guile. Yet it appeared that the Shaman actually wanted that answer.

"Perhaps," Ramsay answered, "because I am not yet ready to be a dead Kaskar as it was your will that I should be. There is that in all of us, Enlightened One, that will always struggle against death."

There was a faint frown, a very shadow of expression on the Shaman's face. His eyes probed Ramsay, who made himself face that searching gaze squarely. He sensed that he presented a problem the Shaman found baffling. And, in that bafflement, Ramsay himself discovered a small strength which made him add: "*Your* Heir has challenged me. Why not let us then settle this matter here and now—openly before what seems to be most of Lom—? I have had my fill of masked assassins ready to cut me down without warning. And I do not think that my sudden death from any cause will aid you now, not after this public affirmation of my right—"

"Your right!" cried Berthal, his voice scaling upward in his anger. "You have no rights at all—you barbarian out of—"

Perhaps Osythes then applied some punishing pressure to the wrist which he still held, for Berthal's protest ended in a grunt of pain. He shot a fierce look at the Shaman, but he was quiet.

Osythes was once more impassive. "Kaskar has been proclaimed, it would seem," he remarked tonelessly, though Ramsay had no faith in such sudden and complete surrender. "It is fitting that His Supreme Mightiness now appear before his court, having already been hailed by his people."

Enter the palace? Yet that, too, would be expected of him, and Ramsay believed he had no choice. He had already delivered a warning, one he knew would be enforced by those of Vidin, maybe also by at least some of these who had cheered him in Lom. Let him die for any cause now and there would be too many questions asked. If he must fight Berthal he would, and he had an idea that custom would decree that to be a very open struggle with plenty of official witnesses.

"His Supreme Mightiness"—Ramsay took a small pleasure in using the grandiloquent title—"agrees."

He glanced at Ochall, who had taken no part in this small flurry of rivals for the throne. In fact, Ramsay decided, the High Chancellor's attitude was one of strict neutrality. But Ramsay was not about to leave Ochall loose to give any orders, not if he could help it.

"His Dignity, our very worth Chancellor, will accompany us," he stated firmly.

So it came about that a meeting, which had begun as a duel, ended—perhaps to the disappointment of many of the spectators—in a uniting of parties. By signal, and with much labor on the part of the combined guards to clear sufficient space, the flyer from Vidin once more set down, and Ramsay, followed by Ochall and, at a slightly increased distance, by the Shaman, who still had his hand on Berthal (now wearing a sulky, much-baffled look) embarked. Moments later they settled on a roof landing, and the Palace of Lom welcomed them with a turnout of the guard.

As Ramsay acknowledged their salutes, Osythes saw fit to abandon his guardianship of Berthal to join the newly proclaimed Emperor. This time he addressed him shortly, without any of the honorifics one might expect.

"Her Splendor Enthroned would speak with you," he stated.

Ramsay smiled. "It is indeed gracious of her," he returned. "But perhaps it is even more gracious of Kaskar—"

For the first time he saw what could only be anger flash momentarily in the Shaman's eyes.

"You have a free tongue!" he snapped.

To that observation Ramsay nodded. "But still I live. Very well, the same trap cannot work twice."

"I do not know what you mean—" Osythes replied.

Ramsay laughed openly. "I did not think you would, Enlightened One. By what I have heard, you folk deal in obscurities upon obscurities. All I would have you understand now is that I shall march to no foretelling of yours."

Now he turned his head and spoke to Ochall. "I am summoned to my grandmother, High Chancellor. Her Splendor Enthroned must not be kept waiting. Whatever matters are of import, those we shall discuss later."

Ochall bowed. Berthal might have made some comment; he had opened his mouth. However, a quelling glance from the Shaman kept him mute. Berthal marched on their very heels as they entered a lift that carried them downward into the Palace that had so many secrets.

Where was Melkolf, Ramsay wondered as he tramped along the last corridor, the one with the secret door that led to the lab. Was Melkolf again at work, perhaps trying once more to match a redundant Kaskar to another victim on a third world plane? At least Ramsay had not had any dream to raise his suspicions. But he was certain now that, if he could put any power into an order, it would be given to destroy the machine squatting evilly below.

Neither Berthal nor the Shaman had said a word since they had left the landing stage. Perhaps their thoughts of revenge, needful action, defense, were as active as Ramsay's own. Berthal was the charge-at-all-obstacles-unheeding-of-the-cost type, so he could be countered that much more easily. But Ramsay was wary of Osythes, not knowing how far or how effective were the powers of these of the Groves. They appeared to be able to use minds in action as capably as the Company used its physical strength and experience in warfare. Therefore—they were to be most feared.

The doors of the Empress's apartment opened at their arrival. Ramsay, summoning up his old anger for a defense, went boldly through. There she sat, cloaked, crowned, small—deadly—in her canopied chair. Beside her, in another seat lacking that shadow-producing overhang, was—Thecla.

Ramsay shot a single glance at the girl. He had, through those days since that attack on the wharfside, kept—or tried to keep—her face out of his mind. She had been a part of the plan that would have left him dead and long since forgotten.

He supposed she would claim, if he ever accused her, that it was part of her "duty." That she owed Olyroun any life, including her own, if it was demanded of her. The odd sensation he had felt when

Lom acknowledged his rule—yes, that made him understand, a little. She had been bred to the belief that a true ruler was a servant of the land, its defender to the death. She would accept any sacrifice the good of Olyroun would demand, and no one would ever know what private thoughts and desires she had set aside. Yes, he could understand, but this was not the Thecla he had held in foolish memory.

He bowed, deeply to the withered old woman in the chair of state, less lowly to the Duchess. Thecla's face was pale, her features set. Ramsay caught a glimpse of her hands, not lying gracefully in her lap, but with the fingers tightly laced together, as if to keep some control on herself.

"Your Splendor Enthroned." He spoke to the Empress.

She wasted no time. "We had a bargain, stranger."

"*You* had a bargain," he corrected her bluntly. "The one offered me in that hour was not the same!"

Thecla's hands flew apart. "What is it that you would say?" she demanded.

Ramsay turned his head deliberately, looked her full in the eyes. Amazing that she could produce that expression of strained surprise. He had always heard that royal personages never could be themselves, that their life of being on constant show must make actors of them from birth, but still her question surprised him.

"Let us have no secrets, at least none concerning the past," Ramsay returned. "My Lady Duchess, you carefully provided the disguise of your kinsman, the Feudman. I warrant that you returned me so to Lom—though your first rescue of me now seems a little strange—or were you then acting on impulse that you later reconsidered? Back in Lom I was able, of course, to discover the futility of trying to counter the act that had brought me here.

"Then"—he once more addressed the Empress—"we have the very timely intervention of the Reverend One." Ramsay nodded to Osythes. "oddly enough, considering the need, he did *not* allow Melkolf to dispose of me. I wonder why the second and more complicated manner of erasing me was tried. There must have been a reason, but I don't suppose any of you are going to favor me with an explanation of it.

"At any rate, you were very frank with me—about the danger it meant to show this face"—Ramsay touched his own chin—"in Lom lest the High Chancellor be alerted and some strange and terrible doom be visited upon an innocent stranger unfairly drawn into your palace intrigues. Therefore I was sent to a carefully arranged meeting with one who, I was later informed, was the highest-priced and most efficient assassin in Ulad.

"It was your misfortune that I, too, have some skills, which are not of your world and so escaped that tidy plot. That I did survive involved me in some other factors—"

"This is what you believe, you truly believe?" It was not the Empress who asked that, but Thecla. Her hands were no longer clenched; the fingers moved on the surface of her rich tunic. Seeing them so for a second, Ramsay was whirled back in time to watch other fingers, perhaps more slender, but no better shaped, flicking down upon a board those five strips with their potent symbols.

"This is what I believe," he replied with firmness.

Her hands stilled, she only watched him dumbly.

He discovered he could not look at her again. After all, in this company, she was perhaps the least of his enemies. That withered doll propped up in the chair of state might be the foremost, unless Osythes held that position.

There was a sound from the Shaman, but the Empress raised her hand in a quelling gesture.

"Let be, Reverend One. We have no time for the unraveling of old tangles. There is the present one facing us. So you have gone to Ochall, and you are Emperor in Lom—and in name—" Her eyes burned fiercely in her face. "And how are you the better for such a choice?"

Ramsay shrugged. "Perhaps I am not—but I am alive—"

"He who yields to Ochall has no life that will matter!" She attacked in force.

"Have I yielded then?" Ramsay returned.

He was aware that those three—for he did not count Berthal, who stood, still sulking, near the wall—had centered probing gazes upon him. And he stared as stealthily back. Did they not have the clarity of sight to understand that when they tried to manipulate events in the future they were only slightly removed in truth from the High Chancelloor who had manipulated a man?

"If you are not yet his tool," said the Empress at last, "you cannot escape." But the tone of her voice was troubled. Her eyes shifted from Ramsay to Osythes, as if asking some unvoiced question.

"I have been told," Ramsay said deliberately, seeking to strike some involuntary reaction from the three, "that in this game I stand as the Knave of Dreams."

The sound of sucked-in breath—Thecla's hands

were now pressed against her mouth; above their masking her eyes were wide and frightened. But it was Osythes who spoke:

"And who did this telling?"

"One Adise," Ramsay replied shortly, and then elaborated, wishing to see the effect of his words upon them. "Fear and Fate, Fear and the Queen of Hope. Does that mean anything to you, Enlightened One?"

Osythes nodded slowly. However, when he spoke, it was to the Empress rather than in answer to Ramsay's question.

"Your Splendor Enthroned, *there* lies the answer! There—"

She interrupted him. "I do not understand your secrets, Reverend One. All I know is that in this hour this—this Kaskar who is not Kaskar rules Ulad. And at his right hand stands the dark one who will pull us all down! Well, we meddled with fate, and this is our reward. But while I live"—now her words were directed to Ramsay fiercely—"I shall fight for all my lord wrought here! And I promise you, I am no mean enemy!"

With lifted chin, and those eyes as bright and menacing as some bird of prey's, she offered him battle, showing far more dignity and purpose than Berthal's dramatics with the sword of ceremony.

"You do not know Ochall." Ramsay knew at this moment, enemy or no, he could not allow her to remain ignorant of what the High Chancellor planned. "He has already dealt with the Merchants of Norn, and what he has gained thereby—listen and believe." In bald, terse words he outlined the Battle of the Ridge, sparing them no detail that might clarify the horror that could be turned against Lom itself.

"In Yasnaby—" Thecla cried out. Now her hands covered the whole of her face, and she was shuddering as if he had produced before their very sight not just spoken the words but the whole scene of that massacre. "In Olyroun!"

"Monstrous!" The Empress's shoulders sagged a trifle. It would seem that more years had gathered in those few moments to weigh her down. "And yet you company with this man! Why do you then reveal his works? Do you mean to use fear as a weapon intended to cow us into a quick surrender?"

"I say only what I have seen—felt—" Absently Ramsay raised his hand to his cheek where the searing fire had left no scar but memory. "If it was my intention to invade Lom, I would have given Ochall his five days—"

"What do you want of us?" Thecla cried now.

"What I have always wanted—my own place."

"But we—Melkolf cannot give you that!" Thecla was flushed; her back stiffened, and she faced him as she might a threat she must not openly acknowledge.

"Yes," agreed Ramsay. "Therefore—we are left with a problem. I am Kaskar now and cannot return. And who is Kaskar?"

"You play with words!" The Empress showed open anger. "The girl is right—what do you want of us?"

"I do not know—yet," Ramsay returned. "But I warn you—I play no more of your games. Nor"—he hesitated for a second to give emphasis to the rest—"will I play Ochall's. That he has power beyond my reckoning—that you had better believe. That he intends to hold Ulad, one way or another—that also you are aware of—"

"You accompanied him here—" began the Empress.

"I brought him because here he can be watched. Had I left him in Vidin—would you have the fog and flame come upon you?"

For the first time Osythes broke into their exchange. "Knave of Dreams—" he repeated slowly. "And what have you dreamed?"

"Nothing—yet."

"Adise—" Thecla hesitated over the name and then continued with more confidence. "She is the Great Reader—"

"Take no comfort from that!" snapped the Empress. She gave the Shaman a hostile glance. "I begin to think, Reverend One, that Ulad's cause did not attract a true supporter in you. Rather we have all been blind yet once again and have been manipulated, even as Kaskar was ruled by Ochall, into this situation because of some decision of the Enlightened Ones, which will do us no good at all! Blind! Blind!" She raised one hand to cover her eyes. "Old and blind and worthless! And so Ulad falls because I have failed."

"No!" Thecla moved to catch the Empress's other hand. "Do not think so!" She glanced up at Osythes. "Reverend One, tell her that is not true. You—all of you—could not be so cruel!"

"Ulad shall not fall." The Shaman said those four words deliberately, as if they did not form an assertion, but a promise.

"Another foreseeing?" Berthal came away from the wall, his lips bent in a sneer. "Well enough—let this—this outlander answer me blade to blade and I shall make sure of that!'' His hatred was hot in his boast.

"A foreseeing"—Osythes again spoke in that measured way—"can only indicate probable events, which may be changed by the choices of those concerned. All of you are aware of that. But—" He paused as if to think his way thorugh some web of mind. "There is a pattern—and it is far-reaching. Ulad is a necessary part of that pattern—the first stable government seen in this land since the Great Disaster. Thus Ulad is the foundation upon which we must build anew. No, Ulad, because of our actions, in spite of our actions, will not fall. Yet that does not resolve our separate fates—"

The Empress had been watching him, her one hand clasped in Thecla's, the other now lying limply on her knee as if her outburst of moments earlier had exhausted even her indomitable strength and will.

"Be Ulad safe," she said now in a low voice, "and I care not that fate rises in my path."

"I care!" Berthal came a step closer to Ramsay. "True blood will rule here! Ulad is the House of Jostern! We made this land in the past, we shall maintain it now! And you"—he fairly spat at Ramsay—"are none of us. Live as Emperor and you will speedily die—"

Ramsay suddenly laughed. "For yet another time, Prince?"

But Berthal nodded as if that had been an accepted truth. "Yes."

"Enough!" The Empress's old authority was once more vibrant in her voice. "We do not bait each other here and now. Rather do we seek to come to some accord. You have made yourself Emperor," she said to Ramsay. "Do you hold to that?"

"Would you accept me so?" countered Ramsay wonderingly.

"I will accept everything—all—that preserves this land. You say that Ochall is not your master. If this proves true—then—"

"No!" Berthal's denial cut across her words. "He is not the Heir, he is nothing—a man who should rightfully be dead! Let *him* wed with Thecla, sit upon the throne? You are old! You are mad!"

Thecla was on her feet between the Empress and Berthal, who again had the appearance of one maddened to the point of losing all control, even as he had been at the Place of Flags.

"Be silent!" Like the Empress's voice earlier, hers now held the whiplash of unquestioned authority. "Her Splendor Enthroned remains the Head of the House of Jostern—"

"I need not your liege words, my dear," the Empress said. "And I am not shaken in my wits. Ulad must come first. We do not plunge this land into war with man against son, brother against brother, over any question of heirdom. If Kaskar proves that he is not Ochall's creature—"

Ramsay was the one who interrupted now. "Your Splendor Enthroned"—he gave her her title—"I am no man's—no woman's creature. What I decide shall be of my own free will. Since I was unwilling and unwitting player in your game for power, I now reserve my own decision."

He bowed to her, to Thecla, ignoring both the Shaman and Berthal, who made as if to step between him and the door of the chamber and then thought better of it, meeting Ramsay's gaze. Then, leaving them to think about his declaration of independence, Ramsay purposefully left the room.

Where Kaskar's apartment might be within this pile, Ramsay had no idea. But he was not subjected to the humiliation of trying to find out, for in the corridor beyond awaited Jasum and two of the Vidin guardsmen. Almost, Ramsay thought, as if they expected to be called upon to protect the person of their sworn lord. And with their escort he reached a richly furnished chamber not unlike that in which he and Thecla had sat to exchange stumbling words the first night of his life here.

He dismissed his liege men with courtesy, wanting to be alone. Where was Ochall in this pile, and what might the High Chancellor be doing? If he, Ramsay, only had someone at his back whom he could wholly trust! The half promise of the Empress to support Kaskar—how much could he depend upon that? Very little. He should know that from his former betrayal. And to be Emperor—he had never intended that!

There was a tray on a table, bearing a stoppered, thin-necked bottle of cut crystal, a waiting matching goblet, and with these a plate of cakes. Ramsay sank into one of the piles of cushions, which here took the place of chairs, and began to eat ravenously, suddenly conscious of the fact that it had been a long time since he had last dined. He would rather have had a more substantial meal, but his own need to think in private kept him from summoning a servant.

Having wolfed the cakes, he sipped the liquid with more caution, wanting no unexpected potency to cloud his mind at this moment. Outside, the dusk cloaked the windows. A single lamp burned on a far table. And the radiance from it was very limited, so that he was well hidden in the swiftly gathering shadows.

There was an ache beginning above his eyes. He was tired—so tired—to try to sort out any impressions of this day was now a wearying task. That he had begun this wild venture at all—why?

Dreams—

No dream could be any wilder than this.

Ramsay longed with all his might to awaken, to know that this was merely a prolonged adventure born out of his own imagination. Dream—they had told him that—the Enlightened Ones.

Suppose he could dream himself awake in the right world? For all the proof they had shown him—perhaps that was as false as other things they had said and done.

No! He could not allow himself to be disarmed. Ramsay sat up straighter, glanced sharply about the chamber. He had that small subtle hint to alert him. Ochall—was the High Chancellor bending on him now some unbelievable power of will to lead him into this particular path of thought? He had to cope with the reality, not allow himself to drift into the dream again.

And in the Palace of Lom he had no one to trust. In all this world he had—

A face formed vividly in Ramsay's mind—Dedan! The mercenary had no company now. If he had survived his terrible injuries he would be left without resources. Dedan—

The thought of the First Captain was like a tonic. Ramsay nodded, though there was no one there to witness the gesture which approved his idea. Dedan would be sent for, through the Enlightened Ones—

that need was as sharply clear as if Ramsay could see it all laid out in print before him. Dedan was also Ramsay's witness against Ochall—therefore this must be done in secret. And who was better able to handle secrets than Osythes?

He would—

Again Ramsay tensed. He had not heard that door open behind him. But hunter's instinct, sharpened by circumstances, told him he was not alone any longer. In the shadows he shifted about to see who had come so silently and perhaps—for good reason—secretly.

SIXTEEN

VEILED, HIDDEN, she advanced. But he knew her. This was the guise she had worn beside the bier of a dead prince, a newly risen man.

Ramsay arose.

"What do you want?" His voice was even more brusque than he intended. She had presented him with two faces in the past—her concern, the reason for which he had never understood, then the false concern when she had set upon him that near-fatal disguise of Feudman.

Thecla stood just within the farther reach of the lamp rays as she lifted her long veil.

"Why did you say such things—that you were marked for death by our will?" she asked simply.

He wondered that she would try to keep up a pretense of innocence—or ignorance.

"Because that was the truth."

Thecla came farther into the light, her intent gaze upon his face.

"I see that you believe it," she acknowledged.

"But how can you? The Empress, Osythes, they do not deal so—"

"They did before," he reminded her deliberately. "What of Kaskar—and me—were we not intended to die together under the influence of Melkolf's machine? What did my life weigh then against their needs? And does it weigh even less now when I stand in Lom to refute, by my presence, all their plans?"

Under the warm brown of her skin there arose a flush. "They—they did not know you then. You were an abstraction—something far removed—not real—"

"So then when by some slip I became real," Ramsay retorted, "I was even more a menace. Is this not so? I have learned something, my Lady Duchess, your strength is duty, and to that you are prepared to sacrifice all. Is that not the truth?"

"It is the truth," she agreed tonelessly.

"Therefore, as duty bid, you found a plausible story and those other two improved upon it. An anonymous Feudman slain on the wharfside by a known assassin for hire. Such an occurence as would bring about little official investigation—and I am well removed."

"*No!*" Her protest was quick, hot. Now there was anger in her tone. "That was not the way of it! I—I demean myself to come to you, to beg you to listen." Her chin lifted. She drew about her not the physical folds of her veil, rather the inborn authority that was bred in her.

"It is only because—" She hesitated and then continued, all her pride displayed by her straight back, her flashing eyes. "It is because I will not have such a slur put upon Olyroun, for I am Olyroun—if you can understand that—I am here. The attack on the wharf was *not* of our planning—''

''Then whose?'' Ramsay prompted when again she paused.

It would appear that she was loath to answer. He saw her hands twisting, wringing the edge of her veil.

''I am not sure, and I will accuse no one unjustly,'' Thecla said slowly. ''But this I will swear by any Power you wish, the Empress, and Osythes, and I—we did not unite to send you to your death. I knew not that you had gone until later. And this is the truth which you can discover for yourself. That guardsman who was to see you safe on board the ship—he did not return to the palace. Her Splendor's Eyes and Ears have been busy—but even they could not find him.''

''This, too, you will lay on Ochall?'' Ramsay was more than half convinced that whatever intrigue had been aimed at him had not included Thecla. Perhaps because he wanted to believe that, he decided in a flash of insight.

What was this girl to him? He could not have honestly answered. With her burden of rulership she was unlike any of her sex he had known. Still, in spite of that burden and difference, he realized now that he had been drawn to her from those hours when she had sheltered him in her chamber, been so efficient in arranging his escape.

''Ochall?'' Thecla repeated the High Chancellor's name with an accent of surprise. ''No, he would not want Kaskar dead.''

''He knows Kaskar is dead,'' Ramsay informed her. ''Though he accepts the fiction that I am Kaskar.'' Of that he was now as certain as if the High Chancellor had had told him so.

Thecla nodded. ''He doubtless plans to make you

is Kaskar. Your life is more precious to him now
han any treasure—''

''So,'' Ramsay persisted, ''we are now left with a
nystery. If it was not the Empress who arranged my
inal disappearance, and Ochall could want nothing
ess, who remains?

She was silent, there was a shadow of obstinacy
about her lips. Ramsay thought that she would not
give him more. Yet he must—somehow he believed
hat Thecla was in earnest—learn what she suspected.

Who would benefit by the death of Kaskar the
second—and who had even been aware that there
was a Kaskar the second? Thecla, Grishilda, the
Empress, Osythes—and Melkolf!

The scientist had been ready to kill him out of hand
when he discovered the lab. Somehow Ramsay could
not associate Melkolf with the devious attack on the
wharf. But Melkolf could have been a link—with
whom?

There was only one other—Berthal! Yet Ramsay
would have thought after that exhibition of reckless
temper the Prince had shown in his challenge, that
Berthal, too, would not have been party to a complicated plot. He would have been far more likely to
have made an open attack under some rule of the
nobility—even as today he had delivered that challenge that Osythes had interrupted before most of
Lom.

However—a last suggestion struck Ramsay—the
Enlightened Ones? But he had a strong impression
that, though they might stand aside and let death
strike down a man if they thought that necessary,
they would not actively arrange for a murder.

Watching Thecla closely, Ramsay made his choice

and spoke two names aloud, hoping that the girl would reveal whether his guess was right or wrong.

"Berthal—and Melkolf?"

By an ebbing of her color he had his answer. "Berthal," he continued, "wants Ulad. Melkolf—perhaps he resents the failure of his experiment so much that he must erase the result—"

"I did not say so!" Her answer was too prompt. "Only—watch yourself—Kaskar." For the first time she used that name. "This much I know—the Empress has ordered that the exchanger be dismantled. Melkolf—he is gone and no one can find him. With him he took things even Osythes has not been able to understand. He knew—knows—more of the Old Knowledge than we suspected."

They only needed that added to the rest, thought Ramsay grimly—Melkolf resentful and hidden, and with him, and untold, unmeasured amount of what might be as fearsome knowledge as anything the Merchants of Norn brought into their dread market. His mind made a sinister leap, and he felt a cold shiver run through him. Melkolf would have only one market for his product—Ochall! In Berthal's present state of mind, that Prince might also be added to a dark company, willing to make peace with the enemy for Ulad.

Not only had Ramsay's thoughts marshaled those surmises into good order, but he had an odd sensation that this was what had happened. He believed this fact, though he could not state why.

If the Empress, as she had already proposed, supported Kaskar—Ramsay—rather than cause any dissension—yes, he could conceive of Berthal's being driven by hatred and a sense of injustice to the strongest aid he could find—Ochall. If only Ramsay himself had those he could depend upon—

Ramsay realized that he was striding up and down. Thecla was watching him. As his eyes met hers she spoke.

"You have the foretelling of Adise. Did the Enlightened Ones give you no other word?"

Dedan—Dream— He shook his head. Why had he begun to believe in impossibilities? Perhaps because he was caught in something beyond all the logic of his own world.

"They told you nothing?" Thecla must have taken that shake of his head as answer to that question.

"Something," he answered absently. Then he turned and regarded her narrowly. Would Thecla help? To allow himself to dream—here— unguarded? There was a danger in that which he sensed as one might suddenly sniff an evil stench.

"I must," he told her, "dream—and dreaming—"

He saw her hands close tightly on her veil. "You must not be disturbed," she stated firmly, as if she knew exactly what he propsoed. "Dream—I shall wait."

She moved to the door, and now, with her own hands, she shot home the bolt to lock them in. Ramsay had a last weighing of his trust in her. He had to believe—after all, their purpose was now nearly united.

Stretching himself on a divan, he closed his eyes. Dream—this was not what he had done before, a bringing to the surface of memory-old dreams to wring them of impressions and facts he needed. This was an attempt to reach out, to form a dream born of his own need and desire. And he did not know how to do it.

Dedan—in his mind he held a picture of the Free

Captain. Not as he had seen him last in the litter, but as the mercenary had been at their first meeting, assured, vibrant with life and ambition. Dedan—he centered on that creation of his mind—Dedan!

He concentrated on creating Dedan. Was he dreaming—or merely exercising his imagination? He dared let no doubt trouble his thoughts—Dedan! The very intensity of his struggle to maintain that mind image, reach out to the personality it signified, was such an effort as no physical action had ever seemed to be. Dedan—

Ramsay—was—elsewhere! Not in any chamber such as he had had in the Grove of the Enlightened Ones. No, this was a state of being that was divorced from all he had known. He entered it with a sharp, breaking sensation, as if he had bodily leaped through some fragile screen to reach it.

There was—nothingness—

Then, up through the nothingness, as a plant might grow from the ground, arose—Dedan! First he seemed as Ramsay had striven to picture him. Yet there was about him a lack of response. His eyes were closed, he was more a puppet—a statue.

Was Dedan—*dead?*

Ramsay's concentration faltered. He saw that figure begin to sink again. No—Dedan!

His urgency of thought was like a shout to hail the personality he sought. There was a slow lifting of those eyelids in a face wiped free of all emotion, a face not of earth. The eyes were alive, if the face that framed them was not.

Dedan—to me! To me, at Lom!

Ramsay hurled that thought feverishly, afraid that any moment he would lose this contact, if contact it was. Now he saw the pale lips of the Free Captain open, move in words he could not hear. Feverishly he fought for the other's answer. But there came only the movement of lips. Then—

The nothingness changed abruptly. It formed a swirl of alien veiling, cloud, he was not sure, and Ramsay knew that in that cloud others moved, listened, were startled by his invasion. From those others he shrank. His will shriveled; he wanted only escape lest he see what would come out of nothingness.

His desire for escape was as sharp now as his need to reach Dedan had been. He gasped, fought, broke free. And was awake.

There was still only the low lamplight warring against the dark. But he had awakened once to an overpowering scent of flowers, so now there was also a fragrance, more delicate and elusive. Then he was conscious that hands gripped his, as if they had drawn him back—or anchored him—to safety.

The hands were Thecla's. She sat on cushions by his side, watching him. There was a measure of relief in her eyes when she saw that he knew her.

"You have dreamed." The girl stated that as fact, not as a question.

Ramsay croaked an answer from a mouth still dried with the fear of those last moments in the nothingness. "I—I do not know. This was different." Yet there would be proof—if Dedan came to him, then he would have his proof that he could exert a measure of control over this strange new faculty—whether it was "dreaming" or something else.

"Who is Dedan?" Thecla asked.

Ramsay levered himself up on one elbow to face her more squarely.

"How did you know—?"

"You called upon that name, she returned quickly before his question was half voiced.

So he had called aloud! But in his dream—vision—he had only thought. Real—unreal—Again he shook his head, trying to throw off the dazed feeling that closed about him.

"He is—was—a Free Captain of the mercenaries, one who will have good reason to hate Ochall when he learns the truth. If I can reach him—"

He was talking too much. Why let Thecla, anyone within Lom, know that he felt the need for someone he believed he could implicitly trust?

"Any enemy of Ochall's," Thecla returned—she had risen from her cushions; about her once more she had drawn her cloak of pride and dignity, "should be useful at this moment. I hope that he comes to your calling—"

Somehow she had moved farther from him than one could measure. Now she was draping her veil once more about her head and shoulders in a way that made Ramsay sense that a barrier had risen between them. He had not consciously voiced his doubts. Perhaps she had guessed in some fashion—that a mercenary First Captin had his full trust over all others in Lom.

Before Ramsay could sort out his tangle of thoughts and surmises, blurt out thanks, Thecla had released the latch, was gone. He pulled himself up from the couch. Waveringly, feeling nearly as weak and unsteady as he had when the Enlightened Ones had drawn him and the others to the grove, he gained his feet. He staggered across the room to set that latch firm once more. Thecla had come upon him earlier without warning; who else might be prowling the corridors of the Palace, eager to have a private meeting with Kaskar?

His head ached with a steady throb that made him queasy. And he had to steer a way with caution back to the divan, afraid at any moment that he might go down again. Melkolf—Berthal—Ochall— The names followed him on and on into troubled sleep.

Ramsay woke with a sense of disorientation. There was a pounding—voices— He moved sluggishly, stiff, his body aching. The noise continued, he turned his head. Daylight swept through windows, though its brightness was filtered by drawn curtains. There was a door, latched—and the noise came from beyond that.

He could make no sense of that gabble of sound, but the urgency of those beyond his door he was now able to feel. Getting up jerkily, he was relieved to discover that the sickness he could dimly remember no longer plagued him. He was able to walk firmly to the door, lift the barring latch.

For a moment or two he half believed that he was under attack, for three of those outside had been backed against that door. Jasum, in the uniform of Vidin, was the centermost of the trio, while opposing him were two differently clad. At the sight of Ramsay the two drew back, saluted, relieving him of the suspicion that a palace revolution might be in progress.

"What is this?" He raised his own voice. Jasum turned smartly, about to salute.

"Your Supreme Mightiness, these men say they

have news of importance—that they must speak with you. But it is not fitting that those not of Ulad intrude upon the Emperor unannounced and without stating their reason for their coming—not even if they are of Olyroun.''

"Olyroun? Admit them—alone!" Ramsay added when he saw signs that Jasum was preparing to play not only court usher but bodyguard.

"As the Throne speaks—so shall it be!" the officer returned, but when he stood aside there was an uneasy shadow on his face. And he closed the door behind the Olyroun guardsmen with what Ramsay thought was reluctant slowness. Was Jasum perhaps Ochall's man? Again that feeling that he could truly trust no one plagued Ramsay.

Once the door was closed, he turned to the two standing at strict attention.

"This so important message—?"

"Supreme Mightiness, it is our lady! She cannot be found—and there are—"

Ramsay stiffened. "Cannot be found? What say her ladies—the Lady Grishilda?"

"Supreme Mightiness, the Lady Grishilda sleeps and none can wake her. The Reverend Osythes has been summoned and—"

"Let us go!" Ramsay wasted no more time. One of the guardsmen leaped to open the door, nearly sending Jasum flying with the force of his push, so close had the Vidinian been to the portal.

"Attend me," snapped Ramsay as he strode by, keeping pace with the Olyrounians who had sought him out. If this was some further intrigue, then he would resolve it here and now! No longer was he going to accept secret upon secret. Yet he had a

growing premonition that this was no act planned by
Thecla. To arouse the palace and cause an open
search was not her way.

"When was this discovered?"

"Our lady had audience with Her Splendor Enthroned. When she did not come and sent no
message—then Her Splendor Enthroned inquired.
The door of our lady's inner chamber was fast locked.
There was no answer to any summons. Then
Fentwer"—the speaker pointed to the other
guard—"swung from the balcony of the outer presence chamber. He found the Lady Grishilda lying
upon the floor deep asleep. Our lady's bed was
empty. There was no sign of what had happened to
her, but neither is there any other way out, except the
door where we stood guard—and the balcony. We
cannot believe our lady would have gone that
way—"

No way out, thought Ramsay as his pace increased
to a half trot. Yet Thecla had come to him, and he did
not believe that anyone, except perhaps Grishilda,
was aware of that visit. He dismissed the thought that
Thecla would have been a party to any drugging or
other interference with her own senior lady-in-
waiting. They were too much in each other's confidence.

Which meant that Thecla might not have returned
to her own chamber after she left him— And someone, for some reason, had made sure Grishilda would
not be able to testify to facts. At least not for a while.

His memory reached back to his first awakening.
Thecla had in some manner then either hypnotized or
dazed the guardsmen by the bier. She was reputed to
have some of the natural gift of the Enlightened

Ones. But Grishilda—could the lady-in-waiting have deliberately submitted to such for some reason to benefit her young mistress?

No, again his knowledge, though that was small, of the bond between Thecla and the older woman denied that possibility. Osythes? He also possessed those "powers" so vaguely defined, and held in awe by most. For what reason?

Ochall? Kaskar's enslavement was attributed to some abnormal control. Ochall wanted Olyroun—needed its ores—Where was Ochall at this moment?

They crossed from one corridor to another, turned into a third. Halfway down there was a door Ramsay recognized. Thecla had once more been given the same chambers in which she had concealed him. There were guards about, some in the tunics of Olyroun, others wearing the eagle-like badge of the palace. They drew to either side as Ramsay came into their sight. Then he was through the outer presence chamber and into Thecla's bedroom.

On a divan to one side lay Grishilda and over her stood the Shaman. As Ramsay entered he glanced up.

"Well?"

Osythes shook his head. "I do not understand, Supreme Mightiness. The Lady Grishilda is in the Deep Sleep which it is believed only an adept can provoke. It cannot be broken, she will so slumber until some hour, already determined upon and imprinted upon her mind, arrives. And that we cannot know—"

His concern appeared honest. But the Enlightened Ones were masters and mistresses of subleties. However, Ramsay could perceive no gain for Osythes here.

Did the Shaman have the power to read thoughts? For now Osythes regarded Ramsay intently and said with a compelling note in his voice: "Supreme Mightiness, this is no doing of the Grove Fellowship. It is rather a trick, perhaps played to induce such belief—to sever confidence and sow discord between those who should be allies, weakening defenses—"

Logical, good sense. Still Ramsay had his reservations. The old reputation of the Enlightened Ones, that they would turn against an ally to further some project of their own, might make any word Osythes was willing to swear suspect.

Ramsay could see only one action possible now. He wheeled on the men who had followed him, Olyroun and Vidinian palace guard alike.

"I want," he said grimly, "such a search of this palace as not even a fly on the wall will be unseen! I want each and every person questioned—and any who has seen—or heard—anything out of the ordinary is to be brought directly to me, here in the Duchess's presence chamber. You will begin at once!"

There was an advantage in standing in Kaskar's boots at that moment, and he would make full use of it. The guard saluted, scattered. When they were gone, Ramsay spoke once more to the Shaman.

"Ochall, Melkolf, Berthal?" The names that had haunted him into slumber came readily enough. But men could not be arrested on suspicion alone, nor could Thecla be found by merely listing possible enemies.

He had been bold in so naming two of Osythes's own party. However, the Shaman showed no surprise.

"We must have more than just suspicions—" Now that they were alone, he omitted, one part of Ramsay's mind noted, the wordy title.

"I am told Melkolf has not only disappeared, but that he took with him knowledge unknown to others. Berthal wants to rule. And Ochall wants not only Ulad but also Olyroun. If they took Thecla to bargain—or to wed Berthal—"

"That cannot be done—the wedding, I mean—while there is another Emperor in Ulad," Osythes replied. "Such a union could not hold—for she was betrothed in the name of the Emperor. But that they might hope to conclude a bargain—yes. And it is true that we do not know the complete sum of what Melkolf learned and can put to use. The Merchants of Norn deal in the antiques of war. Others seek to salvage different knowledge. Where Melkolf has sought—it was thought that he was well overseen—but—" Osythes shook his head. "In all lie error. And in this case error has in turn become danger. There are those now set on Melkolf's trail—but we know only this: that he learned more than was good for the state of Ulad—or perhaps of this world. He is being sought diligently—"

"Time may run out," Ramsay interrupted. "Ochall wanted five days—already those have shrunk to four. How many days may Melkolf need to produce something worse than a flamethrower or a blinding fog?"

He slammed his fist against the frame of the door with bruising force. Thecla—he had let her go into the night—let her go believeing—he was sure—that he had no trust in her. Now she was gone where no one could find her. The palace might be busy as a well-stirred ant hill, but that anything concrete might come from all their endeavors at searching—that he doubted.

SEVENTEEEN

"—THE WORTHY Prince sent his own body servant to our station, Supreme Mightiness. He bore the seal ring of Prince Berthal and said that this was a matter of grave import, ordering that we have ready a distant flyer completely fueled. We had no reason to believe that there was any wrong intended.

The man standing to attention before Ramsay was obviously nervous. He was one of the attendants of the landing areas where were parked the private flyers of the Family and the highest officials of the palace.

"And when did the Prince arrive?" Ramsay's headache had returned full force. Pain ringed in his eyes as he sipped from a glass Osythes had slid before him. Ramsay barely knew what he did, intent only on sifting all the scraps the intensive search of the palace was providing.

"We do not know, Supreme Mightiness. It was in the Prince's message that the flyer be readied for instant use, and left unattended."

"The pilot?"

"The Prince is often his own pilot, Supreme Mightiness."

"And no one saw who came to the ship? That I find very hard to believe." Ramsay kept his own voice level, his impatience under what control he could muster. "There are guards on duty, are there not?"

The man swallowed visibly. "Always, Supreme Mightiness. But—but the Prince Berthal has often been angered by too close a watch. He had before ordered that the guards were not to be on hand when he sent a private message. He—he said something once about not giving the Eyes and Ears a chance to meddle—" The man was half stammering now. "Supreme Mightiness, believe me, I only repeat what the Prince said in anger when he found guards by his flyer some months ago."

"So this flyer is now gone you know not where, bearing you know not whom—" Ramsay summoned up the gist of what the other had told him.

"Supreme Mightiness, we are under command. It is for us to do as we are bid," the man returned.

Ramsay sighed. He was right, of course. Yet there was something—a feeling—perhaps because this answer was too much of a direct defeat. Was that why it was so hard to accept? Berthal's seal ring and a message to be obeyed. A takeoff witnessed right enough, but no knowledge of who had winged into the night.

"You may go," he told the landing attendant. But before the man had thankfully disappeared, Ramsay appealed to the one who had come with this witness. "There is no way of tracing the flyer's course?"

"None, Supreme Mightiness. The director had not been set. But this is not unknown. Those about private errands sometimes neglect that ruling."

"Especially," Ramsay said, allowing some of his rising anger to color his words, "if they are of sufficient rank, is that not so?"

The other made no answer, which was an answer in itself. Ramsay rubbed his forehead. There was sun bright in the room. He could not have told the hour, but it seemed more like days since he had come to find Thecla gone.

In the bedchamber Grishilda still slumbered, always under the eyes of the Empress's own trusted maid, who would report the first sign of waking. For the rest—what did they have?

A handful of bits that he could not fit together. A flyer that had taken off—the fact that Ochall was certainly not to be found anywhere within this palace—a report from a guard on the second level of the tower that he had challenged something and from that time could not remember what happened until discovered by his commandcng officer standing at his post in a state bordering on sleep.

Ochall—Berthal—Melkolf—none to be found. Slowly Ramsay raised the glass he suddenly realized he was holding, drank the rest of its contents. The stuff was bitter enough to give him a slight shock. Was the Shaman drugging him now—?

"What—?" He looked to Osythes, who in turn was watching him intently.

"A cordial only, Supreme Mightiness. And food is being brought. You cannot drive yourself past the point where your mind still rules your body. If the body falters—then what may you do?"

Ramsay leaned back in his chair. There were no more possible witnesses waiting to be interviewed. He fought the wave of fatigue that was a part of the ache in his head, the frustration of his useless efforts.

Perhaps Osythes's remedy was already beginning to work. The throb over his eyes was certainly less strong. And he was suddenly conscious of hunger. As he rested his head against the back of the chair, he asked: "What do you make of this coil, Enlightened One?"

"What do you?" Osythes countered.

Ramsay frowned. He had fought to piece together bits, rule out wild surmise for more definite evidence. Yet now all he had was a hunch, and that was so strong that he could not shrug it aside.

"It would seem," he said slowly, "that they escaped—that they can now be anywhere in Ulad—or out of it. With a world to search, where do we start?"

Osythes said nothing in answer as Ramsay paused. Did his silence mean agreement with what seemed to be facts, or did he also have some premonition that that was all too easy, too direct? Ochall might wield a club, but it was not his nature to proceed too directly to his goal. Ramsay could not be certain of his own deductions—he might be guessing wildly because he wanted to believe in his hunch—he did not dare to think that what he had stated was the truth—that there was no hope of pursuit now.

What had they managed to discover about Ochall in their hours of patient and impatient questioning? That there was absolutely no witness to any communication between the High Chancellor and Berthal. Which did not mean, of course, that such had not taken place.

The High Chancellor had gone at once to the chamber always allotted him when he stayed at Lom on matters of state. He had dismissed even his body servant—who had been the most severely interrogated of all those questioned today—with the comment that he had urgent need to study certain reports which the new Emperor would soon be calling for. The guard swore that he had never come forth from that chamber.

Which report meant nothing, Ramsay knew, with his own experiences of guards under what might be termed control. However, when summoned to attend the conference concerning the disappearance of the Duchess, his apartment had been entirely empty.

Melkolf, the third of their trio, was perhaps in his own way as dangerous as Ochall. His disappearance had come first, several days ago. And there was plenty of evidence of a strong tie between him and Berthal.

Ramsay was shaken out of his thoughts by the arrival of a tray of food. He ate quickly but cleaned each plate. Either the food or the cordial had given him new vigor. With that inner renewal his confidence rose once more.

"What did Melkolf take—instruments, machines—records—?" he asked as he pushed away the last dish.

"None of the machines," Osythes replied. "But the location beamer of the exchanger was gone. And we discovered indication of records hastily combed—including two empty hiding places— neither large."

"The exchanger?"

"Her Splendor Enthroned ordered that destroyed. I myself saw that it was done."

"Could it be rebuilt?" persisted Ramsay.

"Such a task would require great resources— time—"

"But it could be done?"

"With Melkolf's knowledge, yes." Agreement came reluctantly.

"Could Melkolf then operate it as before?"

"No! Not alone," Osythes was quick and emphatic with his answer. "The machine makes the actual exchange, but it cannot be used to locate the proper personality pattern."

"No, that you do with your dreaming," Ramsay returned flatly. "So even if Melkolf reproduced his exchanger, he could not activate it without the aid of those extra powers your fellowship exploits. *Would* they aid him?"

"No!" Osythes leaned a little forward.

"You are very sure—"

"It is decreed so. We want no more variables to upset our patterns for the future."

"One thing I have accomplished at least, merely by being," commented Ramsay. "Then why did Melkolf see fit to take with him the most important part of the exchanger?" He stood up. "I think I want to see the lab."

His hunch pointed him into action as might the keen nose of a hound picking up a faint but traceable scent. He could not put aside a strong feeling that the departure of the flyer was only a screen—a ruse— that what he sought now was not so far beyond their reach.

"Supreme Mightiness—"

Ramsay, for a moment, found it difficult to answer to that title. Half engrossed in his speculations, he blinked at the guard waiting in the doorway.

"Yes—?"

"One has come, he says he was summoned. He was dropped from a flyer of the Enlightened Ones—"

So much had happened since the night before that

Ramsay took a second to remember. Dedan—could it be—?

"Admit him!"

The guard stepped aside for the man in the plain mercenary uniform. He was pale and had lost some of his assured air of command. His face appeared aged by several years, and had undergone another subtle change; yet this grim-countenaced man was indeed the First of the Company.

Ramsay moved forward quickly. "You came!" Until this moment he had not been sure that his meeting in the place of nothingness would bear any results.

Dedan gave a shadow of his old shrug, but there was none of the old warmth. "I have come, Supreme Mightiness. Why—"

So now there existed a barrier between them. Dedan's eyes might not be shut as they had been when Ramsay fronted him in the dream, but his face was closed, perhaps his mind also. He was as stiff as the guardsman who admitted him.

"Leave us!" Ramsay ordered the guard. Only when the door closed did he speak again, though the sharp change in the only man he thought he could claim as friend daunted him.

"Dedan, I speak now as Arluth. Do you want vengeance on the man who sent the flamers to wipe us out?" Was that the promise that could strike through the shell of the First Captain now?

Dedan's blankness of expression vanished in an instant. "You know him?" His demand was harsh, but he was alive, as if only the thought of vengeance could reach through some cloud horror had laid upon him.

"I know who and why. Listen—" Ramsay swiftly

outlined what he had learned from Ochall—of how the Company had been used in the callous, horrible experiment to test the new weapons out of Norn.

Dedan's mask tightened again, only his eyes burned in his gaunt, worn face. When Ramsay had finished he said briefly: "In this matter command me—and I shall follow!"

"Then do so now," Ramsay returned. "For we seek a private place in which other strange things were once stored. There perhaps we can find the beginning of a trail that will lead to Ochall—"

Osythes was already at the door. "You have something in your mind," he said to Ramsay. "You do not believe that we must seek the flyer."

"A feeling only." Ramsay could not defend that feeling, but it was so strong in him now that he felt driven to find some proof.

"A feeling may be more valuable in the end than any fact," the Shaman replied. "And you are the Knave, trust in your feelings, in your dreams."

Once more Ramsay found himself in that well-hidden room which he had not been given a chance before to explore fully, the others crowding in his wake. But now the chamber was in a state of utter chaos. Apparently the Empress's orders had been carried out with great thoroughness and also muscle. For the machines he remembered standing in square rows had been literally smashed, as if sledgehammers had been used with force and fury.

The floor was littered with shards of equipment, broken glass, twisted metal, so that one had to pick a careful way, yet still crunched bits under boot heel. Whoever had been at work here had made very sure that nothing was salvageable.

Osythes took over the lead, gathering up skirts of

his robe in one hand as if fearing contact with the wreckage. He ushered them past the flattened, dis-emboweled exchanger, from whose wrecked casing trailed coils of fused and tangled wire, to the far side of the chamber where there were a number of small cupboards.

The doors of each had been sprung, and now either lay free of their hinges on the floor or swung open to show masses of blackened stuff within, from which arose chemical stenches.

"This," reported the Shaman, "was not done at the Empress's orders. These records were destroyed before our men went to work here. And"—he came to the end of that row of cupboards to show a rent in the wall itself, behind which they could see two bare shelves—shelves—"this part was entirely secret—we never knew of it at all."

Ramsay's mind since the meal, the disappearance of his headache, was clearer. He now felt as alert as if he had had a good night's rest with no worries to trouble him. "Then you do not really know what Melkolf looted before he went. Where did he—did you—get the knowledge to set up this place in the beginning?"

For the first time Osythes wore an uneasy expres-sion. "Not all the knowledge of the Great Era was lost. There were those who were farseeing and estab-lished caches which might and did enable them and their civilization to survive. We have found some of them. Now I believe that Melkolf has also discovered in the records we showed him some hint to others which he plundered in secret. His ability to handle our notes, which are often vague, was too sure, too ready—"

"Who *is* Melkolf?" Ramsay asked.

Osythes seemed unhappy in his answer, which he gave slowly and with obvious reluctance. "He is from the Grove in Marretz. Not all who seek the Way of Enlightenment are fitted by temperament to our training. Yet they may have a brilliance in one thing or another that makes them of potential worth in the outer world. Thus, if they cannot take the full vows, still they are encouraged to develop such talents and work with the Fellowship in other ways. Melkolf's talent was"—he swept his hand about to indicate the well-wrecked chamber—"centered in experiment with ancient equipment. He showed a genius for being able to read the cryptic notes we have discovered. But he had not the spirit to make him acceptable in the Inner Circles.

"Thus he left Marretz and wandered for a while. It is during that time perhaps that he did discover some secret cache of knowledge. He was in Yury and there met with Prince Berthal, who was hunting. It was Berthal who brought him to Lom, and what he had to offer then—" Osythes shook his head. "Her Splendor Enthroned was impressed, she summoned me in turn. It had been ordained that Ulad be protected—" Again he hesitated.

"It is the sworn duty of my Fellowship to raise mankind again to what our species once was. In Ulad there has been a beginning of lawful and peaceful government. To preserve that we were willing to advise. Also—the research into ancient knowledge—to that we are pledged."

"Did Melkolf or the Fellowship suggest the exchanger?" demanded Ramsay. He was more than a little surprised at this explanation. He had never expected Osythes to speak so freely.

"The principle of the exchanger," Osythes

answered, "was known to us. Melkolf was able to build from the study of those principles. Also—" He faced Ramsay now squarely. "We had a foreseeing—we had to learn concerning the power of dreams. When it was proved that dream and exchanger together could work—that was knowledge we needed—"

"Lord Emperor," Dedan interrupted abruptly, as if impatience to be in action whipped him sorely, "who is this Melkolf of whom you speak? Was it he who gave the order that ended the Company?"

"No. But he is a part of all that lies behind that order," Ramsay returned. He was standing still, his eyes on the stinking mess of destroyed records.

There was something—idea—hunch—? Just as he had been convinced, against concrete evidence, that Melkolf and Berthal had not fled Lom in that flyer, so now this new sense of something of importance here grew in him.

He walked to the first of the cupboards. Picking up a broken metal rod from the debris on the floor, he stirred the sodden mass of the stuff within, awaking only a stronger odor, enough to make him cough, but discovering nothing, except that which had been systematically destroyed. It was like the old, old game of childhood when one hunted for a hidden object directed by the cries of "hot" or "cold." Except that those cries did not come now from his two companions, but were generated within his own mind.

That this section of the lab was the most important—of that Ramsay was sure. Yet as he sought to find a clue his instinct told him was there, sweeping out the destroyed records to the littered floor, pulling the remains apart with his rod, he came no closer. It was not until he reached those hidden shelves that his inner monitor assured him that he had come near "hot." But there was nothing here, not even debris.

The hidden section was a narrow panel rising from the floor for about four feet, containing two entirely bare shelves. Ramsay thumped those—perhaps a secret within a secret—? But he could tell nothing by the noise that he had heard.

He turned again to Osythes. "What lies beyond this wall?"

The Shaman shook his head. "Nothing. This place was known of old—a treasure room and secret prison which dates back to the days of Gulfer, when Lom was the main city of the old Kingdom of Ulad."

But that hunch within Ramsay was not satisfied. Somewhere here still lay the clue that would lead them to Melkolf. And he believed that with Melkolf there would also be the Prince, Ochall, and—Thecla.

Once more he thumped the interior of the hiding place. He could see that the backing was stone, solid, with the air of having been set for ages in those blocks. He might put men to tearing down the wall and finding nothing, but the feeling was strong here, that at this one point was the beginning of the trail.

"I want"—he made up his mind—"this wall stripped! If there is anyone who knows the ways of this building, get him here!"

Dedan had gone to examine the space. "Lord Emperor—" Having armed himself also from the wreckage on the floor, he was prodding industriously into the cavity as Ramsay had earlier done. "This is stone that has no crevice. If you seek a hidden way—only such flamers as slew the Company might be able to cut a path for you—"

"Cut a path—" Ramsay repeated slowly. "We

cannot waste time in cutting a path—we must know
the direction!"

"And only you can find that, Supreme Mighti
ness!" Ramsay gazed at the Shaman.

"Yes," Osythes nodded, "only you. And already
you know the way that you must go."

Ramsay hurled his prodder from him. "I give no
man such power to meddle with my life again!" he
said grimly.

"You need no man, Knave. The power is yours if
you will have it so."

The place of nothingness again? But his attempt
had brought Dedan to him. Could that world
again—"

Now he spoke to the First Officer. "You know
what we seek. Now I tell you plainly, Dedan. In this
palace I can trust no man, except perhaps yourself.
For your need now is as mine—to find a murderer,
not of one but many. This Enlightened One says that
perhaps it can be done—not with fire or any tool or
weapon one holds in hand. If I so essay this search
will you be my shield man, seeing that none ap-
proaches me?"

"Lord Emperor, if the trail you seek brings down
that murderer, then I am your liege man—for so
much!"

Ramsay nodded, reassured by what he knew to be
a promise as strictly given as a blood-oath, even
though the man who offered it was this Dedan he
hardly knew.

"Well enough. All right, Shaman. I shall take the
dream road. Yet from you also must I have a
promise—on what you hold sacred enough to blind
you. I will have no aid from you—or any of your ilk.

This I do alone, and free, or not at all!''

"So can it be done," Osythes returned. "You are the variable. We could not if we would—control or direct the future for you.''

Though his suspicion of the Shaman and his kind ran deep, yet at that moment Ramsay thought Osythes's assurance was as empathic and to be accepted as Dedan's had been.

"Then let us to it—" He turned away from that plundered cupboard that still was in his mind a door of sorts, though he did not know the trick of it.

Back they went to that chamber where Ramsay had waited for the reports of the searchers. He saw that the sun was almost gone now—night advanced quickly on Lom. And night somehow seemed better for the task he set himself.

Osythes gave certain orders which brought more food, drink. Ramsay waved Dedan to join him while the Shaman himself would sip only from a brew served him in a small, curiously fashioned flask.

"We eat for strength," Ramsay said. "You, Dedan must watch the night—or as much of the night as is needed. For I am to sleep—and—dream—"

"Dream?"

"Dream true. Believe me, Dedan, in dreams do lie truths. This I have proved.''

The Free Captain eyed him thoughtfully. For a fleeting moment Dedan seemed shaken out of his obsession. "You wear the face of Kaskar, the Emperor, you seem to rule here in Lom. And now you speak of things that are said concerning the Enlightened Ones. What manner of man are you?"

Ramsay laughed. Perhaps the Dedan he had known was not yet dead. That meeting of their eyes assured him even more than the other's words. "The tale is a long one, comrade, and not easily credited. But I am neither Kaskar nor an Enlightened One—I am myself—and perhaps only a true dreamer. This I must discover. I lay upon you, Osythes"—he spoke secondly to the Shaman— "to make clear to this promised liege man of mine that what I attempt may come true."

Osythes put aside the small glass from which he had been sipping his cordial.

"There are many truths," he said. "And there are secrets that are better not disclosed—"

"Except to those who have the right to hear them," countered Ramsay. Within him confidence was growing. He was about to turn to his own this trick of the Enlightened Ones—no wonder the Shaman was reluctant.

"Dedan"—Ramsay did not wait for Osythes to reply to that thrust—"this is the way of what I would do. I must sleep—a sleep so deep that perhaps I shall not be easily awakened from it. And while I sleep, so shall I also dream—and learn how thus to open that door I know lies below. Your part is to stand guard that none wake me before my time."

"This you believe you can do?" the Free Captain replied in a wondering tone. "Well, if it leads as you say, then I am willing—"

Ramsay went to the divan, stretched out upon it. There was a faint spicy scent which seemed to come from the pillow under his head. Thecla—as he had concentrated on Dedan to summon the mercenary, now he would fasten on the Duchess. He closed his eyes and began to form Thecla, not as he had seen her last slipping from his door, that barrier rising between them, but Thecla as he had known her at the lodge among the trees, free, sometimes laughing at some mistake he made in speech. Not a Duchess locked in the tight formality of a court, but a girl who had somehow found a place in his memory—his mind—which no one else could or would fill.

Thecla—thus she was—would always be—

EIGHTEEN

RAMSAY WAS floating—not as if he were enclosed in a flyer, but rather as if he were free to wing the air; the art men had so long envied the birds that they had sought for generations to equal it. At first about him was the nothingness—the absence of all. Then, out of that nothingness, arose a shadow, taking on solid substance as he winged toward it. Only this was not Thecla as he had expected.

A wall—block upon thick block.

Ramsay hung suspended in the space of nothingness, facing that barrier. No door, not even a promising crevice or crack. In him surged his will, strong as rage—he was not to be easily defeated.

There was a way through, he determined upon that. A way through—

Just as he would have used his hands in the world he had left behind to test and examine each of those ghostly gray blocks, so now he drove his will, a spearhand of force against each block in turn. Through!

As his will touched, here and there awoke small points of light—not on each of the stones, but rather on two that were set one above the other. Those points of light looked as if they had sprung from the imprint of fingers—five above, five below.

When the last flashed into life, the stones began to turn, slowly, with great reluctance—but they turned. He had found his door and now he sped through it, again a thing of the air. Nor was there nothingness beyond.

Rather here was another lab, which was near twin to that which had been destroyed. It was not quite the same, being smaller, far less crowded with apparatus. In the very middle of that chamber stood once more an exchanger, undamaged. Only from the top was missing the selector.

Movement centered Ramsay's attention elsewhere. He distinguished four figures. But they had not the concrete, vivid representation of those he had sighted in other dreams. Rather they were veiled in a way that made each one blur as he tried to see it clearly. Ramsay fought with all his will to clear his sight, to know—

There was a flickering of light, swinging back and forth like a pendant supported somehow in the air. Ramsay flinched. Remembered— Just so had Ochall swung the key of his office. There was danger in that swinging pinpoint of light.

He tried to avoid watching it, tried to reach beyond to the dim figures. Two were in constant movement, but he could not make out what they were doing. Always as he tried to concentrate that flicker arose. He began to feel drained, confused, for a second or two the force of his will lessened.

Thecla!

Was she one of those ghostly blurs?

Even as he wondered, he saw her—far to one side, her face clearing under his gaze. It was a face such as Dedan had turned upon him in the place of nothingness—a face without life. Nor did she open her eyes in answer to his dream demand.

The flickering had stopped. He was somehow warned by that. They must know of his invasion, they *wanted* him to be sure that they held a hostage. He had only realized that when there was imprinted over Thecla's face, even more clearly, something else—a black object—

It was the selector missing from the exchanger!

A threat—a promise? Either or both, Ramsay knew. Search out this hidden den, try to free the prisoner, and she would be gone—rift away to the death they had tried to give to Kaskar!

He who planned this—who was protected by that flicker of swinging light—Ramsay continued to watch what he had been allowed to envision as if shocked by the implication so easily induced by that other. To open himself to attack—was that what the other sought, to provoke Ramsay into trying to reach the source of the threat?

There was a feeling of vast confidence, so strong it might have streamed visibly from behind the flicker. The mind, the will, hidden beyond, believed his position impregnable. He alone would state terms, all others must surrender.

Let him believe so!

Ramsay relaxed his will, withdrew— And sensed the high roll of triumph, following him as a hound might be dispatched to snap at the heels of a beggar, hurrying the hopeless on his way. Once more he hung in nothingness, the wall closed before him.

Something he had learned, but not enough. To force the issue now when he was too ignorant—no. He relaxed his will again—and awoke.

Dedan's face, then Osythes. He was back. But he did not try to rise.

"I know where—" he said slowly.

"Yes, but that may avail us little," the Shaman answered him. "There has come a message. Grishilda roused moments ago, nearly out of her senses with fear. If we do not surrender to their demands, the Duchess—"

"Will be sent to her death," Ramsay interrupted. "Then they will begin on the rest of us, no doubt. There is a second exchanger—behind the wall. They are still in the heart of Lom, and one of them has knowledge that may equal yours. Ochall I think."

Osythes muttered, but his words were not plain enough to hear. Dedan merely watched Ramsay's face, his eyes narrowed.

"Which is the murderer?" he demanded, intent upon his own dark hunting.

"Ochall. But he is not the one we can easily take." Ramsay lay still. "Shaman"—he put into his voice now the crack of a demand from equal to equal— "what forms a defense against a dream search which appears as a flickering light? You have the resources of the Enlightened Ones, and surely you know enough to find explanations. Let me warn you—in your dream searching you have unloosed what perhaps cannot be controlled, a weapon worse than any out of Norn, put into the hands of one ruthless enough to use it at will."

Osythes seemed to shrink in upon himself. He had always been an old man to Ramsay; now he was a withered remnant of the one he had been only hours earlier. His lips parted as if he would answer, then shut again; his fingers plucked feverishly at the folds of his robe.

"These—" His voice came as a ghostly whisper, grew only a little stronger as he continued. "These are forbidden things—you are not of the Grove. I cannot reveal to you, an UnEnlightened—"

"Then prepare to have your own weapons turned against you," Ramsay returned. "Do you think that Ochall will spare any of us now? He apparently has some power of his own, he has the secret of the exchanger. Be ready to dream yourself into death, Shaman. For you he may now consider the most important of his resident enemies."

"I have not the authority," Osythes made answer. "I must consult with—"

"And while you are consulting," Ramsay pointed out, "Ochall may be on the move. Your secret is no longer any secret to him!"

Dedan got to his feet. "You say, Lord Emperor, that this burner of men is behind the wall? Then it is simple enough, we tear down that wall—"

"I wish it *were* so simple." Ramsay turned his head wearily. Again he was drained of energy. "The fact is we do not know what defense stands beyond. Would you send more men to face flames?"

Dedan grimaced. His fist struck into the open palm of his other hand.

"Then what *will* you do, Lord Emperor?"

"Bargain—" Osythes began.

"*No!*" Ramsay returned. "Ochall would use the

time to concentrate his own position. He will yield nothing in any bargain, merely play with us to his pleasure. You know him, Shaman—can you say that I am not now speaking the truth?''

Osythes was silent. Then, as if the words were dragged from him one by one through some torture, he spoke?

''I will be breaking oaths that are beyond your understanding if I do as you wish. There are great matters to which men are nothing—''

''You have said,'' Ramsay broke in, ''that the safety of Ulad is a part of the plans of your Fellowship. Very well, where will that safety be if Ochall achieves his purposes?''

The stricken look Osythes had worn earlier was going; the Shaman sat straighter in his chair, his head erect, will and a gathering determination about him.

''You are the Knave,'' he said. ''And as the Knave you have such power as no one, not even one who is outside the disciplines and restraints of the Grove, can in the end defeat. But what you draw upon can be lessened by lack of confidence in yourself. To battle you must commit all that is you, body, mind, spirit. And this is also true, that in such a struggle you may lose mind, body—spirit I do not know, for though we can measure two of the possessions of men, the third is beyond our understanding.

''If you are willing to risk all that you are, then you can drag Ochall down. But there is no promise that you will not also fall. This I say because once more yours is a choice no one else may make for you.''

Ramsay's gaze lifted from the earnest face of the Shaman. He lay now with his eyes on the ceiling overhead. To commit himself utterly—never in his life had he made such a choice. There was a finality to this that threatened a part of him now rising to active rebellion. Though he could not understand to the full Osythes's warning, there was that in it which chilled his tired body.

When he had been proclaimed Emperor he had touched upon a choice, but that was only a pallid shadow when compared to this. He knew that there would be no return—

Still, he had, in a manner, already gone well down this road.

"You will tell me now"—he did not look to the Shaman as he said that, but continued to stare upward—"what I must do."

"You must confront Ochall both as a dreamer and one who wakes," Osythes replied. "You must hold on both planes against all his powers, believing in yourself strongly enough to defeat him. How this may be done no other can tell you."

Ramsay pulled himself up. His weariness was a weight, and now he made another demand of the Shaman.

"I must have strength—"

Osythes nodded. "First"—he spoke to Dedan—"unite with me!"

He held out his hand, and Dedan, looking puzzled, clasped it. Then Osythes leaned toward Ramsay and, with the fingers of the other hand, he touched the younger man's forehead.

Ramsay felt that flow, first slowly, then feeding into him—energy that spread downward through his body, banishing that burdensome languor that was a part of waking from the dreaming.

Rising as the Shaman broke contact, he knew that he was ready, as ready as he would ever be.

"To the lab." He drew a deep breath. "Let those guards *you* can trust the most," he added to Osythes, "come. And comrade"—Ramsay turned to Dedan—"you are at my back, armed. I will not deny that we may meet death beyond that wall, for I could not see their weapons, and they may have worse than we met, even at Yasnaby."

Dedan showed his teeth in the grin of a wolf. "Comrade." For that first time he used the warmer address as if the promise of action were indeed a fire. "You need not waste words in such advice. I am ready." He reached behind him and plucked a needler from beneath the pile of cushions where he had been sitting.

Once more they descended to the hidden chamber that had been Melkolf's domain. Ramsay led, with Dedan at his shoulder, Osythes behind, and following the Shaman, those of the latter's choice from the guardsmen. Ramsay went directly to the secret cupboard.

"Rip out the shelves," he ordered. One of the guards moved instantly, using strips of metal to pry and pound out the wooden lengths, clearing the ancient stone behind.

Ramsay closed his eyes, bringing to mind the picture from the dream. There—there—

His hands were outstretched, fingers crooked. Just so must he finger the well-concealed lock.

Beyond—Thecla's dead-alive face before his eyes—that black threat of the box blotting it out. Ramsay fought away that vision. He dared have no doubts now, nor allow any fear for himself or another to deflect what force of will he could summon.

There were no visible spots on the blocks he chose, but when his fingers were on the stone he felt out a double set of depressions. Pressure— It was as if now his flesh were sinking into the rough rock, being swallowed—Pressure—

Along with the strength of his arm, Ramsay exerted his will, for it seemed to him that the resistance of the stone was amplified by another, more subtle thing. As if Ochall and the others were reinforcing the holding of that physical barrier with their own force of projected power.

Slowly, even as it had in the dream, the blocks slipped back, showing light beyond. Ramsay spoke. "Be ready—!" He delivered a last vigorous thrust and jerked aside, out of the path of any weapon that might be set to cover that doorway.

The flash of fire, or projectile he had expected, did not follow. With caution, after a long moment of waiting, he slid back to the opening, stooping to peer into the hole.

Beyond—no, not the nothingness of his dream— but a haze that did not quite have that turgid look of the yellow fog that had rolled across the dunes at Yasnaby but was as hard for the eye to penetrate.

Ramsay pushed his way through that opening, into the haze. Though he could not now depend upon his eyes, he had another guide. Some unknown sense that was allied to the dream told him those he sought were here.

On the other side of the opening he stood, his hands consciously half raised to ward off attack, his head turning slowly from right to left. Then he caught that flicker of light, seeming less strong than it had been in his dream, but, he guessed, nonetheless deadly to his purpose because of that.

Behind that glinting of light was the enemy, believing himself safe. For it was something in the flickering that was both shield for defense and weapon poised for attack. And it was the light which Ramsay must face in its unknown strength, beating down the defense, warding off the attack.

He took one step and then another into the swirl of the mist. If any followed him now, he was not aware of it. All his senses, both the five of his physical body, and the new one of his mind, were centered only on what was before him.

Out of the mist loomed a solid shape. He thought it the corner of the exchanger. But he heard no sound. If they did shelter here, they were using a cat's trick of freezing, waiting for its prey to approach within striking distance.

The flicker—it was playing with his mind, weakening his will. But there was only one way he could reach the one behind it—and that was to force him out of ambush into the open. That mist, it swirled— Did or did not the forms stride through it? He glanced from the light to the solid edge of the exchanger, riveted on that for the space of a breath to steady himself. Then once more he looked steadily at the swing-dip-swing that reached not only into his eyes but his mind, weaving a web to entangle his will.

Behind that light—reach behind that light!

The man—not his weapon—reach the man!

He knew what was to be done, but to accomplish that—

Ramsay fought to see beyond the flicker, to reduce it to something that mattered no more than perhaps the glass of a window. He must break the pattern of the flicker, yet let him concentrate on the seeing and he saw only that. With sudden inspiration he closed his eyes. See the dream—he ordered his mind— SEE!

Spin—swing—dip—He was dizzy, fear rising in him. SEE!

Into that one thought he poured his strength.

Behind the flicker—yes! There was now a form, dim, hardly to be parted from the swirls of the mist. But it was there!

Then—

"You die!"

No cry that rang in his ears, but rather a blast that clawed at his mind.

"Look—and die!"

Ramsay held against the blast. "OUT!" he countered. "Out to face me. I am the Knave—" From somewhere flooded those commands. "I am the one outside the pattern Out to face ME!"

"You die!" That was like a scream torturing his mind with its lash of red fury.

"I live! Out—" And into that command Ramsay poured for an instant every trace of his own will, of the strength that was Ramsay's life and identify.

The flicker was still spinning, more and more furiously. But behind it—behind it now a face. Only not the face he had reached for. So that the very identity of his enemy nearly shocked him into making a fatal slip.

"You die!"

"I live!" Ramsay rallied before the other could take advantage of that half-breath length of shock. "Out!"

The flicker spun now as a corruscating cloud, but it could not hide that face again, no matter how hard it tried. There was a spouting of maddened, fiery particles, like an explosion.

"No-o-o-o—!" The scream that came to his mind

was not now that of fury, but rather fear, fear which accompanies fate.

"Yes!" Ramsay held. The fiery particles shot out at him. He opened his yes. There they were, as visible to his sight as they were in his dream state. A mad whirl of sparks to envelop him. But he looked beyond and held that gaze level.

The fire enveloped Ramsay; there was a scorching heat around him. This was not real; to that belief he held firmly. And he who tried so to trick that attacker was—

Aloud, Ramsay spoke a name.

The fiery particles were snuffed out, the mist tore raggedly. He faced the enemy clearly for the first time. In the other's hand—

Ramsay leaped. He was past the exchanger as his hand shot out and down. The edge of his straight, firm-held fingers met a wrist with an audible crack.

There was a cry of pain and the selector fell to the floor. Then the other was clawing for his throat, yammering like an animal, the very wildness of the attack driving Ramsay back until his shoulders were pinned against the exchanger. He dropped to the floor, confusing the other, heard a shout which he knew was a warning though he could not distinguish the words.

The crackle of a needler warned him to remain where he was. But only inches beyond his hand lay the box which brought the exchanger to life. Ramsay grasped at it. Above him someone cried out. Ramsay threw himself to the right, the selector tight in his grip.

Once more the needler cracked as Ramsay fought to his knees. Another bore down on him, gas gun ready. He had only time to strike forward with the box. It met flesh, wringing a grunt from his new attacker. But muzzle of the side arm had been deflected. Mist shot to the roof, not directly into Ramsay's face.

He drove his fist into a belly where muscles stiffened to meet the blow, took a jolt in return against his cheekbone, one that had enough force to send him reeling back. His boot heel caught and he crashed down, falling prone over a body on the floor.

Then Ochall gave a strangled whoop, his hands rising to his chest, and went to his knees, to fold up, his head against Ramsay's boots.

"Enough!" Ramsay only half heard that voice. His head was still spinning a little from that one good blow the High Chancellor had landed.

He was struggling to get once more to his feet when he heard a scream. Not this time in his mind, but ringing in his ears. And he wavered around to see—clearly, for the mist was now gone—Berthal backed against the wall, in his arms Thecla, not now any blank-eyed, mindless captive, but a raging, struggling fury, fighting against the Prince's grasp so that he could not hold her and bring his weapon to bear on Ramsay. Even as Ramsay faced him he stopped that attempt. The barrel of his side arm pointed into the girl's face.

"Move—" he panted. "Give us a free road out, or by all the Blood of Jostern in me, I will fire!"

Ramsay froze. He glanced toward the door. Osythes was there, Dedan also, with that needler that had taken out the greatest of their enemies. Then he looked back to Berthal—there was madness in the Prince's eyes. He was on the edge of killing from fear alone.

In that instant Ramsay used the only weapon left to him. For the second time in this hidden room he summoned the full force of his will and sent an arrow straight into another's mind.

Berthal's mouth jerked, he shook his head. But his arms fell limply. Thecla broke from his grasp with a force of her own that almost sent her sprawling. She half fell forward and Ramsay caught her, steadied her gently.

"Take him!" he ordered, and guardsmen moved to Berthal's side.

As they led the Prince away, Ramsay looked to the Shaman.

"We were wrong. Ochall must have been *his* man, not the other way around—"

It was still hard for him to believe that one with the High Chancellor's supreme confidence in himself, possessing that aura of raw power, could have been second to anyone—no matter what strange knowledge that other might use.

"Not wholly." Osythes had knelt by the crumpled body beside the exchanger, had shifted it so that Melkolf's face was turned uppermost. "I believe that they were rather partners. We judged Ochall to be the complete master because of his outward nature. However, I do not think that, even had they won, he would have easily ruled in Ulad. Not with all Melkolf knew." Gently the Shaman touched the forehead of the dead man. "So much this youth knew, yet not enough. He wanted everything, in the end even what little he had was reft from him, and he was left naked to a storm of his own raising."

Ramsay felt Thecla shiver. "You do not know what they planned—" Her voice was ragged. "They would have sent you—us—all who opposed them to other level deaths. He"—she glanced at Melkolf and then quickly away again—"boasted that he could do it now without a dreamer. He said—that dreaming had no force compared to that of the machines he could master—"

"And so he died," Osythes answered, "because he disdained self-mastery and trusted most the work of his hands, rather than that which lay within himself. That was the Great Sin of the Ancient Ones, and one that we are very prone to—valuing the visible always above the unmeasurable."

"Lord Emperor—" Dedan brushed aside the Shaman's words as if they had no meaning. "Here we had three men. Which of these gave the order for the Company's slaughter?"

"He—" Ramsay indicated Ochall. "Or so he told me."

The First Captain went to look down at the High Chancellor.

"It was my hand that ended him. I am content," he said slowly, half as one waking from a nightmare. "Those of the Company will now rest well."

"There is one thing more, comrade," Ramsay said.

Dedan looked up. "What is that, Lord Emperor?"

Ramsay nodded toward the exchanger. "That—and any more such apparatus as may be found here. Will you see that it is left so no man can once more attempt to solve such secrets?"

"Well enough—"

Content, Ramsay turned to the door, supporting Thecla who shivered and stumbled as she walked. The girl did not speak until they were out in the wreckage of the outer lab.

"Melkolf and Ochall—" Her hand had a wondering note. "They—they are finished. And Berthal—what will be done with Berthal, Kaskar?"

He noticed the name she had given him.

"He will have justice—"

"From whose hand?" Once away from that hidden room she seemed to revive in strength. Her trembling had stopped, she walked more easily, but she made no attempt to draw out of Ramsay's hold.

"I suppose—from those who deal with justice in this world."

"He is of the House Royal—justice comes from you, Kaskar."

"I am not—" Ramsay began and then stopped. Thecla had turned her head, was watching him intently.

"What are you not?" she asked, when for a long moment he had stood in silence, unable to finish that statement.

"I do not know what I am not, but perhaps I know a little of what I am," he said slowly. "Once I was one man—it seems I have become another."

Ramsay Kimble was dead. He was dead in body in his own time and world; here he had died slowly in another way.

"You are Kaskar who shall rule in Ulad," she said softly.

"Am I? Or am I a dreamer who has gone too far into his dreams to return?"

"If the dream is Ulad," she replied confidently, "then you have dreamed true. Are we so poor a dream that you would seek waking from it?"

She raised her hand and drew her fingertips along his cheek.

"Tell me, Kaskar—Knave of Dreams—are we so poor a dream?" she pleaded.

His arm tightened about her. "Never so—!" he said with the same firmness with which he had faced Melkolf.

Thecla laughed softly.

"Then dream on, Kaskar, and never wake!"

"So be it!" His lips met hers, and the last of Ramsay Kimble died forever.

ANDRE NORTON

*37290	Iron Cage $1.50
*41553	Judgment on Janus $1.25
*43673	Key Out of Time 95¢
*47163	The Last Planet $1.25
*49237	Lord of Thunder $1.25
*54103	Moon of Three Rings $1.25
57753	Night of Masks $1.50
*66834	Plague Ship $1.50
*67556	Postmarked the Stars $1.25
69683	Quest Crosstime $1.25
74983	Sargasso of Space $1.25
75697	Sea Siege $1.25
75832	Secret of the Lost Race $1.25
75992	Shadow Hawk $1.25
*76802	The Sioux Spaceman $1.25
77552	Sorceress of the Witch World $1.25
78013	Star Born $1.25

Available wherever paperbacks are sold or use this coupon.

- - - - - - - - - - - - - - -

SCIENCE FICTION from the GREAT YEARS

*01570	**Alien Planet** Pratt	75¢
*02938	**Armageddon 2419 A.D.** Nowlan	$1.25
06713	**The Blind Spot** Hall & Flint	$1.50
07690	**The Brain-Stealers** Leinster	$1.50
07840	**A Brand New World** Cummings	$1.25
27291	**The Galaxy Primes** Smith	$1.25
52831	**Metropolis** Von Harbou	$1.25
53870	**The Moon Is Hell** Campbell	95¢
70301	**The Radio Beasts** Farley	$1.50
70320	**The Radio Planet** Farley	$1.50
75431	**Science Fiction—The Great Years Part II** Pohl	$1.50
75894	**Sentinels from Space** Russell	$1.50
*84331	**The Ultimate Weapon** Campbell	$1.25
87182	**War Against the Rull** Van Vogt	$1.50

Available wherever paperbacks are sold or use this coupon.

ace books, (Dept. MM) Box 576, Times Square Station
New York. N.Y. 10036

Please send me titles checked above.

I enclose $................. Add 35c handling fee per copy.

Name ....

Address ....

City.................... State............ Zip........

EDGAR RICE
BURROUGHS

THE CASPAK SERIES

*47022 **The Land That Time Forgot** 95¢

*47023 **The Land That Time Forgot** $1.25 Movie Tie-In

65944 **The People Time Forgot** $1.50

64483 **Out of Time's Abyss** 95¢

VENUS SERIES

*66505 **Pirates of Venus** $1.50

21563 **Escape on Venus** $1.50

49504 **Lost on Venus** $1.25

*09203 **Carson of Venus** $1.50

INNER WORLD NOVELS

03324 **At the Earth's Core** $1.25

*65854 **Pellucidar** $1.50

*79794 **Tanar of Pellucidar** $1.25

79854 **Tarzan at the Earth's Core** $1.25

04635 **Back to the Stone Age** $1.50

*46999 **Land of Terror** $1.25

*75134 **Savage Pellucidar** $1.50

Available wherever paperbacks are sold or use this coupon.

---

ace books, (Dept. MM) Box 576, Times Square Station
New York. N.Y. 10036

Please send me titles checked above.

I enclose $. . . . . Add 35c handling fee per copy.

Name . . . .

Address . . . .

City. . . . . State. . . . . Zip. . . . .

16J